THE
KANSAS CITY
COWBOYS

Center Point
Large Print

Also by Johnny D. Boggs and available from Center Point Large Print:

And There I'll Be a Soldier
Top Soldier
Return to Red River
Hard Way Out of Hell
Summer of the Star

**This Large Print Book carries the
Seal of Approval of N.A.V.H.**

THE
KANSAS CITY
COWBOYS

Johnny D. Boggs

CENTER POINT LARGE PRINT
THORNDIKE, MAINE

This Circle Ⓥ Western is published by
Center Point Large Print in the year 2017 in
co-operation with Golden West Literary Agency.

First Edition
June, 2017

Printed in the United States of America
on permanent paper.
Set in 16-point Times New Roman type.

ISBN: 978-1-68324-418-9

Library of Congress Cataloging-in-Publication Data

Names: Boggs, Johnny D., author.
Title: The Kansas City cowboys / Johnny D. Boggs.
Description: First edition. | Thorndike, Maine : Center Point Large Print,
2017. | Series: A Circle V western
Identifiers: LCCN 2017005583 | ISBN 9781683244189
    (hardcover : alk. paper)
Subjects: LCSH: Large type books. | GSAFD: Western stories.
Classification: LCC PS3552.O4375 K36 2017 | DDC 813/.54—dc23
LC record available at https://lccn.loc.gov/2017005583

In Memory of John G. Rose Jr.,
of Timmonsville, South Carolina,
who, as my friend Bobby Gibbs said, took
"the time to teach us the game of baseball—
how it was supposed to be played as a kid."
Mr. Rose and his father, a World War I
veteran, always treated me kindly, and always
encouraged me, even though I couldn't hit,
run, throw, or field worth a nickel.

"Baseball is the very symbol, the outward and visible expression of the drive and push and rush and struggle of the raging, tearing, booming 19th Century."

Mark Twain

". . . losers are as important as winners."

H.L. Dellinger
One Year in the National League:
An Account of the 1886
Kansas City Cowboys

PREFACE

I've always found many similarities between the American West and baseball, and I've always loved both. Baseball and the West are larger than life. Both have fascinating histories, and often those histories are overshadowed by myths of epic proportions.

Several names, most places, and a very few facts are true. The story, however, is a bald-faced lie.

PROLOGUE

My favorite year? Well, that's easy. It was 1886, when I met my beloved wife. Yet there's another reason my dreams often take me back to that wonderful but tragic spring and summer.

Baseball.

Yes, baseball has been another love of my life, and I guess I should mention two other things dear to my heart. Cowboys. And Mother.

Cindy, my wonderful bride, understands. More than anything, she loved baseball and cowboys when she was seventeen, too, and just like me, she still does. Besides, during that summer of '86, she grew to appreciate, tolerate, and even stand by Mother.

CHAPTER ONE

RULE 47. A Substitute shall not be allowed to take the place of any player in a game, unless such player be disabled in the game then being played, by reason of illness or injury.

"Rule say nothing about player being dead." Gustavus Heinrich Schmelz waved his copy of *Playing Rules of the National League of Professional Base Ball Clubs; 1886* under the nose of umpire Klaus Klein.

"Christ a'mighty, Gus!" Dave Rowe didn't reach for any rule book. Instead, his hand stretched toward the Smith & Wesson pocket pistol he kept tucked in his belt near the small of his back, but the umpire grabbed Rowe's hand, shaking his head sternly, saying: "*Nein, nein,* Rowe, none of that."

May 8, 1886, found us, the Kansas City Cowboys, playing the Maroons at Union Grounds in St. Louis. We had lost our first five games, and were about to see our record drop to 0-6 if Gus Schmelz got his way and persuaded the umpire to rule a forfeit. Seeing Rowe reach for his pistol, and knowing our manager's fierce temper and quick trigger, the Maroons' manager took a step back, bringing up his fists into the stance a pugilist might take, but the German's fists, big as they were, would be no match for that .32 Dave Rowe carried.

Rowe seemed to be trying to determine which man he should shoot first, Schmelz or Klein. The rowdies in Union Grounds stands started hissing, cussing, and hurling beer bottles toward the diamond. National League rules prohibited the sale of any intoxicating spirits at ball parks, but, this being St. Louis, fans brought their own suds to the Union Grounds. Backing up, moving his arms up and down, Schmelz tripped over Grasshopper Jim Whitney's big feet, and Schmelz landed with a thud on his backside. That changed the hisses and cusses into cackles, but the beer bottles—empty, of course—kept flying.

The players on our bench started laughing, too. All except me. I didn't see anything funny. St. Louis outfielder Jack McGeachey had just lined a baseball that cracked pitcher Jim Whitney in the head, sending a geyser of blood into the air, then onto the dirt. Whitney landed on the pitcher's lines long before the blood, which hung in the air like a weak pop-up, splattered in the dust beside him. McGeachey now squatted on second base. Egyptian Healy stood on third.

No outs, no score, bottom of the eighth inning.

And Grasshopper Jim Whitney lay dead.

Likely you know all about Grasshopper Jim. He hailed from Conklin, New York, and had been playing in the big league since 1881, when he broke in with the Boston Red Caps. Back in 1883 when he played for Boston, he had even led the league in strike-outs. Boston had released him after the 1885 season, but Rowe had brought him to Kansas City. And now Grasshopper lay dead.

"Chhheee-rist!"

Sitting beside me, Stump Wiedman almost swallowed his tobacco juice, Jack McGeachey shot to his feet, while Gus Schmelz scurried to his, and the German ump crossed himself.

The crowd fell silent. Even the beer bottles stopped flying.

Grasshopper Jim had raised his arm, brought it to his nose, and turned his head. His eyes opened. They weren't focused, but they blinked three or four times, and I heard him say: "That gun ain't loaded, is it, Horace?"

"He ain't dead," Dave Rowe said. "Now can I bring in a substitute?"

Speechless, his face paler than Grasshopper Jim's, Klaus Klein nodded, put on his cap, and headed back to home plate.

The crowd began booing. That's a St. Louis fan for you. Booing the opposing pitcher because he wasn't killed by a line drive to his noggin.

"Dave wants you, Silver," Stump Wiedman said.

I blinked. Sure enough, our manager kept crooking his finger at me. Jerking my cap down low, I shot off the bench like a cannonball, pulling the glove over the fingers on my left hand. Nervous, sure, not for Grasshopper Jim, but for me, just our days past my seventeenth birthday, about to play in my first National League baseball game. I ran onto the diamond, head bobbing, looking first for the ball, then at Dave Rowe, waiting for his words of encouragement.

"Grab his feet," our manager/center fielder said. "I'll get his arms."

"Huh?"

"His feet. We got to get his carcass off the field before we can finish this game." Rowe looked toward our bench. "Conway! I need you to pitch!"

My stomach soured. My face flushed. I heard my teammates laughing at me, but I sucked in a lungful of putrid St. Louis air, and grabbed Grasshopper Jim's long legs. We hauled him off the field, his butt dragging across the infield dirt, and deposited him behind our bench. Stump Wiedman leaned over and wiped the blood off Whitney's face, and I propped his head up with his glove and hat.

"We ought to get him to a hospital," I said.

"After the game." Dave Rowe stared at Pete Conway. "Move your arse, Pete. You gotta pitch."

Conway lifted his face, the only part of his body that moved. Then he opened his mouth, which took some doing, and said: "Sure . . . D-Dave . . . p-p-pitchhhhhh!"

His breath smelled of forty-rod whiskey. If

someone had struck a Lucifer in front of Conway's face, Union Grounds would have been blown across the Mississippi River.

Dave Rowe unleashed a string of every cuss word I had ever heard. That was one of our manager's specialties. He could turn Jesus-son-of-a-bitching-pig-shitting-asshole-damn-it-all-to-hell-bastard-loving-Christ into one word. Dave Rowe pulled the bottle from between Pete Conway's legs and flung it onto the first-base line, where it shattered against empty beer bottles.

"King!" Rowe jabbed his crooked index finger at me. "Get back out there!"

As I returned to the ball field, Rowe shouted at the umpire: "Silver King's replacing Whitney!" Rowe picked up his own glove, and trotted back to center field.

The crowd, and the Maroons, laughed so hard some of them doubled over. "Silver King! Ain't that a handle for a ballist!" someone yelled. Heckles followed.

"Silver? Why not gold?"

"Hey, there . . . Silver Queeeennnn!"

"Silver ain't king. Maroon's the color to be in Saint Louis!"

Tom Dolan knocked the mud off his shoes with his bat, and stepped into the batter's box. After a curt nod in my direction, our catcher, Fatty Briody, stuck out his ham-size glove, and I put my arm into a windmill and fired my first pitch in an honest-to-goodness National League ball game.

The ball bounced four feet in front of the plate, and Briody had to scramble six yards to stop it from caroming toward the backstop.

Behind me on second base, Jack McGeachey howled with laughter, slapping his thighs. The rowdies filling the Union Grounds seats echoed his enjoyment.

More heckles followed.

Briody threw the ball back to me.

He had to leap to keep my second pitch from sailing over his head.

I tried a spitball next. Dolan's bat didn't budge. Klaus Klein announced: "Ball three."

Then . . .

"Ball four."

"Ball five."

"Ball six."

"Ball seven."

Behind me, Dave Rowe unleashed another string of cuss words, these all directed first at my incompetence, then at Pete Conway for having the audacity to get so roostered he couldn't stand up, let alone pitch.

Dolan tossed his bat toward the Maroons' bench, and trotted to first base. The bases were loaded. No outs.

As second baseman Sam Crane came to the plate, Fatty Briody trotted, all two hundred fifty pounds of him, from home plate to me. He smiled this broken-teeth smile, then asked, none too friendly: "Kid, what the hell are you doin'?"

"I . . . uh . . . well . . ."

"Spitball?" He shook his head. "Fade-away. Shine ball? Tricks? You got to be a Colossus to stand the gaff. You ain't no Colossus, and you ain't no Pete Conway nor Grasshopper Jim, neither." He put his arm around my shoulder. I cringed, expecting him to break my neck, but his touch was gentle, and I felt him squeeze my shoulder. "I seen you pitch, boy. Just throw the ball like you do when we's practicin'. Only harder. Speed. That's what's gold to you, Silver. Your speed. Show 'em your cyclone stuff."

"But . . ." I swallowed down the bile. "Remember . . . Denver?"

In April, we had played some exhibition games in Denver, and how I dreaded bringing up those memories.

"Sure," he said, and patted the big glove on his left hand. "That's where I got this pillow." The St. Louis crowd, and quite a few Maroons, had hammered Briody relentlessly during this series because of that monstrosity of a glove. "And I got it, because of how hard you throw, kid." He lowered his voice. "Sam Crane'll take his time. He likes a low ball, and that's what he'll try to call. But as soon as he steps into the box, you fire your best pitch at him. Savvy?"

I understood. Baseball rules allowed a batsman

to call his pitch—low or high—and the pitcher was obligated to deliver the pitch in the requested spot. If the batsman made no such announcement before the first pitch, however, he could not change or call his pitch.

"Crane can't hit nothin' high," Briody said over his shoulder as he trotted back to the plate.

As soon as Briody squatted behind the plate, Crane stepped into the box, shifting his quid of tobacco from one cheek to the other, and as he started to lift the bat, I shot a pitch faster than Wild Bill Hickok could pull a trigger. It was a ball, and so close to Crane that he stumbled back with a yelp. Once he had recovered, he pointed one end of the bat at me, yelling: "The hell you doing, boy?"

I didn't answer, just caught the ball Fatty Briody threw back to me. Briody grinned.

"Give me a low pitch, boy!" Crane called, and started to step back inside the box.

"*Nein.*" Klaus Klein shook his head. "No call after first ball delivered to home base."

Crane muttered something. I delivered my next pitch, just above Crane's belt.

"Strike."

He swung at the next pitch, right below the shoulders, but caught nothing but air.

He spit a river of brown juice in my direction, brought the bat up, glaring at me angrily. My arm went into a windmill, and I blew my pitch, aiming for something chest-high but delivering something right at his knees. A perfect pitch for a low-ball specialist like Sam Crane, but by the time he started to swing, Fatty Briody held the ball in that massive mitt.

"The striker is out," Klaus Klein announced.

The crowd hissed, booed, and cursed, only this time at Sam Crane.

Fatty Briody threw the ball back to me. Then he shook his stinging gloved hands, and laughed out loud.

I struck out Patsy Cahill on seven pitches, and then pitcher Charlie Sweeney came to bat.

Sweeney had started out with the Providence Grays back in 1882, but had been expelled from the National League in 1884. I never knew exactly why, although Dave Rowe said it was because "Sweeney's a horse's arse." Sweeney had signed with the Maroons, who at the time played in the Union Association, but when that league folded, St. Louis joined the National League, and here was Sweeney, back in the league that had booted him out. Well, National League officials always had short memories. By the eighth inning, Sweeney was drunker than Pete Conway, yet still a menace at the plate and between the pitcher's lines. He had held us to no runs so far, and already had five hits himself.

"High pitch, girlie," he announced, and stepped to the plate.

He drilled my first pitch, a belt-high fast ball, but Dave Rowe ran it down and caught it on the fly.

Three outs. No runs. As I trotted off the field toward our bench, third baseman Jim Donnelly and shortstop Charley Bassett both ran over to me, and clapped my back. Clapped it pretty hard, almost knocking me to my knees. Mox McQuery spit out tobacco juice, waiting for me on first base and saying—"Nice goin', kid."—as I trotted by.

We gathered at our bench.

Pete Conway began drunkenly slurring the lyrics to "Oh, My Darling Clementine". Behind the bench, Grasshopper Jim Whitney spit out a broken tooth as he cried out for his mother.

"Mox," Dave Rowe announced. "You're up."

McQuery spit tobacco juice into his hands, rubbed them together, and grabbed his bat.

A minute later, he was back on the bench. Charlie Sweeney had struck him out on five pitches.

Sweeney struck out Jim Donnelly, too, but Dave Rowe managed to punch a single just over first baseman Alex McKinnon's head.

"You're up, Silver," Fatty Briody told me.

That bat felt like lead. The crowd booed. As a beer bottle whistled close by my ear, I ducked, tripped, and fell to my knees. Laughter filled the stadium, and Charlie Sweeney laughed the loudest.

"Strike this petticoat out," McKinnon said.

19

I dusted off my pants, and walked to the plate. "High," I said.

"Speak up, girlie." Charlie Sweeney tossed the ball from one hand to the other. "I can't hear you."

"High!"

He waved. "Howdy, yourself. Welcome to the National League."

Even Klaus Klein giggled.

I missed the first pitch. Missed the second. Almost swung at the third, but let it curve outside, and sighed with relief when Klaus Klein said: "Ball."

The crowd hissed.

Sweeney started his wind-up in a windmill approach that mocked my delivery, then fired a ball that came toward my left shoulder. I started to back out of the way, but made myself stay, waiting. Sensing the ball would curve away from my person and toward the plate, I swung.

My hands stung at the contact as I watched the ball sail. I saw Charlie Sweeney's lips mouth an obscenity, and heard the crowd groan.

Suddenly Dave Rowe's string of cusses reached my ears, along with his instructions. "Run, boy. Don't just stand . . . !" Rowe had stopped running, stopped coaching, too. Turning, he stared, watching the ball sail, and sail, and sail.

My first hit in my first National League at-bat landed over the fence—yes, the wind blew hard that afternoon, but, still, knocking a ball over the fence was rare in any baseball league, and even rarer for me. Suddenly I was being pounded at home plate by all of my teammates. Well, all except Pete Conway, who was now slumped in drunken oblivion on our bench, and Grasshopper Jim Whitney, who appeared to be begging his grandmother not to whip him for playing with matches.

And not, of course, Dave Rowe. "This game ain't won yet, boys," he announced, "and can damned sure still be lost."

Bottom of the ninth inning, with shortstop Jack Glasscock waiting at the plate.

Likely you know all about Pebbly Jack Glasscock, too. The Maroons' team captain, he would hit .325 in 1886. Like many corncob-tough catchers, Glasscock refused to play with a glove, and the previous year he had shattered Arthur Irwin's record by making three hundred and ninety-seven assists. That new sporting journal, *The Sporting News*, called him "the greatest player to ever trod Missouri soil, and, perhaps, the best hitter and fielder to play on any diamond anywhere."

Pebbly Jack Glasscock didn't bother to request a high or low pitch. Instead, he said: "I can hit anything you can throw me, boy."

He didn't.

I walked him on seven consecutive pitches.

But I struck out Emmett Seery, and then Alex McKinnon dribbled my fifth pitch. The ball went past me, but second baseman Al Myers scooped it up, touched the bag with his right foot, and, leaping over a sliding, cursing Pebbly Jack Glasscock, fired the ball to Mox McQuery at first base. McQuery caught the ball a good two steps ahead of McKinnon, and the Kansas City Cowboys had won their first National League ball game.

My teammates were all professionals, veterans for the most part, but they acted as if we had just won the championship, or beaten the American Association's St. Louis Browns and not the National League's lowly Maroons. Screaming, tossing gloves and caps into the air, they raced toward me—me!—and carted me off the field on their shoulders. After depositing me by the bench, they ripped off my cap, and sauced my curly hair with St. Louis beer, which several players had sneaked into the stadium.

"Welcome to the National League, kid," McKinnon said.

They pushed Pete Conway off the bench, pounded my back, and someone thrust a bottle of beer into my right hand.

"You got the makin's, boy," Fatty Briody said.

"We need to celebrate," Al Myers said.

"At Dixie Lee's in the West Bottoms," Mox McQuery said.

Dave Rowe cut our celebration short by firing a pistol shot that shattered one of the beer bottles along the first-base line.

"First," he said, "maybe we ought to think about carting Grasshopper Jim off to a doctor."

CHAPTER TWO

"You were born to play baseball," Mother frequently told me. "It was meant to be."

You see, I was born on May 4, 1869, the day the Cincinnati Red Stockings, the world's first professional baseball squad, defeated Cincinnati's Great Westerns, 45-to-9.

No spinning tops or lead soldiers or a—*sigh*—pony for me. I grew up with a baseball in my hand, and likely gummed the end of a bat while teething.

For the record, my parents met in 1867, married the following year, after which they departed western Missouri for St. Louis, where I was born. When I turned eight, we headed back across Missouri, back to Kansas City, where Papa went back to work for the Armour Packing Company, one of our city's seven packing houses, when he was not laying bricks. To be closer to Mother's folks. They didn't slaughter beef at Armour or work as brick masons—Mother's folks, that is—but lived in nearby Independence.

My parents never truly explained why they left Kansas City in the first place, although my gut tells me that such a move was ordained once the Antelopes baseball club folded. St. Louis had provided Papa with a job and plenty of baseball. In 1875, professional baseball arrived in St. Louis.

My father sold lemonade at Brown Stockings' games when he wasn't butchering beef, pigs, and sheep at Fischer & Kronenburger, or slapping mortar on bricks. Indeed, I might have come of age rooting for the Brown Stockings, but in 1877, authorities linked the Brown Stockings to a gambling scandal. Players on St. Louis's first professional baseball team, and one other from Louisville, Kentucky, were charged with fixing games, and both the Brown Stockings and the Grays went out of business. Of course, St. Louis had a lousy team and record in 1877, which might have had more to do with the team's bankruptcy and expulsion from the National League than gambling. Anyway, we moved back to Kansas City, where there wasn't a professional club, but one could find a lot of baseball.

Did I mention that the Armour Packing Company had its own baseball team? Fischer & Kronenburger never fielded even a muffin squad.

Papa wasn't good enough to make the Armour's first nine, but he occasionally landed on the muffin squad, usually in right field, and Mother always cheered him on. Once, he even tried to coach me about how to swing a bat. I happened to be holding the bat at the time and swung it as he instructed me to do. The meat of the bat landed in his ribs. After that, Papa left the coaching to Mother.

For a lady who hadn't attended a ball game until she turned nineteen, you see, Mother developed a keen grasp of the game, and kept up with the ever-changing rules. She could quote Henry Chadwick verbatim.

As an infant and toddler in St. Louis, I have been told, I would sit on her lap as we watched amateur teams play. By the time the Brown Stockings were formed, I'd sit beside her while Papa sold lemonade. Once we had returned to Kansas City, I'd still sit beside her, or take part in games with other children.

As we watched Papa's team play (and usually lose) against teams fielded by firemen, or constables, or saloonkeepers, or other muffins, she would tell me about strategy and position and how to play the game. I always paid attention. Especially when she would say: "You were born to play baseball, Silver."

Born to play baseball? I don't know about that. I liked the game well enough, loved spending time tossing the ball with Mother, or hitting with Papa, yet, at that time, I didn't want to be a baseball player. I wanted to be a cowboy.

Now, Kansas City never became wild and woolly like those true cattle towns to our west such as Dodge City, Abilene, Caldwell, Wichita, or Ellsworth, but it had certain elements. The stockyards, rail yards, and packing houses brought in cowboys and cattlemen, not to mention butchers, skinners, horse traders, muleskinners, and hog merchants. Lewd women, too.

When you couldn't find me practicing baseball with Mother, or with my nose stuck in a *McGuffey's Electic Reader* at the subscription school, or helping Papa lay bricks, everyone knew I'd be around the Armour Packing Company—and not just waiting for Papa's shift to end. For me, I couldn't think of a better area of town that I'd rather visit than the packing houses.

More than one hundred thousand people lived in Kansas City, but the city brought in more than five times as many cattle each year—and roughly two million hogs. I didn't care about pigs and, truthfully, didn't hold much interest in beef.

But how I loved watching cowboys herd the doomed cattle, voices sounding musical though hardly human as they chided the beeves, popping them with the ends of hemp ropes or slapping their dusty chaps with even dustier hats. Granted, they usually worked afoot, but every now and then you'd find a man horseback.

One of those men was Daniel E. Dugdale.

I was fifteen years old in the autumn of 1884 when Dan entered my life. He stood better than six-foot-two in high-heeled boots that were adorned with spurs whose jinglebobs chimed when he walked. Long arms, broad shoulders, a Roman nose and a sun-bronzed face, a well-groomed mustache and sandy hair upon which rested a Boss of the Plains that appeared to have been trampled by a thousand buffalo. A striped pillow-ticking shirt, crimson britches, and a tan vest with a pocket stuffed with a Bull Durham sack and the makings, he had cowboy written over every part of his body.

He saw me staring at him as the last longhorn disappeared, then eased his dun gelding over toward the fence where I sat. Swinging one leg over the saddle horn, he fished out tobacco, rolled a smoke, stuck it between pencil-thin lips, and struck a Lucifer on his thumb.

"You a real cowboy?" I asked.

Smoke blew out of his nostrils as he looked down. He fingered the cigarette, flicked ash, and said: "You think a real cowhand would be working at a packing house?"

I ignored the question.

"Could you teach me how to rope?"

His laugh held no mirth. "You're a forward one, ain't you?"

"I just want to learn how to rope."

"That's some hair you got, boy."

I flushed. Even when you've sported a mane of white hair since practically your birth, you never quite get used to folks commenting on it. My hair wasn't blonde. It was white. Gleaming white. Mother and Papa had named me Charles, but I'd never been called that as long as I can remember.

"My name's Silver," I told him.

"I see why."

After pushing back his hat, he studied me a

bit more carefully, and his face changed from irritation to interest. "That's a baseball you're holding, ain't it?"

Glancing at the ball I had carried with me, I nodded. "My father works for Armour," I said. "We play toss when I meet him before we walk back to our house."

Sort of.

"What time does your pa quit work?"

"Eight o'clock."

He snorted, and took another long drag on the cigarette, looking up at the sky. "I'd say it's . . . oh, three o'clock or thereabouts. You planning on waiting here five more hours?"

I shrugged.

"Shouldn't you be in school?"

"It's Saturday."

"I see."

"How about teaching me how to rope?"

He didn't answer. Instead, he asked: "What was the name of that professional baseball team that played here this past season?"

"The Kaycees." Now, it became my turn to look at him with a certain amount of curiosity. I was relieved when the conversation had moved away from my silver hair. "Some people called them the Unions," I explained. "The newspaper often called them the Onions." I laughed at that, and the cowboy snorted again, grinning this time.

"Played in the Union Association, didn't they?"

I tried to mimic his snort. "Not very well."

Still smiling, he drew on the smoke again.

Kaycees, Unions, Onions, or "lousy muffins" or "consistent losers", they had been Kansas City's first professional team. They had joined the league after the Altoona Mountain City's team folded in Pennsylvania. Kansas City didn't play well that year, winning only sixteen games and finishing last in the Union Association—sixty-one games behind the St. Louis Maroons. Even the Philadelphia Keystones finished ahead of Kansas City. Still, the team sure drew a crowd, and I don't mean just Mother, Papa, and me.

"You like baseball?" he asked.

I nodded. "But I'd rather be a cowboy."

He shook his head. Dust flew off the brim and crown of his hat. "You ain't never cowboyed. What position you play?"

"I started out in center field," I said. "But when they changed the rules, started letting pitchers throw overhanded, I moved to pitcher. Mostly. Moth- . . . uh, some folks say I have a gift for pitching."

"Pitcher, eh? Well, you got the hands for it. Arms, too."

Now, I have always been self-conscious about these hams I have for hands. And my long arms. Way too big for someone my size, way too big for anyone who wasn't a gorilla. But Papa had that side job laying bricks, and when I came

30

of age, I went to work with him. Brick masons don't have hands but calloused giant mitts. Whenever I carried bricks or mortar in a "hod", Papa joked that hauling those heavy loads had stretched my shoulders so much that my arms and hands grew abnormally—which made me a better pitcher.

This cowboy, however, didn't seem to be saying this to me, but to himself, and he ran his tongue over his dried, cracked lips, and flicked more as . The horse began peeing, and the cowboy unhooked his leg, stood in the stirrups, stretching, and pretty much ignoring me. I thought: *This is the rudest man I've ever met.*

Finally, after another drag, he said: "Tell you what, kid. Here's a deal for you. We toss that ball around some. Then I'll try to teach you about roping. That suit you?"

My wide grin answered. He smiled back, opened the gate while still sitting in the saddle, and eased the dun through the opening, closed the gate, and dismounted, wrapping the reins around one of the fence posts. He flicked the cigarette's remnants over the top rail and into the dust and dung inside the corral.

We walked away from the horse to a spot where he drew a line in the dirt. Next, he started walking toward the walls of the Armour Packing Company, counting his steps. When he reached fifty, he stopped, turned, and held out his hands.

Idiot that I was, I told him: "If I'm pitching, you need to squat."

"Not until we loosen our muscles, kid."

So for ten minutes, we threw the ball. Softly at first. Then a bit harder. Finally, he threw the ball to me, then pushed back the brim of his hat. "I'd say that's enough." He squatted, held out his arms, and said: "Let me see what you got, kid."

I showed him.

"Criminy!" The cowhand rose, leaving the ball between his spurs, shaking his hands, biting his bottom lip. Tears welled in his eyes. He rubbed his palms against his chaps, and stared at me for the longest while.

"Who taught you to throw so hard, Silver?" he asked.

I almost answered "Mother," but thought better of it. Instead, I shrugged.

He picked up the ball again, threw it back to me, and fished a pair of gloves out of the pocket on his chaps. Shaking his head as he pulled on the gloves, he looked into the cloudless blue skies, and said: "Lord, don't let any ballist I know see me using these." He squatted again.

For more than an hour, I pitched and he caught.

By my final pitch to him, we had both worked up a sweat. Jutting his jaw toward his horse, he said: "That's enough of that, I warrant." Then he strode bowlegged toward his mount, where he fetched the coiled hemp rope dangling from the saddle horn.

"Not much of a ball game, was it, Danny boy?" someone behind me said.

I hadn't noticed how our throwing session had drawn a few spectators. Three dusty cowboys sat on the top rail of the fence. In front of the gate stood a woman with disheveled hair and wearing only a camisole that barely contained her ample breasts. Two more men—one in a bowler hat and patched britches, the other holding a rake—leaned against the fence on either side of the brown-haired woman.

I stopped and stared. At the woman, of course. And not because she had been the one speaking. No, she was smiling at my catcher, a cigar in her mouth. My mouth dropped open. I'd never seen a woman smoke before, especially not a foul-smelling cigar.

That got the cowboys sitting on the top rail to laugh, and spit, and point at me.

The woman laughed, too, once she had noticed me. She removed the cigar, saying: "Why, ain't you a big, strong boy."

I could barely swallow.

"You do everything as hard as you throw that little ball?"

My face flushed crimson.

My catching partner ignored the laughing men, when he returned with the rope.

33

I couldn't take my eyes off the woman.

"Boy. Hey, boy!" My pard's words finally reached me, and I turned. "You want to learn about roping, or you want to spend time with Molly? My lesson's free. Molly charges six bits."

I wet my lips, bobbed my head, staring at the rope in his hands.

"That's a big rope," I said, just to see if I could still speak.

"It ain't a rope. It's a lariat."

"Lariat." I tested the word.

"Hold the loop lightly," he explained. "About a foot or so from the honda."

"What's the honda?"

He shook his head and rolled his eyes. He pointed at the finger gripping the rope near the coil toward the eye the rope was pushed through. Stepping away from me, he turned and started swinging the rope over his head. "Think of the loop as a wheel," he instructed. "And your wrist as the axle. Swing the loop toward the target. Let your palm open . . . and let 'er fly." He did that.

The loop flew gracefully, and fell over Molly, who had stepped a few rods away from the fence toward us.

My pard then stepped back quickly, pulled the rope, and the loop tightened around the woman's waist. Again, the men chuckled. Molly cursed as she was jerked to her knees.

Suddenly, the rope—*lariat,* I mean—rested in my hands.

"Now you try it," my partner said. "First, you gotta free Molly."

"Or use a piggin' string on her!" shouted the leanest of the cowboys, who sat next to a black cowhand wearing the biggest cowboy hat I'd ever seen.

I didn't need to free Molly who was already on her feet. Still, I walked over to her as she stepped out of the loop. She handed me the lariat, but wasn't looking at me. Her eyes glared at my partner as she said: "Dug Dugdale, I'll whip your arse."

Me? I dropped the rope so I could pick up the cigar she had dropped. Before handing it to her, I tried to blow off the grime and dust that coated it. That got her attention, and she smiled at me, revealing crooked, stained teeth, and not too many, at that.

I looked away, but found my eyes coming back to stare at her breasts. Couldn't help it.

Anyway, that's what I was doing when Mother called out my name in a shrieking voice.

CHAPTER THREE

No point in boring you with the details of the scene that transpired, and no sense in embarrassing myself. Suffice to say that my roping lesson ended abruptly, the cowhands, bums, and harlot vanished, while Dan "Dug" Dugdale tipped his hat back and watched with this smirk on his face, which I would have dearly loved to have made him lose. By the time I got back home, my left ear, having been pinched and twisted by my mother, was inflamed, aching, and redder than my face had been after Molly had spoken to me.

Mother instructed me never to tell Papa what I had seen, or what might have come to pass had she not come along when she had, and that I was never, ever, to go to the corrals of the Armour Packing Company again.

Naturally I returned the next afternoon. After church. And after helping my father on a brick job for a neighbor.

I found no one there, however, just unfortunate cows. So I drifted back to the front yard of our ramshackle house, and began tossing the ball with Papa, while, inside, Mother and her parents fixed chicken and dumplings for supper.

Monday found me back in the subscription school, the oldest, tallest, and strongest of the twenty-seven children under Mr. Stokes's instruction, but as soon as he rang that bell, I gathered my lunch pail, *Reader*, and baseball, and hurried back to the Armour corrals. The cowhands had returned to work—without Molly—but I did not see Dan Dugdale. I walked past the wagon yards, and across the railroad tracks, and then strode past the rows of saloons on Main Street. And the cribs behind the saloons. No Dan. No Molly, either.

Back home, sitting at our supper table, I could only pick at the boiled potatoes.

"Off your feed, Son?" Mother asked.

I moved the fork from the first-base position on my plate to second, and dragged it back past the pitcher's lines to the batter's box as if the fork had hit a long fly ball that resulted in an out.

"You need to eat."

My eyes wandered up from the plate to Mother's face.

"We weren't doing anything," I said.

"What?"

"That cowboy. On Saturday. He was . . ."

"I'll hear none of that." She stiffened, straightening in her chair, and looked around the dining room with a thank-goodness-your-father-is-still-working-and-not-here-to-listen-to-such-shameful-talk look etched in her face.

"He was teaching me to rope."

Her tiny fingers balled into iron fists. Through

clenched teeth she said: "I saw what you were roping!"

"He roped her."

"Indeed."

Silence.

After an eternity, Mother let out a breath. "God did not put you on this earth to be a cowboy, Son." She was trying a different approach. "You have a gift, and an arm meant for striking out batsmen, not lassoing . . . strumpets." The last word came out in a whisper.

"I think he's a ballist."

"A ball . . . a what? Who?"

"Dug Dugdale."

"Who?"

"The cowhand with the lariat."

Those tiny fingers of Mother formed fists again while her arms, resting on the table on either side of the plate, remained as rigid as baseball bats. Her eyes hardened. "Ballist indeed. Cowboys are nefarious scoundrels, Silver. Unkempt, unkind, with no redeeming social graces." She sighed. Heavily. "Not gentlemen like baseball players. Mayhap we never should have left Saint Louis. It is not as rancid a cattle town as Kansas City, and . . ."—a dreamy look replaced her iron countenance—"the Maroons. If only we had known."

The Maroons had replaced the Brown Stockings. They won the Union Association this

38

past season with a 94-to-19 record. Beat the dickens out of K.C.'s Onions every time they met.

Mother's stone face returned. "You stay away from those corrals, young man. You stay away from bad eggs."

Loving my mother as I did, I obeyed her wishes. On Tuesday, I did not go anywhere near the Armour Packing Company corrals. That's because Mother had arranged a muffin game behind the schoolhouse. The weather had turned a little chilly for baseball, but I pitched a good game, and my team won, 33-to-9. That satisfied Mother greatly, and, honestly, I felt pretty good about it, too.

Wednesday, however, I backslid my way to the corrals. Molly wasn't there, but Dan Dugdale sat in the saddle of his dun gelding, slapping the lariat against his chaps, urging longhorns through the doors where a number of Armour employees, my father among them, awaited with sledge-hammers, axes, saws, and knives.

"You're back." Dugdale smiled as he swung from the saddle, wrapping the reins around the fence post.

"I never got a chance to throw the rope," I informed him, and immediately corrected myself. "Lariat, I mean."

"I warrant you didn't." He rolled a cigarette, looking up as he licked the paper. "How's your ear?"

39

Instinctively, I reached for the ear my mother had grabbed and twisted.

A grin spread across Dan's face. "I feared she might have ripped it plumb off."

He didn't light the smoke, just stuck it over his ear, took the rope—lariat, darn it, *lariat!*—from the saddle horn, and stepped away from the horse and corrals.

"You bring the baseball?"

I shook my head sadly.

"That's all right." He handed me the lariat. I felt like the king of Prussia.

"Guess it's harder than it looks." I was sweating despite the autumn chill and a wind that smelled of rain as I handed the lariat back to Dan Dugdale some thirty minutes later.

"So's throwing a five-and-a-quarter-ounce baseball," he said.

That surprised me, but Dan Dugdale had astonished me more than once during our lariat-roping and baseball-throwing sessions. The only other person I knew who could quote the weight of a professional league baseball, without thumbing through the pages of the *Playing Rules of the National League* or *Beadle's Dime Base-Ball Player*, was Mother. Well, I knew it, of course. So did Papa. Mother had drilled it into our brains.

Dan Dugdale secured the lariat to his saddle,

found his cigarette, and fished a Lucifer from a vest pocket, saying: "Speaking of which, why don't we throw some, boy?"

"The name's Silver. Not 'boy'. Silver. My name's Silver King." I didn't say that angrily, I just wanted him to know my name.

He blew smoke across the saddle. "That's one hell of a handle."

"Well, I didn't pick it. It's on account of my hair."

He grinned. "Didn't pick mine, either. Hair color or name. I've known some who have, though. Picked their own names, I mean. Dan Dugdale. So just call me Dug. You can imagine the jokes I've heard about my name."

"Try being Silver King for a week."

His smile widened. Shaking his head, he put the cigarette back in his mouth, removed his hat, which he draped over the saddle horn, and began unbuckling the straps to one of his saddlebags. "How about a catch?"

"I told you," I reminded him, "I left my ball at home."

"Well," he said, lips still holding the smoke, "I might be able to remedy that." His right hand disappeared inside the leather bag.

That's when we heard . . .

The Voice.

I whirled, my face paling, watching my mother charge down the alley, umbrella in her left hand, raising a right hand at me. "Silver King," she said, verifying my name to Dan Dugdale, "I warned you. I told you . . . you . . . about this . . . this . . . this . . . wayfarer. You come home with me this instant, young man."

My right ear began aching, even though she hadn't tried to tear it off, yet. I moved away from the horse, trying to think of an excuse, trying to explain. After all, Dan and I were the only ones around. No cowboys. No Molly or any other soiled dove.

"Best listen to your sister, Silver," Dan Dugdale's voice drawled.

"Sister!" Mother spun. Words choked in her throat, and the umbrella slipped from her fingers. "Sister?" she repeated, but this time much, much softer. "I . . ." Her fists unclenched, and she began brushing the dust off her skirt, then smoothing her hair, before pushing away a stray bang. Next Mother did the damnedest thing. She smiled.

I turned around to face Dan Dugdale, to explain to him that this was my mother, that I was an only child. But words caught in my throat.

He stepped away from the dun, throwing a baseball from left hand to right. On his head was a white cap, two brown stripes on the crown. The type worn by a baseball player. Oh, that cap had stains all over it, dirt and mud and maybe some blood, and I knew those stains had gotten there

42

bouncing around in a leather bag behind a saddle.

"I'm . . . his . . . mother," Mother whispered.

Dan Dugdale's right hand touched the brim of his cap. His left still gripped the well-worn baseball. "I find that hard to believe, ma'am. But it's pleasure, Missus King, to make your acquaintance. I'm Dan Dugdale. Call me Dug."

"Call me Samantha," Mother said.

Honest. That's exactly what she said.

"We were going to have a catch," Dan Dugdale said, and tossed the ball to me. I muffed it, my attention solely on my mother. Truthfully, had I not spotted the ball sailing my direction out of the corner of my eye, it would have knocked my teeth down my throat.

"Well, goodness, it's a nice day for it," Mother was saying as I chased down the ball before it rolled under the fence and into the corral.

He had just turned twenty in October, and had spent the past summer playing for his hometown club in Peoria, Illinois, and later for a team in Keokuk, Iowa. Now he was drifting.

"I got a lethal case of the fiddle-foot," he said, and shoveled a forkful of potatoes into his mouth.

"Where you bound?" Papa asked.

Dan Dugdale swallowed and shrugged. "Wherever I hang my hat. I like baseball. Like cowboying. And gold."

"There aren't any gold mines in Kansas City,"

I told him. *And,* I thought sadly, *not that much baseball. Or cowboys.*

"You're a nice young man," Mother said. "You should settle down, find a nice young girl. You're a good ballplayer. Have you considered trying out for the Unions?"

He reached for his glass of tea. That's right, Mother had brewed tea, and it wasn't even Sunday. She also had brought out our best blue enamel plates, the ones without chips, dents, or rust.

"You've never seen me swing a bat, Missus King." He mopped up the remnants of his plate with cornbread, and Mother didn't scold him the way she would have done had it been me. Hitting is not my strong suit." He laughed. "Some say it's not even in my wardrobe."

I said: "You mean you're not a real cowboy?"

He reached over to tousle my hair. "Not many trail herds or ranches in Peoria, Silver, but our stockyards are impressive."

My heart sank.

"But I've done some cowpunching. Probably will do some more. It struck me when I was down in Sedalia, working in the yards there, that roping was a mighty good way to keep my arms and shoulders loose. That's something I learned from our manager in Keokuk. I haven't been playing baseball as long as some, but I've seen plenty of players come down with the rheumatism. Dead arm. You don't want that. No sir. 'The human arm,' our manager in Keokuk said, 'is not meant to throw a baseball.' That's why I told you, Silver, that we needed to loosen up those muscles with a little soft toss before getting down to serious business. Roping keeps my arm going, and, I warrant, sitting in a saddle toughens up my backside so I can squat behind the plate."

"Maybe you ought to be a doctor," Papa said. "Hang your shingle somewhere."

"I'd be better at it than that pill-roller we had in Peoria."

"How many ranches have you worked at?" I asked.

Mother asked if he wanted any lemon cookies. He did.

Thus, Daniel Edward "Dug" Dugdale became a fixture at our home, supping with us four nights a week, practicing baseball and roping with me, enjoying a pipe with Papa on the porch, and talking baseball with Mother, all through the rest of November and into December. When we were alone, however, Dan Dugdale would regale me with tales of Dodge City—the wickedest cow town of Kansas—of poker games, saloon brawls, and Kansas lawmen. Of panning for gold. And of harrowing escapes from Indians.

By Christmas, however, he was gone.

Silver, the note read, *the fiddle-foot has taken me westward. Best to your folks. See you on the diamond one day maybe. Your pard, Dug.*

• • •

In January, the management of the Kansas City Unions traveled to Milwaukee for the Union Association meeting. Only one other team showed up besides Kansas City, and that was Milwaukee. That's how they found out that the Union Association had dissolved. In St. Louis, the Union Association's Maroons had been accepted into the National League, and that news certainly put Mother in a funk. St. Louis had a National League team, and Kansas City was suddenly without professional baseball even though the Unions seldom played like a professional squad.

In February, however, the Western League of Professional Base Ball Clubs announced that it would field teams in Omaha, Indianapolis, Cleveland, Milwaukee, Toledo, and Kansas City.

Secretly I hoped Dan Dugdale's fiddle-foot might lead him back to Kansas City to try out for the Kansas City Westerns, but it didn't happen.

We cheered the team, anyway. Even when the manager chased the umpire out of town. Even when they played games on Sundays, which riled the Baptists and Catholics and Methodists but not so much the Lutherans or the Israelites or the Presbyterians who preached that baseball wasn't work and indeed was a good way to relax—after Sunday school and preaching, of course, the Presbyterians and Lutherans sermonized. Luckily for us, Mother was Cumberland Presbyterian. And Papa was a backslider.

We even cheered when Keokuk—which had replaced Omaha, which had gone belly-up in June—came in to play our team at Pastime Park. I had hoped to find Dan Dugdale on the team, but, alas, he wasn't there. Keokuk did have Bud Fowler, a Negro, on the team. We cheered him, too, when he turned a double play, and Mother ignored the hisses coming from behind us. Well, no, Mother didn't ignore anything. She turned to face the crowd of Sabbath beer-drinkers and said: "If you cannot appreciate a good play, even when it is turned by our opponent, you lack gentlemanly qualities and perhaps you would be better suited to attend a cockfight rather than a game of skill like baseball."

The hissing stopped.

Shortly after that, so did play in the Western League of Professional Base Ball Clubs. Cleveland and Toledo folded. Kansas City's police force, whose chief was a Baptist, put an end to Sunday games. Indianapolis sold its best players to the National League team in Detroit. Milwaukee quit after Bud Fowler led Keokuk to a three-game sweep of the Brewers. That left two teams in the Western League, and although I didn't think Kansas City could beat Keokuk, a runner-up finish would have satisfied Mother, Papa, and me.

'Twas not meant to be. In July, the league folded. That marked the beginning of a long, bitter summer in which a deadly tornado pretty much destroyed what was left of Pastime Park.

No baseball. Unless you counted the Armour Packing Company's muffins playing the Long Brothers wholesale grocery house. Or Keystone Iron Works versus Yates Ice Company. No roping. No cowboying. No Molly.

Grandma Hollister died in August, and Mother started dropping hints that maybe we should move back to St. Louis.

What saved us was an important announcement by a couple of brew *meisters*, Joseph Heim and Americus McKim.

CHAPTER FOUR

On February 5, 1886, the National League voted to admit a team from Kansas City into its ranks. Professional baseball would be returning to our city that summer, and not just any professional baseball league, but the National League—the old boys, the real pros, the league that had been established in 1876 and replaced the old National Association of Professional Base Ball Players. It was the home of our country's first truly professional baseball team, the Cincinnati Red Stockings, who had won their first game on the day I was born. Well, it had been home to the Red Stockings, but the National League had kicked Cincinnati out of the league back in 1880. It seems that Cincinnati sold beer, and played games on Sundays. Papa told me—when Mother was out of earshot—that the leaders of the National League came straight out of the Old Testament.

Times must have been hard for the National League. Not only did they bring in Kansas City, but also the Washington Nationals and the St. Louis Maroons—making that three cities, or even teams, that had played in the rival Union Association.

Now, what you need to know about Mother is

49

this: she was not the kind of mother who would pull her only son out of school, unless something dreadful had happened. So when she came to get me this day, tears froze on my cheeks as I kept asking her: "What is it? Is it Papa? What's happened?"

"Hush," she said as she let the Negro help her, and then me, inside the hack.

"Take us to the East Bottoms. . . ."

I stopped crying. The driver lifted his head, his eyes widening.

"The Heim Brewing Company," Mother clarified to him.

His mouth went agape.

"Now, sir. Before we freeze to death."

The cabbie whisked us away.

"Joseph Heim?" I asked Mother.

"Of course," she said, and placed the carpetbag on my lap. I knew what I would find inside.

You might not know Joseph Heim personally—which, trust me, is nothing to regret—but likely you have tasted his beer. Or the lager brewed by his brothers, Ferdinand, Jr. and Michael. Or his father, Ferdinand Heim, Sr. Long before I had been born, Joseph Heim's father had left Austria and opened a brewery in Manchester—about twenty miles west of St. Louis—and made a fortune, as residents of St. Louis love their beer. He bought another brewery in east St. Louis, and, back in 1884, his three sons had taken over the

Star Ale Brewery in the slums of Kansas City's East Bottoms.

Mother could forgive a man for producing ardent spirits as some slight foible if he had other redeeming qualities, and Joseph Heim did. He had been one of the owners of the Union Association's Kansas City Unions, and now he and two partners had raised the money and had been accepted into the National League.

When we arrived at our destination, she paid the hack, and practically pulled me up the steps to the Heim Brewing Company office. The place smelled sour, but Mother did not seem to notice. The place felt drab, the walls bare except for a few plaques. One read:

FIRST PLACE
LAGER
Heim Brewing Company
St. Louis Fair
1884

Another announced a second-place finish for bottled beer from the same fair and same year.

Mother found a small, bespectacled man sitting behind a desk and told him she desired to have an interview with Joseph Heim.

The man, chewing on a pencil, looked up. "How 'bout Mike?"

"Joseph," Mama said.

"What's your business?" he asked.

"Mine," she told him, and the man removed the well-dented pencil from his mouth. Leaning back in his chair, he looked my mother over, not even noticing my presence it seemed. When you have a mother who still looks maybe thirty and a lot like Lilly Langtry, you get used to that.

"You got a name?"

"Samantha King."

He glanced at me, but looked back at Mother before I could open my mouth to tell him my name. Not that he had any interest in my name. Or me.

"Lady . . . ," the man began, but a string of profanity cut off his statement.

"You call this barley? I call it horse shit, you flim-flamming son-of-a-bitch!" Not a trace of an Austrian accent.

Turning, we saw Joseph Heim for the first time. We also got a glimpse of a man in a white coat, who ducked as a jar passed just over his head, and shattered on the floor. The man in the white coat disappeared behind another door, and Joseph Heim walked out of that room, and toward us.

He didn't look rich. If he had arrived at the office in a suit, the coat had been removed. His sleeves were rolled up, his tie loosened, and his yellowed teeth clamped a well-chewed cigar. I would not have guessed him to be a brewer of beer or an owner of a professional baseball team. He wasn't small, but you would not call him big. He did wear an impressive cowboy hat and high-heeled boots, which got my attention, but I wouldn't say he looked like any of the cowboys I had seen with Dan Dugdale, either.

Joseph Heim did not notice Mother, or me. He didn't acknowledge Pencil Chewer, just made a beeline for his office. Until Pencil Chewer called out: "Mister Heim, this here Samantha King desires an interview with you!"

The beer brewer whirled, tossed his soggy cigar to the floor, and roared: "Who the hel-*lo.*"

Beaming, he swept off his ten-gallon monstrosity and bowed in front of my mother, took her hand in his (the one not holding that $5 hat), and brought it to his lips. When he released my mother's hand, he stepped back.

"Missus . . . ?"

"King," Pencil Chewer informed him.

"Missus King," Joseph Heim said. "How may I be of service?"

Mother gave the beer king her most Lilly Langtry-ish smile. "This is my son . . ."—the word "son" caused Mr. Heim's smile to fade—"whom you need to sign to play baseball for your National League team this season."

By the time she had come to the word "sign", Heim's hat had returned to his head. At "baseball", he was scowling at Pencil Chewer. By the time Mother finished her introduction, Mr. Heim's face had turned red.

"Criminy . . . what do I pay you for, you worthless bastard?" The beer brewer was speaking to Pencil Chewer, whose face paled—especially compared to Heim's face—as he began stuttering one of those I-didn't-know-what-she-wanted excuses.

"I pay you to . . . never mind," Heim began, but then whirled back to Mother.

"Distillers. Farmers. Everybody in this brewery . . . Folks I don't even know and never wish to know. They all come with some sure-fire, bona-fide professional ballist that I just have to sign. I had to pay twenty-five thousand dollars . . ."

"You and your partners," Pencil Chewer whispered, but Heim did not hear, perhaps because Pencil Chewer only mouthed the words to Mother and me rather than speaking them aloud. Not that Heim would have heard anyway, as loudly as he kept roaring.

"I pay all this money to the National League . . . and that's not all. Twenty-five thousand, plus another five thousand for some stupid-ass fund those rich bastards decided they needed to cover some lame expenses and . . . ahem . . . as a guarantee against violations of any club against the league's constitution. Five grand . . . but only one thousand a year. Installments, you see. Do you know how much beer I have to sell to be able to own this National League team? And then there are people like you coming in off the street to tell me who I need to sign to a contract for another thousand a year? Or more? When I can't even sell my beer at the stadium that I'll own?"

Heim whirled and pointed a thick finger in my face. "Look at this monstrosity. Pimples on his chin and hands the size of . . . Jesus, look at those mitts. How old are you, kid? Don't answer. Let me guess. Twenty-one. Every kid whose pa . . . I'll give you this, lady, you're the first woman who came peddling her boy. Every kid brought in here is twenty-one."

"He's eighteen," Mother said.

Which was a lie. I was seventeen. It didn't matter. Joseph Heim didn't hear as he kept right on raging.

"But that don't even bring into account the one-legged Civil War veteran who swore he could swat the tar out of a baseball. Or the blind Negro. You think I'm gonna put a colored boy on my baseball team? Well, I ain't. And I'm damned sure not gonna put this galoot you call your son on my team. I'm not out to win no damned championship, lady. I bought this team to make me some more damned money!"

He caught his breath. Had to. Or drop dead of an apoplexy right then and there.

As he retrieved a handkerchief to mop his

sweaty brow, Mother gave him a courteous bow and said: "Well, Mister Heim, I thank you for your time, and now I shall go see Mister McKim."

Americus McKim was one of Heim's two partners in the National League team. He was a beer brewer, too. I hoped he wasn't a shouter like Heim.

"Do that, lady. Tell that old college boy that I sent you."

He was inside his office by then. The door slammed.

We left without saying good bye to Pencil Chewer.

From the Heim Brewing Company, Mother and I walked to McKim's office.

Americus McKim had arrived in Kansas City about a decade earlier. In polite society, people noted that he was a player in Kansas City's malt and grain business, which meant that he brewed beer, too. I understood what Heim meant when he had called McKim a college boy. His diploma hung on the wall behind his desk. Franklin College. Athens, Ohio.

He looked fit, slim. Photos of his wife and children lined the desk of his office. I saw nothing about him that reminded me of Joseph Heim, except for a cowboy hat, lying crown down, on the left side of his desk.

"Your partner," Mother told him as his secretary,

a young man with red hair, brought mother a cup of tea, "is quite rude, sir."

"By that," Americus McKim said, "I believe you mean Joseph Heim, and not James Whitfield." He grinned.

Whitfield was the other partner in the new National League team. I read his articles all the time in the Kansas City *Times*.

"Indeed." Mother sipped the tea. "This is fantastic tea, sir."

From behind his desk, Mr. McKim bowed. "I know more than beer, Missus King. And there's one thing you need to know about Joseph Heim, Missus King." Mr. McKim pointed to the diploma hanging on the wall. "If you go inside Joe's office, you'll find one portrait hanging on his wall. It isn't Abraham Lincoln, Napoleon, or his mother or father. It's P.T. Barnum."

Mother set the cup on the side table. "Barnum? The showman?"

"Yes, ma'am. Tom Thumb, Jenny Lind, freaks . . . The Prince of Humbugs himself. My partner wants money, ma'am. And he likes gadgets. Hooks. Something that, in this case, will pull a crowd into a baseball stadium."

McKim turned and examined me. "Your son's far from a dwarf, Missus King. Those hands . . ." His head shook. "I don't think he's another 'Swedish Nightingale'. And despite those large hands, I would not call him a freak, either.

In fact, he's a rather nice-looking young man."

"Thank you, Mister McKim," Mother said.

"Every day after work Joe complains to me that he is deluged by passers-by and friends and acquaintances and total strangers who want to play for our baseball team. I get a few myself. I'm sure Jimmy Whitfield can't get away from any ballist, as editor of the *Times*' sports section. But, ma'am, the day after our purchase of the franchise was announced, a bookmaker told me that our odds of winning the championship were fifty-to-one. I'd like to win, Missus King. Winning means having good baseball players."

"Silver can throw a baseball harder and with more accuracy than any ballist I have ever seen, sir," Mother said, "and, before you ask, I have been watching baseball since Eighteen Sixty-Seven, before Silver was even born."

"Silver . . ." McKim tested the word. "Silver King." He grinned. "Joe Heim would love that name. It might sell tickets."

I held my breath.

"But right now, ma'am, I am busy with the business of getting ready for a baseball season. Getting our stadium in order. Built, I might say. Besides, Heim's the president. My title is vice president and treasurer."

"Meaning that you control the money," Mother said. "Who gets paid and how much."

"In time. But baseball affairs will be left to

Jimmy Whitfield and our manager, Dave Rowe."

"You've hired Dave Rowe?" Well, I had found my voice.

Americus McKim and Mother stared at me. "You've heard of Dave Rowe?" the beer man asked.

I swallowed, but made myself talk. "More about his brother, Jack."

They both waited for more, so I said: "Jack's a catcher, mostly. Been playing with Buffalo. Dave played with the White Stockings in 'Seventy-Seven, but he was with the Maroons in Saint Louis the past two years. I think the National League blacklisted him . . . but for just a year." I caught my breath and, with a grin, added: "They say he has a bit of a wild side."

Mr. McKim grinned at me. "Well, you know a bit about some of the players, I see. Rowe will manage and play center field for us. And his brother Jack has been signed by the Detroit Wolverines. I'm sure that'll please Heim whenever Detroit visits us. Brother against brother. A way to promote the game. Gimmicks. That kind of thing. That's what Joe loves."

The humor left him, and he looked at my mother. "I seriously doubt if even Joe Heim will try to stage some open try-outs. We are, after all, in the National League. We are a professional baseball team, not a bunch of muffins trying to play ball. And right now, my business is coming up with a name for our team. Anything but the Onions."

"Cowboys." I had been admiring McKim's hat.

Again, I found myself being stared at.

Again, I swallowed. "Well, we are in Kansas City. There are a lot of cowboys here. At the packing houses, I mean. Rail yards. There won't be a National League team farther west. West. Cowboys. That's . . ."

"Synonymous," Mother said.

"It is," Mr. McKim agreed. "Quite."

"Mother's first ball game she ever watched was here in Kansas City," I told Mr. McKim. "Wild Bill Hickok was the umpire."

"Indeed," Mr. McKim said. "That's a story I have never heard."

He heard it now. Mother told him the story that she had told me many times. It was her first date with Papa.

"A beautiful afternoon in August back in . . ." She gave Mr. McKim that fabulous wink that was the envy of any coquette. Mr. McKim laughed, and Mother went on without telling him the year.

I knew the year. 1867. I knew the story by heart.

How the Antelopes of Kansas City played their biggest rivals, the Pomeroys from Atchison, Kansas, on a vacant lot between Fourteenth and Oak. How Wild Bill Hickok wore a wide-brimmed sombrero as he called balls, strikes, and everything else. How no one disputed any of his calls during

60

or after the Antelopes' 48-to-28 victory—because Wild Bill wore a brace of Navy Colts stuck, butt-forward, in his sash during the game.

"It was the first, and the greatest, baseball game I ever saw," Mother concluded. "And afterward, a nickel-plated Columbus phaeton drawn by two of the most beautiful gray Connemara stallions ever born, pulled up behind home plate. And Wild Bill turned to face the crowd, tipped his hat, and climbed into the carriage."

By then, she had closed her eyes, picturing her gallant hero. The only thing missing from her version of the event that day at Mr. McKim's office was Papa's epilogue that he would typically add with a wink: "Wild Bill weren't alone in that carriage. No, sir. He had a soiled dove hanging on each arm."

"Fascinating," Mr. McKim said. "A story for the ages."

"So you see, Mister McKim," Mother told him, back to business now, her eyes open and hard, "there is a connection with cowboys to our city. And we are the West. Besides . . . the Kansas City Cowboys . . . there is a ring to it."

"Not the Onions," I said. "Not the Unions."

"The Kansas City Cowboys." Mr. McKim tested the name on his tongue, and then he found a sheet of paper and a pen and wrote down the words. He stared. He looked at his hat. He picked up the Stetson and placed it on his head.

He looked like a clown, but I just nodded with approval.

"What are you doing on Saturday the Twentieth of this month?" Mr. McKim asked.

"Nothing," I said, before Mother could answer.

He wrote something on another sheet of paper, which he handed to Mother. "Ten in the morning, Independence and Lydia. Show this to the guard. And Dave Rowe."

"Independence and Lydia," Mother repeated.

Mr. McKim's smile returned. "That's where we're building our baseball stadium," he said. "League Park. Short for *National* League. The home of the Kansas City Cowboys."

CHAPTER FIVE

March 20, 1886. Cloudy, warm, humid. Mr. McKim had told us to be at the ball park at ten in the morning. Mother and Papa drove me there in their buggy. We arrived at seven-fifteen.

Of course, the place looked deserted—no Mr. Heim, Mr. McKim, not even the guards—and since League Park remained under construction, my parents and I just walked in.

"Criminy," Papa lamented, "they done drained Ranson's Pond."

"It's in the name of progress," Mother told him.

Progress. Baseball. No difference.

Yet Papa was right. For a number of years, this had been a popular swimming pool—named after some old-timer who had settled here back before Kansas City became such a metropolis. When the city decided to build Independence Avenue, the workers had used tons of dirt for the roadbed. That left the hole, which soon became a pond, and now was a baseball field. Loosely speaking, if you asked me.

Granted, my first view of what would become my first professional home field, came before League Park had been finished, but I could see some problems. The playing field lay about twenty-five feet below the ground level, and a high hill surrounded the area. Mr. McKim and Mr. Heim both had said how much they wanted to make money, but I could visualize people parking up on the hilltop to watch the ball game so they didn't have to pay 50¢ to sit in the ball park. Not a good view, maybe, but many Kansas Citians were . . . well . . . skinflints.

"Hey," Papa said, looking around, "we could take the buggy up the hill, just cut off Admiral Boulevard or Virginia, park up yonder, and watch for free."

Like I said . . .

"You'll do no such thing," Mother scolded.

She smiled at me, though, and pointed at a ladder, apparently left by the carpenters, that led from the grandstands, still under construction, down to the playing field. "Go on, Silver," she said, and pulled a baseball from her purse. "Warm up."

"With whom?" I asked.

"Why that nice-looking man down there."

That's when I noticed some fellow standing along the third-base line, doing some trick with a baseball. Nothing fancy, just tossing the ball up lightly, then knocking it with the inside of his forearm to his biceps, which would kick the ball back to his hand. He was right-handed.

"He must be a ballist, too," Papa said. "Maybe he got invited here to join the team."

"Go down, Silver, and introduce yourself. Get

'loose', as that nice Mister Dugdale always said."

Shyly, I made my way to the ladder, dropped my ball and baseball cap over the side, and carefully descended into the hole. Gathering my ball and placing the straw hat back on my head, I walked across the field—which was dirt, except for a few mud puddles from the most recent rain—and stopped a few feet in front of the other player.

The blond mustache, neatly groomed, made him look older than he was. His blue eyes locked on me, but he never blinked. His ears were big, but I figure most ladies would have considered him handsome, even if he was of average height and rail-thin.

"Howdy," I said.

"Yeah." He kept right up with his baseball trick. I wondered if he could juggle, too.

"You here to try out for the team?"

He didn't answer.

"My name's Silver King," I told him.

That caused him to muff the baseball, which landed a few feet in front of me.

"I got it." After picking up the ball, I held it out for him.

Finally, he blinked. "Gee willikins, look at them hands of yours."

My cheeks reddened. He gaped for a few more seconds, then carefully plucked the ball from my massive paws, but he did not resume his one-armed juggling act.

"Name's Bassett," he said. "Charley Bassett."

Now it was my turn to gape. "Are you related to *the* Charlie Bassett?" I sang out.

His eyes narrowed, and he pursed his lips. "Who the hell is *the* Charlie Bassett?"

So I told him what I knew, not letting on that all I had heard came from those stories Dan Dugdale had told me a couple of years ago.

"Why, he's one of the lawmen who helped clean up Dodge City, Kansas. Helped start the Long Branch Saloon, and played poker with the likes of Wyatt Earp, Bat Masterson, and Dug Dugdale. He was sheriff of the county and a deputy marshal, or something like that. Chased train robbers, too."

He started tossing the ball again. I took that to mean that he was no kin to Dodge City lawman Charlie Bassett.

"You want to get loose?" I asked.

Again, he stopped his trick, but this time he did not drop the ball.

"Huh?"

Before I could explain the idea of muscles and such, a pistol shot rang out in the morning air, followed by the first "Jesus-son-of-a-bitching-pig-shitting-asshole-damn-it-all-to-hell-bastard-loving-Christ" I ever heard, with a few other delicately edited bits of profanity that, alas, Mother heard, too.

"Who the hell are you two buckos and what the hell are you doing on my baseball field?"

He was a tad shorter than Charley Bassett, though much stockier, and while I had him beat in the height and weight departments, he certainly wore more scars on his face than Charley Bassett and me combined. Plus, he held one of those self-cocking pistols, nickel-plated, with smoke still wafting from the barrel, which was aimed in the general direction of Charley Bassett and myself.

"I'm . . . uh . . . Silver . . . King," I said.

I should have kept my mouth shut, because now the barrel trained directly on my nose.

"I didn't ask who you are, because I don't give a shit who you are. What I want to know is what you're doing here?"

Mother was shouting something from the grandstand, and the burly cuss in the baseball uniform turned in her direction. He lowered the revolver, and nodded at my mother, even though none of us could hear what she had said.

His tone changed. He wet his lips with his tongue. "Who the hell's that sweet-looking petticoat?" he asked.

"I don't know," Charley Bassett said.

Blushing again, I managed to find the note Mr. McKim had given Mother, and slowly withdrew it from the back pocket of my trousers. The man turned, saw the note, glanced again at my mother and father, and slid the .32 behind his back. He took the note, read it, and swore again.

"Cowboys."

That was another voice, but this one I recognized, and I also remembered the big cowboy hat as Mr. Americus McKim came down the steps—not a rickety ladder—that connected the playing field with the stands, something neither my parents nor I had noticed. Joseph Heim and a sloppily dressed man, smoking a pipe, followed Mr. McKim.

"Where's your mother?" Mr. McKim asked me as he shook my hand, while looking toward the stands.

"Yonder."

"Oh, yeah," Joseph Heim said. "I remember this punk. The little son-of-a-bitch with a buxomly ma who went behind my back."

"And gave us a great name for a baseball team," Mr. McKim said. He had doffed his hat and was bowing in the general direction of my mother.

"Damn it all to hell," the man with the .32 said. "What the hell is going on here?"

"This is Silver King," Mr. McKim said, "a local talent with a wonderful name that we can market like blazes. Right, Joe?" He put his hat back on his head and nudged his partner, then turned to the man with the pipe. "What do you think, Jimmy?"

Which meant that the man with the pipe was the third partner in this baseball franchise, the great sportswriter for the Kansas City *Times*, James Whitfield.

"It's a handle, all right," Whitfield said. The pipe stayed in his mouth.

"Pig shit," the burly man said. "Ain't I supposed to be managing this team? This is the son-of-a-bitching National League. *Professional.* Top of the world. Don't I get a say in who the hell plays for me?"

"You're Dave Rowe?" I sang out.

The man's right hand reached behind his back, and I knew he clutched the Smith & Wesson, waiting for me to say the wrong thing so he could murder me in self-defense.

"You got a problem with me, boy? I owe you money? Got your sister in the family way?"

"No, sir," I said. "I just admire the way you play. Or what I've read about you in Mister Whitfield's articles in the *Times.*"

"Jesus, Mary, and Joseph!" That came from Charley Bassett. "You'll lick anybody's boots, won't you, boy?" He stopped, dropped the ball, and realized his mistake. Now everyone, including me, was staring at him. The only difference was that I wanted to pound him beneath the ground.

"You got a letter, too, I warrant," Dave Rowe said, but at least he had left his revolver behind his back. "Or at least a name?"

"Charley Bassett," he said.

Rowe glanced at Heim, then Whitfield, each of whom shrugged, but McKim stepped closer, looking the young man up and down. "Charlie Bassett's son?"

I'll give Charley Bassett credit. Seeing Mr. McKim's big Stetson, hearing the comments about cowboys, Charley Bassett learned quickly.

"That's right. From Dodge City."

"By thunder, isn't this something?" In a furious handshake, Mr. McKim worked Charley Bassett's arm like the pump to a dry well. "I knew your father . . . not well, but sold him my beer. He ran the Marble Hall Saloon in our fair city for a year or so, till he sold it and headed back west. Where's your father now, son?"

"Probably chasing train robbers," Bassett said, "somewhere in the West. Maybe playing poker with Wyatt Earp, Bat Masterson, or Dug Dugdale."

"By grab, that's something. Wonderful. Just wonderful." Still gripping Bassett's hand, Mr. McKim turned to explain to Rowe, Heim, Whitfield, and the other ballists who had begun descending the stairs into the hole. "He's the son of a great Kansas lawman. You can get even more publicity out of this, Joe. The son of a Dodge City great . . . he helped organize that Peace Commission in Dodge three, four years back." At length he released Bassett's hand, but kept marveling as he laughed. "Playing poker with Wyatt Earp and . . ." McKim's expression changed. "Who's Dug Dugdale?"

Now it was my turn to grin, but Charley Bassett showed he was no stranger to the world of lies.

"A tough *hombre* out in the frontier," he said, and looked at me, "but he'd lick my pa's boots just so he could play poker."

"Poker?" A giant of a man stepped toward Dave Rowe. "I thought we come here to play baseball?"

CHAPTER SIX

Which is what we did all that morning, through dinnertime, and into the afternoon.

Not all the ballplayers had arrived when we began. After all, Mr. McKim had told me to be there at ten in the morning, and I doubted if it was past eight now. The arrival of the seven or eight ballists that early, though, impressed me. This is what it took to be a professional ballist, I thought. Dedication to the game. Practicing every waking minute.

The fat catcher, though, shattered that dream.

"Most of the boys is still in their cups, Skip," the brute said to Dave Rowe. "And you'll need to bail two of 'em out of jail."

"That's a job for McKim or Heim. Or you, Whitfield." Dave Rowe sneered, not at the owners, but at Charley Bassett and me. "I got my own designs," Rowe said. "To rid us of some rotten eggs."

Luckily for me, Dave Rowe decided to test Charley Bassett first.

"All right, Mister Kansas Shootist," he said. "What position do you play?"

"Anywhere on the infield," Bassett said, "except first base."

"Get to second base." Rowe fetched a bat,

stared at me, then nodded at the big man who had made the poker comment. "Fatty," he said, "this tall drink of water fancies hisself a pitcher. See what he can do."

So while Dave Rowe smacked ground balls to Charley Bassett at second base, I walked to the pitcher's line and began throwing to Charles Briody, a fat man with the pudgy face of a child. Some people called him Alderman, but to most fans and friends, he was simply Fatty, a proper sobriquet for a man who topped two hundred and fifty pounds.

Crack went Rowe's bat. Another *crack* sounded when Bassett snagged the ball and drilled a perfect strike to Mox McQuery at first base. And *slap* went Fatty Briody's hands when I fired a fast ball to him.

He screamed, stood, shook his hands, and hurried to the bench along third base where most of the real professional ballists had left their satchels, baseball bats, sacks of Bull Durham or plugs of chewing tobacco, and liquor bottles. While other players laughed, Briody found two gloves of black leather—one with fingers, the other without—and pulled them over his beefy hands. He was right-handed, so he put the fingerless glove on that hand, for a better grip and dexterity when he had to throw the ball.

Even the players who likewise wore fingerless

gloves (only one glove, of course, pulled over the non-throwing hand) tormented Briody.

"Fatty!" Dave Rowe pointed. "You . . ."—he stopped, remembering Mother was sitting in the stands, and whispered—"you said you wouldn't be caught dead catching with gloves."

"Said I wouldn't be caught dead catchin' a baseball," Fatty clarified. "A cannonball. That's different, Skip."

That stopped Rowe for a minute, and he dismissed Charley Bassett. "Go over to shortstop," he told the young man who was no kin to a Kansas lawman. "Throw with Myers and Donnelly for a bit. I'll deal with you later."

Briody squatted and held his now slightly protected hands a good six feet behind home base, a twelve-inch diamond of white stone.

"Well . . . ?" Dave Rowe was leaning on his bat maybe a foot outside the batter's box. "Throw it, boy."

I did. Fatty Briody grunted, but caught the ball with both hands, pulling the ball into his ample gut. He stood and stared defiantly at Rowe.

"That's heat, Skip," he said.

"And a ball. Eight inches inside."

"Umpire's gotta be able to see it to make that call, Skip. And a batter can't hit what he can't see."

"Bullshit." Rowe straightened, hefted the bat, and stepped inside the batsman's lines. "All right, Silverado, pitch to me."

Holding the ball against my side with my left arm, I wiped the sweat off my palms, and tried to swallow.

"Strike him out, kid!" the big first baseman, Mox McQuery, said with a snort.

"He can't hit. That's why he's playing for Kansas City," came a cry from one of our outfielders.

"Come on, Silver." I stared across the infield at Charley Bassett, who grinned and repeated his encouragement. I guess as a rookie, he had decided that we should join forces, after all. Besides, I hadn't sold him out and let Mr. McKim or anyone know that his relationship to former Sheriff Charles Bassett of Ford County, Kansas, was as close as my relationship to King Arthur.

Briody settled into his stance, and I began wind-milling my arm, then zipping a fast ball.

Crack!

With a grimace, I turned to watch the ball I had just pitched—my baseball, not one belonging to the Kansas City Cowboys—bounce off the fence.

"Can't hit what you can't see, eh, Fatty?" Dave Rowe chuckled.

"I can see that's a foul ball, Skip," Briody said.

"Bullshit."

"Foul," Briody repeated. "By a good ten feet."

Dave Rowe spun, but nods from Whitfield, McKim, and two pitchers standing against the catcher's fence behind home plate, Grasshopper

Jim Whitney, and Stump Weidman, confirmed the catcher's call.

Cursing again, Dave Rowe returned to the plate, bent his knees, swiveled his bat, and glared. "All right, Silver Queen, try it again."

I did, and Rowe swung so hard he practically corkscrewed himself into the dirt.

"Strike two!" Grasshopper Jim Whitney said with a chuckle.

"The Beaneaters don't miss you in Boston, Jim," Rowe snapped at the pitcher. Pushing himself to his feet and brushing the dirt off the knees of his britches, Rowe gave Whitney a cold star. "And you sure as hell ain't been here long enough for them to miss you in Kansas City after I send your ass to the Western League."

Then, lowering the giant bat, Rowe spit into the palms of his hand and dropped to his knees to grind his hands in the dirt. Satisfied, he picked up the bat, tapped it against the ground, and rose to step inside the batsman's lines. "All right, Silver," he said. "Strike me out, if you can."

I couldn't.

Dave Rowe was thirty-one years old, tougher than a cob and meaner than a rattlesnake. He had been playing professional baseball since 1877, in the National League, American Association, Union Association, and on semi-professional clubs from Baltimore to Denver. Besides, I hadn't forgotten that .32 he still kept tucked inside his belt behind his back. Would he shoot me dead if I struck him out? It's hard to pitch when that kind of fear eyes you in the face. And Dave Rowe had one awful stare when he had two strikes on him.

I tried, however. After all, my parents were up in the grandstands. Yet Dave Rowe showed me that he was a pro, and that I was a seventeen-year-old kid out of his league. He fouled off three consecutive pitches, then laid off one I threw, on purpose, far outside.

"You're gutless," Rowe said.

This time, I did the glaring, and threw my last pitch to Rowe. I didn't strike him out, but I sure as hell fooled him. Taking off most of the speed on my pitch, I watched, quite pleased with my cunning, as Rowe dribbled a weak roller toward third base, where third baseman Jim Donnelly fell to his knees laughing hard at the pathetic hit. Dave Rowe wasn't laughing, though, for he was a true baseball player, and as soon as he made contact, he ran as hard as he could to reach first base.

He didn't make it there in time, though.

"Criminy!" Finally the pipe had left James Whitfield's mouth.

Something zipped past my ear, and I realized it was the baseball. Charley Bassett had sprinted from deep at shortstop, and closer to second base, to bare-hand the ball and throw it while his momentum carried him toward Fatty Briody. I turned just in time to see Mox McQuery secure the catch a step ahead of the charging Dave Rowe, who ran through the bag, and turned to see McQuery shaking his head.

Rowe strung together another long curse.

"You're out!" James Whitfield said with a chuckle, and tapped the pipe bowl against the third-base bench.

"Yeah, well I didn't call my pitch," Rowe said. That was another thing that impressed me about Dave Rowe. As hard as he had run, and as old as he was, he did not look winded in the least. "Hell, if I'd called high, I would have sent that ball to Topeka!"

"Which would've been foul, too," said Mr. McKim.

Rowe, forgetting all about Mother in the stands, cursed foully and furiously.

So I made the team. Mr. McKim said he would bring contracts to the park for Bassett and me on Monday. After that first practice or try-out or audition, or whatever you want to call it, however, Dave Rowe let me know that there was one big difference between making a baseball club and actually being a part of a baseball team. "McKim wants you, boy," he whispered. "I don't. I hope your long-handle underwear is tough, kid. 'Cause you're gonna find out how hard, and how many splinters, there is on a baseball bench."

Now, I'm not sure what kind of deal Mother made with the schoolmaster, but it sure wasn't to my liking. I would practice with the Kansas City Cowboys from morning to dusk, come home, and burn the coal oil while I pored through my *Reader*, doing all sorts of ciphering and writing. Mother would take my homework to school the next morning while Papa would drop me off at League Park on his way to the packing house.

For the next three weeks, we practiced as the carpenters finished the stadium, and McKim and Heim thought of gimmicks they could use so Whitfield—and the other Kansas City newspapers—would write stories to bring spectators into League Park, or, as most of my teammates had begun to call it, The Hole.

Eventually we began practicing against other baseball teams. I rarely pitched except at batting practice, so I spent most of the time chasing down baseballs. To Dave Rowe, I was nothing, and my anger festered when I realized that Charley Bassett would likely earn a starting position on the team. On the other hand, I could not deny that Bassett was a wonderful infielder.

So I sat on the bench when we played games against muffin teams from Independence, St. Joseph, and Fort Leavenworth. But during that spring, I learned a few things from my teammates.

William Thomas "Mox" McQuery, a Kentucky-born bear of a man, not yet twenty-five, had played for the Outlaw Reds of Cincinnati's Union Association team in '84 and the Detroit Wolverines the previous year. McQuery loved baseball, but I think another dream drove him. He kept asking Charley Bassett about what it took to be a lawman like his pa. Charley told him, although I knew Charley Bassett had no idea. I wondered what Bassett's real father did.

Second baseman Al "Cod" Myers, another slender mustachioed man in his early twenties, had spent one year in the Union Association (Milwaukee) and one in the National League (Philadelphia). He loved baseball. He loved gin even more.

Third baseman Jim Donnelly, another pro ballist but, like me, not even old enough to vote had spent part of 1884 with the American Association's Indianapolis team and, in 1885, started with the Hoosiers, then playing in the Western League, before joining the National League's Detroit team. He stood out because, like me, he didn't have a mustache. Fatty Briody said he couldn't even grow one.

Outfielder "Shorty" Paul Radford, no taller than five-foot-six, no older than twenty-four, had three National League seasons under his belt, one with Boston and two with Providence.

No one could understand how Shorty's short legs could carry him across the dirt outfield so quickly. The man wasn't built for speed, but he damned sure had it.

Outfielder Jim Lillie, who had spent the previous three seasons with Buffalo in the National League, was always stealing Myers's gin, and getting into fights.

Pete Conway, only nineteen years old, pitched and played outfield, and instead of packing a .32 Smith & Wesson on the field, he carried a flask filled with rye in his back pocket. "Grasshopper" Jim Whitney, our star twenty-eight-year-old pitcher, had recorded one winning season in five years pitching for the Boston Beaneaters. Stump Weidman, who also spent time on the pitcher's line or in the outfield, was twenty-five years old and a veteran of six years in the National League, the previous five with Detroit. Utility player George Baker, a twenty-eight-year-old, had wandered about the American Association, Union Association, and National League. His best trick was polishing off Myers's gin bottle while Myers and Lillie were fighting.

Most of them hailed from the North—Connecticut, Illinois, New York, Massachusetts, Pennsylvania, Rhode Island—where baseball had been born. Mox McQuery was the only one who hailed from the South, if you considered Kentucky the South, and George Baker and I were the only Missouri talent, Baker hailing from St. Louis.

"Cowboys." Dave Rowe spit tobacco juice between his legs. Practice had ended, and Lillie was straddling Myers, punching him in the head, cursing the gin-stealer. Some of the players circled our brawlers, but most, by that time, had grown bored with the usual after-practice fisticuffs.

"That's what we got here, ain't it?" Rowe said to no one in particular, and shifted the quid from one cheek to the other.

"How's that?" I asked, making the mistake of thinking Dave Rowe would actually be speaking to me.

Rowe didn't look at me, but rather Fatty Briody. "Cowboys. Outcasts. Misfits. Sure ain't no base-ball team, is it, Fatty?"

Fatty Briody shrugged. "Season ain't started yet, Skip."

"Bullshit. Damned season's already over."

I sighed, and watched the fight. Mother had told me that a great manager inspired his team to play beyond expectations. Dave Rowe merely bent over, picked up the gin bottle that had started the most recent Lillie-Myers two-round bout, and polished off the gin.

There were other players, of course, but some rarely showed up for practice, and if they did, they were too hung over to offer much help. Two of them, pitchers I kept being told, always sat on the bench playing poker.

James Whitfield showed up on most days, teeth chewing down on the pipe stem as he frowned, his hands deep in the pockets of his frayed, moth-eaten suit. Every now and then he would walk onto the field after practice and chat up a few players, usually Grasshopper Jim or Dave Rowe, but more often he just interviewed Mr. Heim or Mr. McKim about their plans, so I got to read wonderful articles about "hokey-pokeys", which would replace cigars and peanuts as the staples of baseball games.

Of course, ever the good son, whenever I went home after practice, before starting my school lessons, I told Mother and Papa how great we were doing, how friendly my teammates were, how much I was learning about professional baseball.

Then the rains came, and League Park began to revert to its previous form of Ranson's Pond. The poker-playing pitchers took their cards and their money into the grandstands to find some shelter. Soon, we had to join them because The Hole turned into a quagmire.

Yet it was on one of those typical rainy afternoons, too humid, too wet for the spring mosquitoes, that Mr. McKim called out my name at the grandstand where we all sat. An angel stood beside him. My mouth dropped open. He waved his arm at me again.

"If you ain't going up there, I sure as hell am," Charley Bassett said, grinning. Through everything, we had become friends. It must have been a rookie bond. I even forgot how jealous I was that he played more than I did. Hell, James Whitfield played more than I did.

Then Dave Rowe made some vile comment, and, fearing that that foul brute would ascend the steps, I sprang from my seat, and sprinted to Americus McKim, who said the most magical words I had ever heard.

"Silver, this is Cindy, my daughter. She wanted to meet you."

"It's a pleasure," she said, curtseying while blushing.

"Ummm," said I.

She wore a jacket of cream-colored French cashmere, with matching skirt, blue lace stripes at the bottom, black velvet shoulder straps and faceted pearls on the collars. Out of my league, I knew, for I was a seventeen-year-old son of a man who slaughtered livestock for a living when he wasn't laying bricks. Besides, I was playing with a bunch of ruffians and drunks on a National League team.

Mother had once called baseball players "gentlemen" and cowboys "nefarious scoundrels". Ballists sure weren't gentlemanly when you took the field with them.

Cindy McKim looked nothing like Mr. McKim.

Yet even though I had been staring at plug-uglies like Fatty Briody or Mox McQuery for weeks, I knew she was beautiful.

Her blue eyes sparkled, her blonde hair had been delicately curled, and her lips reminded me of strawberries—the fruit, not the scrapes on my thighs I had gotten chasing after a Fatty Briody line drive before the rains started washing out practice.

"I need to chat with Dave and Joe for a minute," Mr. McKim said. "You two stay here, out of the rain. I'll be back in ten minutes, no more."

I guess he left. I wasn't certain.

"Ummm," I repeated.

She nodded back in agreement, and I remained uncomfortably silent.

My brain, of course, kept telling me all sorts of things to say, but my mouth sealed shut and my tongue weighed fifty pounds during the time Cindy and I were alone. I felt certain Mr. McKim had not been gone ten minutes when he came back to where we stood like baseball bats leaning against the railing out of the rain.

"Come along, Cindy," Mr. McKim said. "Else we'll both catch our death out in this weather. Are you faring well, Silver?"

I said: "Ummm."

"Stadium's looking great, isn't it?"

Knowing I had lost all of my vocabulary, I

made my head bob. Later, it struck me that he had complimented his stadium. He hadn't said: "Team's looking great, isn't it?" Which would have been a shameless falsehood.

"Nice talking to you . . . Silver. Maybe . . . I'll see you . . . again . . . real soon."

The angel, Cindy McKim, had said something . . . something . . . wonderful. Then she said something even more remarkable. "I absolutely love your hair. It's beautiful."

"Howdy," I said.

She laughed again. So did Mr. McKim, but like that they were gone, and Dave Rowe was screaming at me to come join the rest of the team on the front row. So I descended the steps into hell, but thought I might climb out if Cindy McKim were to return tomorrow.

Dave Rowe shattered that illusion.

"The hell with this," he said. "We can't do nothing in these turd-floats. We're going to Denver."

CHAPTER SEVEN

"Permanent?" I said.

Everyone, even the card-playing hurlers, laughed.

I felt like the green idiot that I was.

"You dumb oaf," Dave Rowe said. "Barnstorm a bit. Play a few games against the locals. Then come back before the season starts at the end of the month."

"Why Denver?" Donnelly asked.

"Because I like Denver. Been hanging my hat there when I ain't been playing. Played some ball there before. We'll let McKim's boys finish this stadium . . . if it don't sink into the bog . . . and then we can play baseball."

"And drink?" Pete Conway asked.

"And drink." Dave Rowe grinned.

"Gamble?" Stump Weidman asked.

"Yep."

"Run whores?" George Baker asked.

"Now you're talking," Dave Rowe said.

Before we boarded the special train Mr. McKim had leased from the Union Pacific—which had taken over the old Kansas Pacific Railway a few years back—Joseph Heim arrived at the railroad station in a beer wagon filled with trunks, instead of kegs. As his driver set the brake, Heim, like a man either giddy with excitement or drunk on his own beer, leaped into the bed and motioned us, and two Negro porters, to hurry over.

"They came!" he shouted. "They came!"

I looked around, but the only people who had arrived to see us off were Mother and Papa, and a couple of prostitutes from along the East Bottoms, standing in the shadows, who were sad to see some of their best customers disappear for a week.

They, we learned, were not spectators or baseball enthusiasts. *They* were uniforms. Pants and collared shirts the color of chocolate, with large tan letters, K and C, on either side of the four-button front. The belts, like our shoes, were black, but our stockings were maroon.

Then Joseph Heim, who I had found to be the rudest man I'd ever met—before I came into contact with Dave Rowe—pulled out our caps. "McKim," he cried out, unable to contain his excitement like a boy on Christmas morning, "said we ought to wear cowboy hats, but I knew better! Look like a baseball team, play like a baseball team."

He tossed me the first cap out of one of the boxes. A short-visored woolen cap, also maroon like our stockings, that sported four narrow rows of black braid. I took off my straw hat and tried it on. It didn't fit, too small, for, like my hands, my head was also unnaturally huge. Pete Conway snatched it off my head. It fit him a little snug, also, but he did not complain.

"We should have another set of uniforms when you get back from Colorado," Heim said. "Those'll be white . . . blue stockings and belts and caps. That's what McKim wanted. But I figured the dirt won't show up as much on these brown ones."

"Silver's ma'll appreciate that," Fatty Briody said.

Everyone, even Mother, laughed. Everyone, that is, except Dave Rowe. "Like that snot-nose'll ever get off my bench," he whispered in my ear, before he walked to the side of the wagon and hollered at Heim to give him his uniform.

"Brown and red'll hide the blood, too," Mox McQuery said.

Which prompted a few more good-natured chuckles.

Mr. McKim arrived as the other players got their uniforms. He frowned at the brown and maroon uniforms, but said nothing as he tipped another porter to take his luggage to one of the Pullmans. I frowned. Cindy McKim wasn't with him.

Eventually I got another cap, one that did fit, if barely. By then Mother and Papa had come to my side, my mother smiling with so much pleasure that it pained me. Papa merely nodded, and handed me a greasy sack of food to eat on the long train trip to Colorado. I set the sack down near my grip. Papa shook my greasy hand. Mama got on her tiptoes and kissed my cheek.

"You look dashing," she said. "I'm so proud of you. You look just like a ballist."

At least I'll look like a ballist, I told myself, *even if I'm not really a player on this team.*

Never had I left Missouri, and I did not remember much about the train ride we had taken when I was little. I grabbed a seat by the window, excited, forgetting all about my baseball troubles. It wasn't long before I was watching Kansas fly past me. After a few hours, however, Kansas no longer excited me, so I ate the smelly food Papa had given me. By then, darkness had fallen, and the rocking of the coach was making me sleepy.

"Where do we sleep?" I asked Fatty Briody.

He chuckled. "We ain't McKim, Silver. We sleep right here."

I slept well, though on that long train ride west, I would wake at every stop along the U.P. line. I woke up and stared at the pitch blackness that was Dodge City, and wondered what Charley Bassett, the liar, would say if someone asked him to point out the Long Branch Saloon. Charley, of course, kept tossing and turning two rows ahead of me. The only noise coming from our car were snores.

· · ·

When I stepped onto the platform at the Denver depot and saw the mountains, the bright white snow capping their rugged tops like crowns on kings, all I could say was: "Wow!" And see the frost from my breath.

"Wow's right," Mox McQuery said. "It's colder than a witch's teat."

"The son-of-a-bitching calendar says it's April, don't it?" Stump Weidman lamented.

"It did," Cod Myers said, and took a pull from his bottle of gin. "But that was back in Kansas City."

"Yeah." Fatty Briody stretched. "We been on that train since forever."

"Quit belly-aching, you bastards," Dave Rowe said. He pointed. "That's the trolley. It'll take you gents to the ball park to practice. See you turds tomorrow for breakfast before the game. And I do my drinking at the Exchange and at Victoria's Parlor. Remember that."

Our manager and center fielder picked up his grip, pulled down his hat, and strode across the platform to meet four men in overcoats. They shook hands, piled into a carriage, and disappeared in to the bustling city at the edge of the Rocky Mountains.

"Remember that, kid," Fatty told me. "Stay out of the Exchange and Victoria's."

I gave Fatty Briody my dumbest look.

"Dave's our manager. Managers don't drink with players."

"Oh." I had no intention of doing any drinking, and no intention of being anywhere around Dave Rowe. That's all I needed to say, but I kept right on talking. "A cowboy I knew, a good friend of mine, he once told me that trail bosses didn't like to drink with cowboys, either."

"Jesus!" Charley Bassett picked up his grip and walked to the trolley. "You'd rather be a cowboy than a baseball player, wouldn't you?"

The wind felt as raw as Denver looked, so we took our bags and bats and hurried after Charley Bassett to the horse-pulled trolley that had been reserved for us. I knew that by the crudely painted sign hanging from the top.

WELCOME TO DENVER, K.C. BALLISTS
WE'LL KICK THE TAR OUT OF YOU SOBs

"Should we go to the hotel first?" I asked Fatty Briody, who chuckled.

"Hotel? Boy, we're on the road for three games against a Western League team."

"Hotels cost money," Pete Conway said.

Briody laughed. "Hotels is for sleepin'. We're here to do some serious gamblin' and drinkin'."

"No sleep?" I asked. "We're here for two days."

One game Thursday, followed by a double-header on Friday.

"Kid," Shorty Radford said. "You sleep after the season."

But, as professional baseball players, they did want to see the stadium where we would play.

All right, stadium didn't quite describe Larimer Street Base Ball Park, but neither did vacant lot. It stretched out between Thirty-Second and Larimer Streets, but the field appeared level and, unlike Kansas City's League Park, grass covered the outfield. A few blades could be seen poking out of the patches of ice.

Not that we had reason to complain, for League Field had little going for it, but we quickly stopped looking at the baseball field. The players practicing on it commanded our attention.

They donned gold uniforms with red lettering on fancy shield-front shirts, stockings, belts, and striped caps—and they not only looked like a baseball team, they played like one, too.

"I thought this Western League of Professional Baseball Clubs was composed of unprofessionals," Pete Conway stated.

"And that we come to play a bunch of hayseeds," Shorty Radford said. "Miners, you know. Cowboys."

"We're the Cowboys," whispered Cod Myers.

"I ain't afraid of them," Charley Bassett said.

"Hell, kid," McQuery said, "I ain't afraid of

'em, either. But they sure look like they can kick our ass."

One of the Denver players spotted us and ran from right field to greet us. Well, *ran* isn't the right word. The boy flew. I mean, his speed made Shorty Radford look more like Mox McQuery or Fatty Briody.

"Howdy," he said, and starting pumping our hands. "My name's George. George Tebeau. Welcome, fellows. I was born in Saint Louis, so it's good to see some Midwestern boys. Yes, sir. We're sure glad to have you-all come to Denver. What do you think? Lots of big things happening up here in Denver. Big things. I know it's nothing like those big cities where you-all often go to play baseball. Man . . . Playing baseball in New York or Boston or Philadelphia. Gosh. That's just something I've always dreamed of. Well, I'm talking too much, but, golly, I'm just so excited I can't hardly stand it. You probably come here to practice. Well, let me get those fellows off the field. You got a few hours before the sun goes down, then it'll be too cold to play any baseball till tomorrow. Where are you-all staying? Boy . . . A real National League baseball team. Man. I'd sure like to be playing at that level someday. Where's Dave? Dave Rowe? No, don't tell me. He's been coming here since 'Eighty-Three, so I know where I'd find him. Ha! Man. A real National League baseball team. Boy, tomorrow's going to be something." He turned and yelled: "Clear the field, gents! Let a real team show us how baseball's played!" And he sprinted to help usher his teammates off the field.

"Damn," whispered Fatty Briody. "That bastard talks faster than he even runs."

"What'd he say his name was?" Charley Bassett asked.

"Tebeau," Shorty Radford answered. "George Tebeau. Don't look like no Frenchy."

"Don't look like no Missourian, either," George Baker said. "No Missouri boy ever run like that."

Yes, if you know your baseball, you might even recollect the name of George Tebeau. He would help lead the Denver Mountain Lions to the Western League title in 1886. The next year, he would join the beer-and-whiskey league's Cincinnati club, spend two more years with those Red Stockings, another with Toledo's American Association team, and join the National League, finishing his career with the great Cleveland Spiders in 1895 before returning to Denver to manage several Western League teams.

"They's watching us," one of the card-playing pitchers said.

"All right." Mox McQuery took command. "Let's show 'em what National League professionals look like. Intimidate 'em, so they'll fear us tomorrow." So we sprinted as hard as we could to the visitors' bench, including Fatty Briody.

"God . . . A'- . . . mighty!" Grasshopper Jim Whitney pressed both hands against the bench and tried to suck in air. Even Shorty Radford sank to his knees, gasping: "Can't . . . catch . . . my breath." Chests heaving, the two poker-playing pitchers cursed, crossed themselves, and slowly walked toward second base to help Fatty Briody to the bench, or, perhaps, a hospital— if Denver had one. I sat down and lowered my head between my legs, wondering if I would hurl all the coffee and peanuts and Papa's greasy food from my innards.

"We're a mile high!" George Tebeau hollered from the home bench. "The air's real thin. Takes some getting used to."

"Hell," another member of the Mountain Lions yelled. "Could be worse! You-all could be playing in Leadville!"

"Be nice, Darby," George Tebeau told the big cur. "They aren't used to this altitude."

Somehow, I managed to raise my head. The Larimer Street Base Ball Park slowly stopped spinning, and my eyes found that they could still focus at five thousand feet above sea level.

With a hideous laugh, the burly man—whose name we would soon know as Darby O'Brien— led his teammates off the playing field. All except one. That one, who had been catching, pulled off his gloves, stuffed them and his striped ball cap into a saddlebag, and replaced it with a battered old Stetson. After settling onto the bench, he began to roll a cigarette.

Even in my delirium, I thought that he looked familiar.

"Do we practice, Mox?" Fatty Briody asked in a voice that begged for McQuery to forget that foolish idea.

"Got to . . . can't let 'em . . . show us . . . up."

"Give me a minute," I said. I sucked in a deep breath, which singed my lungs with frostbite, and somehow managed to walk down the third-base line, turn at the plate, and stop as the Mountain Lions catcher fired up his smoke, took a long pull, and grinned after he exhaled.

"Dug?" I called out skeptically. It couldn't be.

"Been a long time, kid. You roped Molly lately?"

CHAPTER EIGHT

I took Dan Dugdale over to meet my teammates, who were still trying to catch their breath. Since all of the other Mountain Lions had left the ball park, Mox McQuery decided that we did not need to practice after all.

"Let's find the hotel," McQuery said.

"I thought we didn't have a hotel," I said.

Everyone, even Dan Dugdale, laughed.

"Kid," Fatty Briody said, "you're greener than a cucumber. Not that I plan on sleepin' in it, but we's got rooms at the Albany. You's bunkin' with me . . . if I ever shows up." Fatty nodded at Dan.

"I know where the Albany is," Dan said. "I'll get him there, if that's all right with you."

"Sure." Fatty Briody stuck out his hand, and Dan took it, then made his way through all the men with handshakes. Everyone wished him good luck in tomorrow's game.

"Now," Fatty said as I followed Dan back to Denver's bench, "who the hell can help me to that damned trolley?"

"Where have you been?" I asked.

We sat at the practically empty counter in some ramshackle restaurant on Tennyson Street, which wasn't any more than a corridor for street cars.

"Wherever I hung my hat." Dan smiled at the waitress as she topped off his coffee. He pulled off a corner of a piece of toast, and popped it in his mouth.

"What brought you to Denver?"

"Gold." He laughed. "One of my weaknesses, if you remember. 'Course, I didn't find any pay dirt, but I found baseball." He reached for the cup, blew on the hot brew, and took a sip. "Damn," he said in a whisper, "you're on a National League team. You . . . a kid I met at a packing plant."

"You're a professional ballist, too," I told him.

He drank more coffee before lowering the cup. "Big difference, Silver, between the Western League and the National League. How much they paying you?"

I almost spit out the milk. Dan Dugdale laughed. "You don't have to tell me. I've forgotten my manners."

Green as that proverbial cucumber, I figured that I could tell Dan that. Friends didn't keep secrets. He had asked me. I should tell him.

"Sixteen hundred dollars."

Mother and Papa had decided we would stop renting and buy a house. I didn't tell Dan that. I did whip the napkin off my lap and help him and the waitress, who had hurried back, to mop up the coffee he had spilled on his plate and the counter.

Dan was standing, so I figured I needed to do some explaining. "I mean, that's the contract.

It's spread out over the year . . . I mean, as long as we're playing. I mean, I think Mister McKim liked my mother so much . . . that's why . . . I mean . . . is that a lot of money, Dug?"

He turned, glaring, but the anger died in his eyes almost instantly, and he sat back on the seat as the waitress carried the soggy dishrag and empty cup away. Dan stared at his water-logged toast, shook his head, and began to roll a smoke.

"A dollar a day 'punching cattle. Five dollars a game catching for the Mountain Lions. Yeah, Silver, I'll warrant that, for five months' work, that is a right tidy sum."

I tried to do some arithmetic in my head. A dollar a day. Five months. Thirty days, roughly, per month. Dan would make $150 punching cattle while I was playing baseball. But, he was also playing for the Mountain Lions—$5 a game. That would . . . be . . . if Denver played, say, a hundred games. So . . . $500. But if he also cowboyed at the same time, like I had been going to school and playing professional baseball— well, not really going to school, but at least doing my lessons. I tried to think faster than George "White Wings" Tebeau could talk. Quickly I stopped. Mother, and the schoolmaster, Mr. Stokes, would have been proud of my ciphering. I wasn't. I felt ashamed.

"Maybe . . ." I tried to find the right words. "Mister McKim . . . he's one of the owners . . .

maybe . . . Well, Dug, it's like this. They love cowboys, Mister McKim and his partner, Mister Heim. They like gimmicks, I think that's the word they used. You're a bona-fide real cowboy, Dug, not like that fake Charley Bassett, though Charley's a real good infielder. So . . . well . . . perhaps I could see about getting you on the . . ."

I stopped. Dan's glare had returned. He could stare even harder at a body than Dave Rowe.

"Is that what I am to you, Silver?" he asked. "A gimmick."

The waitress brought over a fresh cup of coffee, but Dan waved her off. Instead, he fished out some coins from a vest pocket.

"Let me . . . ," I started, but Dan snapped: "No!"

He laid the change on the counter, pulled on the hat he had placed on the empty stool to his right, and nodded curtly at me. "Your hotel's at Seventeenth and Stout. Street car can get you there. See you tomorrow, Silver, at the park."

Once again, Dan Dugdale walked out of my life.

If I felt bad at that café, I felt worse when I reached the Albany Hotel. Four stories of impeccable design that seemed to cover the entire block. A Negro in a uniform opened the door for me and offered to help with my satchels, but I shook my head. My misery worsened as I stepped onto the Persian velvet that covered the entire floor of the lobby. Fires crackled, smelling faintly of piñon, in the fireplaces guarded by screens adorned with bronze peacocks.

"Welcome," a bespectacled, bald man said from behind a mahogany and marble counter. "You're the first of the Cowboys to check in, sir. We wish you a most enjoyable stay. Your name, please?"

"His name is Silver," Cindy McKim said. "Silver King. He's our best hurler."

I had not seen her on the train, just her father as he had boarded, but, of course, we players did not have Pullman sleepers.

"Howdy . . . ," I said.

"We've been through that before," Cindy said with a smile. "Haven't we?"

I couldn't answer yet because the clerk had spun around the register, pointing where I should sign. After I had done that, he snapped his fingers, and, magically, another man appeared who picked up my bags and made for the stair-case. "Room Two-Oh-Three," the clerk said, and handed me the key.

"I should . . . ," I said to Cindy, but did not move.

"You needn't go with the bellman. He has a pass key," Cindy told me. "You should tip him."

"Oh . . ." He had reached the stunning stair-case.

"When he comes back downstairs is fine,"

Cindy told me. She walked to a plush sofa that faced the fireplace. "You look down, Silver," she said. "Is it because of Mister Rowe?"

"No," I said, and realized I had actually spoken to her. Yet the conversation ended because at that moment her father walked out of the dining room and, smiling, walked to the sofa, where Cindy and I both stood.

I took his proffered hand and shook it. "Good evening, sir," I said.

"Fine city, isn't it, this Denver?" he said. "I'm not sure even Kansas City has a hotel as nice as this. How's your room?"

"Ummm . . ."

Cindy laughed.

"Well, son, you should get a good night's rest. Tomorrow's an important game for us Cowboys. Come along, Cindy. We'll have a busy day tomorrow, too. Busy . . ."—he was practically beaming—"beating the stuffing out of those Mountain Lions."

The team's treasurer, who was paying me an ungodly sum of money to play a game, led the angel away—and just when I'd begun to start up a regular conversation with her. Worse, the bellman had come down the stairs and was making a beeline right for me.

Me? Who hadn't gotten the chance to ask Cindy McKim just how much I was supposed to pay this fellow.

The next day didn't fare any better. My bedraggled teammates, winded by the altitude and aching from their night of debauchery, played like a bunch of muffins. We lost, 12-to-3. Dan Dugdale, catching, got two hits and tagged out speedy Radford twice when Shorty tried to score from second base on Dave Rowe's line drives into the outfield. Denver's real star that day, however, was Darby O'Brien, who crushed two home runs and added a triple before Stump Weidman learned to just walk him on seven consecutive pitches.

The Mountain Lions proved gracious winners, however, waving us over to where four grateful supporters had deposited two kegs of beer. I didn't feel like drinking, or seeing Dan Dugdale, so I sneaked off and took the trolley back to the hotel. Alas, I didn't see Cindy McKim, either, and so I sadly went up to Room 203, and slept fitfully until Fatty Briody staggered in around two that morning, crashed onto the bed we had to share, wet the sheets with urine, and began some hideous noise that he claimed, the next morning, was snoring.

Pete Conway pitched the first game of our Friday double-header. We lost that one, too, though we played a lot better in a 3-to-1 loss. By we, of course, I mean everyone on our team except me.

I had become nothing more than a water boy, or the kid they sent to chase down a foul ball so we could keep playing the game.

Immediately after that loss, we started the last game with Grasshopper Jim Whitney tossing for us against left-hander Harry Salisbury, who had pitched for the Troy Trojans several years earlier and the Pittsburgh Alleghenys of the American Association in 1882.

"These ain't a bunch of hard-rock miners," Mox McQuery said as he settled on the bench next to Dave Rowe.

"Never said they were," Rowe mumbled.

"They're a damned good baseball team," McQuery said.

Rowe spit tobacco juice onto the ground. "Just because they beat us don't make them a good team, Mox."

We were good, however, that afternoon. So were the Mountain Lions. By the seventh inning, neither team had scored. In fact, the only two hits of the game had come off Darby O'Brien's bat, and both times O'Brien never made it past first base.

In the bottom of the seventh, however, Grasshopper Jim, uniform drenched in sweat, and his face pale, eyes bloodshot, kneeled down at the bench in front of Dave Rowe. His nose poured blood.

"Dave," he said in an ugly whisper, "I'm

finished." He pressed a wadded-up handkerchief against his bleeding nose.

"The hell do you mean?" Rowe demanded.

"It's this . . . damned . . . thin air." Lowering the bloody rag, he held up his right hand and extended the fingers to reveal blisters on the tips of his first two fingers and the thumb. "Besides, I can't pitch . . . with these."

"Blisters?" Rowe spit again. "Horseshit."

Grasshopper Jim turned, spit, wiped blood from his lips and returned the rag to his nose.

"Must be the air," Mox McQuery said. "Snot in my nose is drier than a lime-burner's hat."

"Had a nosebleed last night myself," Charley Bassett conceded.

"Shut the hell up," Dave Rowe snapped.

"Skip," Fatty Briody said as he pulled on his gloves, "this ain't no real game. Real season starts the end of this month." He nodded his two chins at our ace pitcher. "And we'll need 'em fingers of Grasshopper's then."

Rowe stared up at our fat catcher. "Who in the Jesus-son-of-a-bitching-pig-shitting-asshole-damn-it-all-to-hell-bastard-loving-Christ hell appointed you manager of this team, Fatty?"

"I'm just sayin' . . ." Fatty Briody hobbled off to home base.

Dave Rowe bent to lace up his shoes, pulled the cap down on his head, and cursed again. "Rub some butter on those blisters, Jim. Or blood.

Son-of-a-bitching hell." Spinning, he yelled at the umpire, a tall man who worked for one of the railroads in Denver: "Mundt . . . Grasshopper hurt his fingertips, the crybaby. So I'm replacing him with . . ." He stared at the bench, and his eyes finally fell on me. His grin chilled me. "You're right, Fatty," Rowe said, although our catcher had moved far out of earshot by then. "This ain't no real game." He raised his voice. "Silver King. Silver King's my new pitcher."

The men and women who packed the stands and sidelines at Larimer Street Base Ball Park roared so hard, the Rocky Mountains probably trembled.

CHAPTER NINE

When the laughter finally faded, I threw four pitches to loosen my muscles, then stopped. The rumble from the grandstands had resumed, not the cackles and hoots and insults at my name, but rather shouts of approval. That's when I saw, strolling from the Denver bench, the big man, Darby O'Brien.

The Darby O'Brien if you've followed professional baseball for any length of time. Darby O'Brien, a solid, tall, twenty-two-year-old product of Illinois whose time in Denver, Colorado, would end after the Mountain Lions won the Western League championship. The star who would earn the nickname "Flaming" Darby O'Brien while powering the New York Metropolitans and Brooklyn Bridegrooms, losing to the New York Giants in the 1889 World Series but winning the following year against the Louisville Colonels.

"Low," he said, and stepped to the plate.

He did not move, didn't even blink, as my arm went into the windmill imitation, and I released a ball that flew like a bullet into Fatty Briody's hands.

"Chhheee-riiiisstt!" the catcher wailed.

"Strike," the umpire said, and tried not to laugh as Briody tried to shake feeling back into his stinging hands. O'Brien squatted to pick up the ball and throw it back to me.

"Thanks," I said.

O'Brien just nodded, gripped his bat, and waited.

Fatty Briody finally moved back about two feet, pointed at the inside corner of home base, and spit tobacco juice.

Wetting my lips, I tried to control my breathing, tried not to throw up in front of two thousand Westerners. I rifled another pitch, and again O'Brien watched it without moving.

"Ye-ow!" Fatty cried.

"Strike two!" shouted the umpire.

Minutes later, Fatty Briody nodded again, and set up his hands on the inside corner.

I pitched, and, this time, Darby O'Brien swung the bat with speed I'd never seen or even imagined. I didn't hear the contact, but I turned and saw Dave Rowe running toward the fence in center field. The ball did not leave Larimer Street Base Ball Park, but by the time Dave Rowe had caught up with it and thrown the ball to Charley Bassett, Darby O'Brien was walking to the bench, receiving slaps on his back by the rest of the Mountain Lions.

The next batter was Dan Dugdale.

I swallowed. Dan's boots scratched the dirt like a bull's hoofs. Fatty Briody set up outside. I delivered exactly where he wanted me to throw, but Dan Dugdale, unlike Darby O'Brien, did not watch. He swung. And that ball cleared the fence in right field.

Right fielder Bill Mountjoy doubled. Third baseman Frank Meinke sent a cannon blast that should have scored Mountjoy, but Charley Bassett robbed him by knocking the ball to the ground. He couldn't get Mountjoy or Meinke out, but he had saved a run. Not that it mattered. Shortstop Dave Butler sent my first pitch into right-center field, stopping at first base to watch his two teammates score.

"Time!" Dave Rowe yelled, and trotted in from center field. Straight for the pitcher's lines— with murder in his eyes, and his right hand reaching behind his back. I swallowed down fear and bile, but Dave pulled out a plug of tobacco, not his Smith & Wesson, and waited for Fatty Briody to join us.

"Kid's throwin' faster than lightnin', Skip," Briody said. "Exactly where I show'm. Never seen the likes."

Rowe bit off a mouthful and began working the tobacco with his teeth.

"My hands hurt like hell, Skip," Briody whined.

Dave Rowe made an indelicate remark about what our catcher could do with his smarting hands. Then he spit tobacco juice onto my shoes. First he addressed my catcher. "I don't give a damn about your hand, Fatty. Your nose ain't bleeding, and you ain't got blisters, yet, have you? God A'mighty. I remember back when baseball players were tough."

Next, he whirled and jabbed a finger against my chest. "You'll stay on this mound, boy. Till hell freezes over. And if you get out of this inning before we have to catch the eastbound for home, well, that'll be too bad. Because you're gonna come right back out. I don't care if we lose ten thousand to squat. I'm gonna show that asshole McKim just what kind of talent you got, boy. And I'm gonna laugh when McKim tears up that contract and leaves you at the depot. Jesus-son-of-a-bitching-pig-shitting-asshole-damn-it-all-to-hell-bastard-loving-Christ, what a shameful embarrassment you are to the entire son-of-a-bitching sport."

With those words of encouragement, Dave Rowe returned to center field.

"Let's try a curve ball, Silver," Fatty Briody suggested.

The Mountain Lions hit that, too.

Somehow, however, I got out of that inning, and we trailed only 7-to-0. True to his word, Dave Rowe sent me back to pitch in the eighth inning, and I did much, much better. When we led off the top of the ninth, we trailed by thirteen runs.

Baseball, of course, is a funny game. Strange things happen, and they started happening for us in our last at-bat.

I walked. Maybe I shouldn't have. The crowd

certainly thought the last pitch to me was a strike, but Mundt called it Ball Seven, and I trotted to first base. Cod Myers and Mox McQuery reached base, too, but Fatty Briody, his hands still smarting, struck out.

Some man in the stands stood up to shout: "I just want to know who the hell's the National League?"

The folks around him laughed, as did a few on the Denver bench.

Then Dave Rowe came to the plate, and showed the Denver crowd just who the hell the National League was. The second pitch he saw went farther than anything anyone had ever seen in Denver. Four hundred and ten feet, folks said, and I wouldn't argue with that estimate. Dave had cut the Mountain Lions' lead to 13-to-4. Rowe would hit another homer in that extraordinary inning as we just kept piecing together run after run.

The crowd began shifting nervously—13-to-5 . . . 13-to-6 . . . 13-to-8 . . . 13-to-9 . . . Again, Fatty Briody struck out. Two outs. Just one out from a Denver sweep. Rowe followed with his second home run, scoring Myers and McQuery, and we trailed 13-to-12.

By now, the crowd had fallen into a church-like silence.

Jim Donnelly walked to put the tying run on first base, then he stole second base. Shorty

Radford then hit a weak roller to third base, but Shorty knew how to run, and when the umpire yelled—"Safe!"—we had runners on first and third.

Jim Lillie lined a shot that the third baseman, Frank Harris, couldn't snag, but he kept the ball in the infield, and caused Rowe to scream and curse and stomp on his cap. "Donnelly, you dumb bastard! Two outs! You should be running on contact. You son-of-a-bitch. If we lose this game, you're walking back to Kansas City . . . if I don't shoot your sorry ass first!"

Bases loaded, and Charley Bassett at home base, and me swinging a bat on deck.

I don't think I'd ever seen a walk cause so many spectators to curse, groan, and even force a few to walk out of the ball park in disgust. Charley Bassett jogged to first base, and Jim Donnelly touched home to tie the score. We had scored thirteen runs in one inning. That's what a National League team can do. And I, sick to my stomach, approached the plate with the chance to drive in the go-ahead run . . . or runs.

"Come on, Silver!" Cindy McKim's voice did not steady my nerves.

Four balls, two strikes, and two foul balls later, I stared at Harry Salisbury, who did not look tired in the least, even if, in one lousy inning, he had been hammered by our batters.

"You're hanging tough, Silver."

I blinked. Dan Dugdale, catching, was speaking to me.

"He's a good pitcher," I said. "I've never faced a left-hander before . . . not batting, I mean."

"You're a good pitcher, too," he told me.

Salisbury was kneeling now, tying his laces, rubbing his throwing hand in the dirt.

I looked at Dan Dugdale, squatting behind me, holding one fat-looking glove in his left hand, and a fingerless one in his right. He had been catching with those all day, and while the players on our bench had heckled him off and on, Dan didn't seem to mind.

"You are, too, Silver. A good pitcher. Never seen anyone throw as hard as you, kid."

Relief swept through me. Dan Dugdale, who I had angered two nights earlier, was grinning at me.

"Not today," I said.

"Balderdash. Things happen. You had command all day. I saw that. You threw exactly where you wanted to. So we hit you. Hell, we've hit a lot of great pitchers. And that includes Pete Conway and Stump Weidman. Remember. Everyone has a bad day. Some days, I couldn't rope a steer to save my life."

"How about Molly?" I asked.

He spit, snorted, and nodded toward Salisbury. "Best get ready, Silver," he said softly. "Expect a licorice ball."

I did. Salisbury had been rubbing the ball, putting a high shine on it. He didn't discolor the baseball, not even damage it, but it made the baseball do weird things. Kind of the opposite of the spitball. It came in high, which is where I had called it, floating like a watermelon that I couldn't miss, shining like a beacon that begged me to knock it out to Wyoming. But Dan Dugdale had warned me. Licorice ball. I had thrown some shine balls myself. Even today. Which way would it break? Left? Right?

Down, I told myself. *Away.*

I swung.

I knew I'd made solid contact, and immediately dropped the bat and took off running. My teammates on the bench leaped up and screamed. Watching, even Dave Rowe stood. Charley Bassett, Jim Lillie, and Shorty Radford ran around the bases. My eyes tracked down the ball, and I saw it flying deep into right field. I saw something else, too, almost a blur.

George "White Wings" Tebeau had found an angle and chased after the ball.

"No!" I said, and ran harder, as if that would stop Denver's right fielder. As I reached second base, and turned to third, I looked back, saw Tebeau leap into the air, saw the ball fall neatly into his black glove and bare left hand. I heard the crowd erupt in cheers, and I stopped running, turned, and saw Tebeau bounce off the ground, coming up immediately and showing the umpire the ball he had—somehow—caught and held on to.

"The striker is out!" Mundt yelled.

Well, at least we had tied the score. I just had to get us through the bottom of the ninth inning. Fatty Briody came up to me as he pulled on his thin gloves and whispered in a nasal whine. "Curve balls, kid." He blinked. "My old hands just can't take no more of your heat, Silver. Curve balls. That suit you?"

"Sure." How could I argue with Fatty Briody, whose face looked like a chubby infant? Even if he had pissed in our bed and kept me up all night with his God-awful snoring.

The first batsman I faced was Dan Dugdale. The last batter I faced was Dan Dugdale. The first pitch I threw was a curve ball. It hung. And Dan Dugdale knocked it to the center-field fence and scored easily.

"Hell's bells," I heard Dave Rowe say, and I was already walking to the bench, knowing I had just lost the game. The spectators screamed. The Mountain Lions rushed off the bench to congratulate my cowboy pal as he scored the game-winning run on a monster home run that some miner said, after he paced off the distance, had traveled five hundred feet.

"Nice going, boy," Dave Rowe told me. "You lost the son-of-a-bitching game for us." Our manager and center fielder didn't even wait around to shake hands or help tap and drain two more kegs of Colorado beer.

I just sat on the bench, head down, with Fatty Briody.

"Don't kick yourself, kid," Fatty told me. "It happens. Happens to Grasshopper. Happens to everybody. You threw well. They just hit it. They just hit everything. Must be the damned air."

"It is."

We looked up. Dan Dugdale held out his right hand.

Fatty Briody grinned. "Nothin' personal, Catch', but . . ." He held up his reddened palms.

"I've got something that might help out with that." Dan Dugdale pulled out that massive pad he had been catching with . . . the one my teammates had been ridiculing him for using. Fatty Briody studied it.

"They'd laugh at me if I used that pillow, mister," he said.

"They laughed at me, too," Dan told them. "Then they stopped laughing."

Squatting, Dan pulled the padded black glove over his left hand. On his right, he wore the fingerless leather glove that most players wore.

"I was playing on a team in Peoria," Dan explained. "Last year. Harry Decker, my teammate, came up with this idea. Split fingers tormented Harry when he had to catch, so he started tinkering. He started with a fingerless glove . . . like this one . . ." Dan held up his right hand. "He slipped some raw beefsteak between the glove and his hand. That worked, and I tried it, too. Problem was, playing for Peoria, a steak a day proved more than we could justify as an expense. So Harry put shot in the glove's pocket and leather on top of the shot. Next, he added more stuffing, rags and the like, and laced the fingers on the back of the glove. Finally, I told him maybe if we put some felt in it, that would do the job. And it has."

Dan stood, and held out the glove. "It's yours, Briody. If you want it."

"I couldn't take your glove, Catch'," Fatty said.

"You need it. Pitchers here . . . they don't throw the heat that young Mister King throws. And I can make another mitt for myself. Reminds me of when I cowboyed, and spent the winter mending tack."

Standing, Fatty rose and tried on the glove, gently. He looked over his shoulder, waiting for the jokes, but the Cowboys were drinking beer with the Mountain Lions. "Thanks, mister. Those were two hellish hits you rocked today. First one must've gone a mile before it come back to earth. And that one that won the game? Hell, it must be two miles to that fence in center."

Dan Dugdale laughed. "It's the thin air, Briody. Trust me, if the National League ever puts a baseball team here in Denver, folks will be lamenting how far the balls go, saying it's not fair to the rest of the teams."

He looked at me. "Sorry about the other night, Silver. Hell, I was jealous. Cowboys are human. And . . ."

He stopped. Americus McKim had come to our bench. He wasn't drinking any of the Denver beer. He was frowning.

I shot to my feet. "Mister McKim," I said, and pointed at Dan. "This is Dug. I mean, Dan . . . Daniel Dugdale."

"Yes." McKim had no interest. "Fatty, take that . . . um . . . pillow . . . and . . . well . . ." He stopped to study Dan. "Dug Dugdale. I've heard that name before."

"You have?" Dan looked as if he had been run over by an elk.

Mr. McKim shook his head. "No matter. Good hitting today, sir. Solid game you played all the way around." Complimenting an opposing player—after our team had been swept in three games—took a lot out of Mr. McKim, yet I didn't notice any anger in the team owner's eyes.

Actually, I felt excited, thinking, in my ignorance, that McKim might offer Dan a contract. "He's . . . ," I began, but Americus McKim silenced me with a stare that rivaled Dave Rowe's.

"If you two gentlemen will excuse me," my boss said, "I need to have a private word with Master King here."

CHAPTER TEN

I knew what was coming. Truthfully, after giving up fourteen runs in three innings, I couldn't argue that I didn't deserve to be terminated. All I could hope for was that Americus McKim would at least give me a train ticket back to Missouri.

When the malt and grain man sat on the bench beside me, I expected him to put his arm over my shoulder in some fatherly, comforting fashion, but he just stared at the baseball field, vacant, except for our two card-playing pitchers who were drinking from beer steins over at second base, away from the rest of the Colorado and Kansas City ballists.

"There is a big difference between Joseph Heim and myself," Mr. McKim said. "All Joe is interested in is making money. He'd sell his soul if he thought that would bring in more people to League Park. I want to win, damn it." He ground his teeth, clenched his fists, and turned quickly to stare at me with malevolent eyes. "We lost all three games . . . to this . . . bunch . . . of rabble!"

Rabble? Actually I thought the Denver Mountain Lions played like true ballists. They had fun. They knew the game, and played like professionals. They even shared their kegs of beer, and their manager didn't carry a self-cocking

Smith & Wesson and preach drinking, gambling, and consorting with lewd women. Knowing their catcher the way I did, I felt certain that Dan Dugdale did not come into his hotel room at some unholy hour, pass out, and wet the bed.

I did not, of course, contradict Mr. McKim.

Dave Rowe was never fun to be around, at a ball park or on a train. Fatty Briody, on the other hand, was a miserable person to share a hotel bed with, but, on the baseball field, he was a joy, and one of my few defenders on the Cowboys team. Joseph Heim was Joseph Heim, usually angry, but constantly scheming. And here was Americus McKim, who had been so polite, thoughtful, helpful, and patient with Mother and me. Yet now . . .

Baseball, I started to learn, brought out the best in some people. In others, it helped some inner demon take control, and that lust to win had turned Mr. McKim into a monster.

"You stunk today, boy," he said. "Blew the game for us."

I could have argued that Pete Conway and Stump Weidman had done no better in the two games they started, or reminded him that Dave Rowe, our star and our manager, had struck out seven times in the three-game series. But I just made my head bob, and tried not to cry.

He blew out a hot breath. "Your mother," he said, shaking his head, "is a nice lady. Anyway

. . . well, King, we all make mistakes. And I'm afraid that . . ."

"Yes, Father," Cindy McKim said once she had covered the distance from the gate in the fence to the visiting team's bench. "Like that first batch of beer you brewed. Remember?"

Unclenching his hands, Mr. McKim tried to take control of his emotions, but he remained angry, and I feared he would take out his frustrations about my lousy pitching on his beautiful daughter.

"Cindy," he said in a rough whisper, "you need to . . ."

But his daughter just gave him, and me, one of those radiant smiles.

"You see," she said nonchalantly, though I somehow understood that she had come to my rescue. "Father always tells us this story. He says the first batch of beer he brewed wasn't fit for an outhouse." She laughed. "Father can be so salty sometimes."

"Cindy. . . ." His fists had balled again, and, this time, his knuckles started to turn white.

"Yet . . . ," Cindy began as she settled between us. "And this is what Father always says is so important. That's why he always tells the story. That foul batch of beer did not stop him. 'If you don't learn from your mistakes,' Father always tells us, 'then you have no chance to improve. You'll go on to repeat those same mistakes.' " She shook her head, and gripped her father's fist with her left hand and my left hand with her right.

Her hand on mine felt so wonderful that I no longer feared getting kicked off the Kansas City Cowboys.

"Father says we must not let failure bother us. Everyone fails. It's how you respond to such mistakes that makes you better. Isn't that right, Father?"

Mister McKim's mouth moved this way and that without actually opening, and his eyes burned with rage as they bore through his daughter, then me, and then . . . looked up.

Dan Dugdale was back, holding two steins of beer. He held one out to me, and, confused, I took it.

"Sir," Dan said, shaking his head and chuckling softly. "I don't know where you found this young hurler, sir, but . . . well . . . I'll be glad to see him back to Kansas City. That last hit of mine? The one that won the game. Pure luck. I didn't even see the damned ball. Pardon my salty language, ma'am," he added as his eyes darted at Cindy.

His stein clinked mine, and Dan walked back to join the celebration.

"What was his name?" Cindy McKim asked.

I set the beer down. "Ummm. Dug. Daniel Dugdale. We just call him Dug."

"Dugdale." Cindy's father spoke again. "I know I've heard that name before."

"He played for Peoria last year," I said.

Mr. McKim no longer looked angry. The fist that wasn't being held by his daughter relaxed, and he brought it up to rub his nose and eyes. "Well . . . ," was all he could manage to say.

"What did you learn today, Silver?" Cindy asked.

I had to think.

"Yes," Mr. McKim said, but his voice had lost that sharp edge. "What did you learn?"

"Well . . ." It struck me then. I even grinned. "Well, I learned that I can throw a ball exactly where I want to throw it. And that I can throw it pretty danged fast and hard." Then I laughed. "And Dug taught me that if you throw a ball hard enough, and a savvy batsman connects, well . . ." Now Cindy giggled, too, and her father's lips turned upward, though I wouldn't say he smiled exactly. "That a good batsman can send that ball over the moon."

Cindy released both of our hands. "So, what do you do with that bad batch of beer you brewed today, Silver?"

My head bobbed. I thought I understood.

"I . . . toss it . . . out."

"Exactly." That didn't come from Cindy. It came from Mr. McKim. He stared straight at me now, no longer expressing that feeling of doom.

"I have to learn where to pitch to these players,"

124

I said. "They hit today, but they were hitting hard every game. Mix up my pitches more. Like I did when I kept Dave Rowe off his feed that first time, back in March."

Now Mr. McKim laughed. He slapped his knee. "Remember how Rowe looked? He swung so hard he practically drilled himself into the ground?"

Cindy pushed herself to her feet. "Grasshopper Jim Whitney once told me how he did in the first professional game he ever pitched. He said the town pretty much wanted to buy him a one-way ticket back to Conklin."

With a whistle, I shook my head. "He sure pitched well today."

"Yes," Cindy said. "Because he threw out that bad batch of beer."

"Speaking of beer," Mr. McKim said, and he rose, too. "I think I should sample how Colorado makes porter."

So I handed him my stein. He laughed, took a sip, wiped the foam off his upper lip, and began walking toward the Mountain Lions and Cowboys. "If you two shall excuse me. Cindy, I will see you at the Albany. Master King, I hope you will join us for supper before we catch the nine-twenty-seven train back to Kansas City."

For the longest time, I just sat on the bench. Somehow, I still had a spot on Kansas City's roster. I couldn't understand what had just happened, but then I looked up into those lovely blue eyes of Cindy McKim.

"Thank you," I said.

She shrugged. "That Dug Dugdale probably deserves the thanks more than I do. Papa gets into moods like these. He's a different person when he steps inside a baseball park for a game. A total stranger. Says things he later regrets. He might have told you to go to thunder, but tomorrow morning he would have offered you more money to come back to the team."

I smiled. "Maybe I thanked you too soon."

She laughed, and offered me both of her hands. I took them, feeling the tingling that ran from my fingertips to my shoes. She pulled me to my feet.

"Come on," she said. "Walk me back to the Albany Hotel."

She held out her arm toward me, and for once that day I wasn't greener than a cucumber, so I didn't turn down such an invitation.

First though, I looked back, and I saw that Dan Dugdale was gone. That filled me with regret.

"What's the matter?" Cindy asked.

"Oh . . . Dug . . . the catcher . . . he's gone."

"Don't worry," she said. "You'll see him again."

"How can you know for sure?"

"Because a ballist who can hit like that isn't going to be in the Western League forever."

126

I shook my head. "Dug once told me that hitting wasn't his strong suit."

"He lied," Cindy said.

It was a great walk. We didn't take the trolley. We walked, arm in arm, stopping to look at the sights Denver had to offer.

Two miners whaling each other with fists in front of a boarding house.

Two cowboys racing their ponies down a street, while other cowhands and a handful of chirpies cheered. The black horse won.

A confidence man running a shell game. He let Cindy win 50¢, and she took the coins before we walked away. Both of us knew that the confidence man had salted the mine, as one might say. He let Cindy win so he could take the other fools for most of their money. And this is something you need to know about Cindy McKim. The money she had won, she dropped in the tin cup of a blind man who stood on the corner. Yet when I told her that that fellow wasn't really blind, she said softly: "I know. But it doesn't matter."

When we reached the Albany Hotel, Cindy suggested that I go upstairs to change out of my baseball uniform, and meet her downstairs in an hour. It was the longest hour I ever had to endure, because it took me no time to change my clothes, wash my face, and comb my hair. It was worth the wait, though, for she came down the stairs looking beautiful in a lovely evening dress.

We ate oysters and antelope with her father in the dining room, onion soup, and chocolate cake, and the evening ended all too soon. I knew I wouldn't see them on the train. They would be in their fancy car, and I would be with the rest of the Cowboys, probably sitting next to Fatty Briody and trying to sleep despite his snoring.

"We will see you in Kansas City," Mr. McKim said as he shook my hand. "Hard to believe, isn't it, lad, but the season will start before you know it. We'll put this trip to Denver behind us and start the season anew. Victory after victory after victory, and you, I am sure, will be one of the kings of the baseball diamond. You'll make all of Kansas City proud."

Dave Rowe, of course, had other designs.

When we stepped off the train at Union Station in Kansas City, he reminded me that I was worthless, had blown our chance at victory, and that I had better find a comfortable spot on the bench.

"Because," he growled, "that's where you're gonna be till October the Eleventh."

I didn't tell Mother or Papa that. And I didn't have to tell them how I had stunk things up in Denver. James Whitfield's telegraphs had found their way to the Kansas City *Times*, and those newspapers had found their way to my parents. They didn't mention the games, just took me home, and made me catch up with my schoolwork.

Anyway, I think I've almost caught up to where I left off when I began this narrative.

On April 30th, we opened the season to a packed League Park against Cap Anson's Chicago White Stockings. We played them well, too, but fell 6-to-5. From my spot on the bench, I had a good view of the entire game.

On Saturday, May 1st, we played a lot worse. Chicago 17, Kansas City 8.

Dave Rowe's brother and the rest of the Detroit Wolverines came to Kansas City on Monday, and stomped us, 11-to-4. On Wednesday, we played Detroit again, and lost, 4-to-3.

"Good luck in Saint Louis," my parents told me at the train station on Thursday, before I boarded the coach with my teammates, heading off to play the Maroons.

They beat us on Friday, May 7th, 7-to-5.

But on Saturday, May, 8th, I won the game for the team through my pitching and my home run, and felt like a king after that 2-to-0 victory.

Of course, feelings such as that don't last long in the world of professional sports.

Dave Rowe saw to that.

CHAPTER ELEVEN

On Monday, we dropped the last game of the series, 5-to-3, which I blamed on the fact that no one on our team, with the exception of me, belonged on any baseball diamond that day. Grasshopper Jim remained in the hospital—just so the doctors could be sure his skull wasn't fractured and his brain wasn't compromised. Every member of the team reeked of whiskey. Except me, even though during our Saturday victory celebration Fatty Briody and even Charley Bassett allowed me to drink beer—but only two. Novice that I was, those two bottles left me fairly pickled but not hung over on Sunday. I went to the hospital to visit Grasshopper Jim while the rest of the Cowboys returned to Dixie Lee's for more drunken debauchery. By Monday, of course, I had completely recovered, but regarding my teammates . . . well, they weren't fit to play baseball.

Still, Dave Rowe did manage to hit a two-run home run, scoring Charley Bassett. After touching home, he staggered to our bench, leaned forward, gripping the hard wood with both hands, and vomited.

Everyone on the bench slid over, to one side or the other.

Rowe rose, sat down, wiped his mouth with his cap, and shook his head. "Two-day drunk. No one will ever know just how hard that home run was."

The Maroons pitcher, Joe Murphy, laughed, but we had grown accustomed to laughter, heckles, and finger-pointing.

Murphy's teammates, the spectators, and even the umpire had been ridiculing our rough-looking players, but mostly they had been howling insults and jokes at Fatty Briody because of the fat mitt he had been using. Eventually Fatty replaced that big glove and wore his two thin gloves. That got everyone in the stands or on the home bench worked up so much that they began insulting Fatty with other comments.

"Where's that fat mitt?"

"Look at his gut. He musta et it!"

"Hey, Catch'. We don't like that cap, either? Why don't you swap it out for somethin' better?"

"That was a catching glove? Hell, I thought he was just holdin' one of his chins!"

The game remained close because the Maroons stank of whiskey, too. This being St. Louis, if you included the spectators, I might have been the only one at Union Grounds who was neither inebriated nor hung over, because while the National League did not allow the sale of inebriating spirits at the stadiums, saloons surrounded Union Grounds, which made it easy for people to sneak in flasks of liquor or bottles of beer.

After the game, we checked Grasshopper Jim out of the hospital and caught the train for home.

We had more than a week before our next game. "It's our only break, you boys," Dave Rowe told us. "Damned league couldn't figure a way to get the teams back east out here. So enjoy yourselves. I'm going to Topeka. To . . . ahem . . . do some scouting."

I, on the other hand, had no break. Mother threw the ball with me the first day, then sent me back to Mr. Stokes's school, and when I got back home, she and Papa would make me practice. On Friday, after school, I finished my studies and was pronounced an educated man.

"Your schooling is over, Silver," Mr. Stokes said, keeping me in the brick building after he had dismissed all of the others.

I stared at him. School wasn't supposed to let out until June, but I had no good reason to mention that.

"What are your plans?" he asked.

"Baseball," I answered with a shrug.

"Baseball," he said, "is a game, not a profession."

"But I'm . . ." I stopped. Being an educated man, I had learned the wisdom of not telling anyone, not even a friend who was catching for a Western League team in Denver, that the Kansas City Cowboys paid me $1,600 a year. To sit on the bench.

With a weary smile, Mr. Stokes shook his head,

and closed his lesson book. "I know, Silver, that the Kansas City Cowboys pay you to play baseball. But have you given thought to what you will do for a living when you no longer can play this children's game?"

"Oh." I waved away such long-term concern, and in doing so brought my right hand into view. Big hands. What *would* I do? Lay bricks? Then I thought of something else. Dave Rowe despised me. Mr. McKim had been set to release me in Denver before Dan Dugdale intervened, and Mr. Joseph Heim had practically thrown Mother and me out of his office. I remained clueless about what Mr. Whitfield thought of my ability, or of me as I had not read his article about my Saturday victory against the Maroons.

"I have to go, Mister Stokes," I said as I gathered my dinner pail and my books for the last time, and raced out of the schoolhouse. I sprinted to the nearest street car, took it to our neighborhood, ran into the house that we would be leaving soon for a better home, grabbed my baseball gear, and made my way to The Hole.

Yes, Dave Rowe had given us the week off, but I knew I had to work. And work hard to keep alive my dream, and Mother's dream.

"Howdy, Kid. Where you been?"

Fatty Briody sat on our bench, using Dan Dugdale's mitt as a pillow, while he dipped a ladle into a nearby bucket and drank water, refilled the ladle, and drank more. Sweat poured from his every pore, but his sweat did not stink of forty-rod. It was the sweat of hard work, which, you know, smells different than whiskey sweat.

On the infield, Charley Bassett picked up a ground ball Jim Lillie had hit, tossed the ball to second base where Cod Myers caught it, stepped off the bag, and drilled a missile into Mox McQuery's hands. The big first baseman then threw the ball back to Jim Donnelly, who tossed it to Lillie.

"Let's do it again," Lillie said, and hit another grounder to Bassett.

They weren't alone.

Fatty set the ladle on the edge of the bucket, and pushed himself to his feet. "So . . . we wondered if you'd quit us?"

"Quit?" I asked.

"Wanna catch for me?" Fatty asked. "I'm gonna hit some fly balls to Shorty and Petey."

Sure enough, Pete Conway and Paul Radford stood in left field, waiting. Stump Weidman and Jim Whitney were throwing the ball in right field. Even the poker-playing ballists had left their decks of cards in their pockets and were sprinting from the right-field line to the center-field fence, stopping, then running back to right.

"I thought Dave gave us the week off," I said.

134

Fatty laughed. "Yeah. Well, you was at Saint Louey, kid. You saw how we stank. Or how we played against Chicago and Detroit before we even taken that train ride east. Figured we could use some practice. Reckon you did, too. That's why you're here, ain't it?"

"You've been practicing all week?" I asked.

"Well . . . some of us. I showed up Thursday. But I reckon that was only yesterday." Fatty smirked. "C'mon." He grabbed his big Spaulding bat and headed down the base line.

"But, Dave . . . ," I said as I caught up with him, tugging on my fingerless glove. "He's not practicing. He went to Topeka."

"Not to run whores, kid. Well . . . maybe a little. He and McKim went to Topeka to watch the Capitals play the Soldiers, then I think they was goin' to Saint Joe. The Reds is playin' the Tree Planters. You heard what 'Bond Hill' Hart done against the Maroons, didn't you?"

"Uhh . . . no."

"Really? He no-hit those sons-of-bitches. But Leavenworth . . . that's the Soldiers, you know . . . they have some fine ballists playin' for 'em. And we saw just how strong them Denver boys is. Western League ain't a bunch of hayseeds playin' on cow pastures. McKim and Rowe . . . they's lookin' for ballists. Nobody's an untouchable, not on the Kansas City Cowboys' roster, that's certain sure. Not when you're one-

135

and-six and the New York Giants is comin' to town. Not when you's us."

I looked off to center field, where the card players had stopped sprinting, and were now walking slowly, heads down and gasping for breath. One of them stopped, and dropped to his knees.

Certainly we needed practice. I felt like an idiot. All I had been doing that week was playing catch with Mother and Papa, and going to Mr. Stokes's school.

" 'Sides," Fatty said as he fetched a ball from one of his pants pockets, brought the bat up, and prepared to hit. "We's all professionals. And nobody, not even the worst amateur, likes getting his ass kicked."

So we practiced, morning through afternoon, the rest of the weekend, even Sunday—Mother let me miss church.

On Monday, May 17th, we met again, but stopped our workout just after noon as we had to play the Giants the following day. By then, Dave Rowe had returned, fortunately, with not one player from one of the Western League teams. That made us feel a little safer—for the time being. Rowe passed a bottle of Irish whiskey around the bench, saying we looked fit and might be able to hold New York to ten runs tomorrow.

"Hey . . ." Joseph Heim snapped his fingers as

he crossed the gate on the third-base side toward our bench. He kept snapping his fingers, pointing. At first, I thought he wanted the rye, which Grasshopper Jim had not let me sample, but the bottle was back in Dave Rowe's hands, and our team president seemed to be coming toward . . . me?

I swallowed. Maybe Dave Rowe had found a player, after all, and Mr. Heim was coming to fire me. Instead, he stopped in front of Charley Bassett.

"Where the hell do I find a cowboy?" Mr. Heim demanded.

Charley Bassett blinked.

"You're from Dodge City, Bassett," Mr. Heim said. "I need to have a cowboy. A real cowboy. And I need him for tomorrow." Heim grinned like a villain in some melodrama playing at the Opera House. "Well . . . ?"

From talking with Charley Bassett on the train ride, I knew he had been born in Central Falls, Rhode Island, and had attended Brown University.

"You know, Charley," I said. "The stockyards."

"Uh . . ." Charley swallowed, and tried to mask his New England accent. "Yeah. Stock-yards. Or . . ." He snapped his fingers, a pretty good imitation of Mr. Heim, though our boss did not notice. "Or . . . ?"

"Packing house," I said.

"Which one?" Mr. Heim asked.

137

"Armour Packing Company." I figured I owed my father's employer that much.

Mr. Heim turned to Bassett. "That right?" he asked.

Charley Bassett breathed a sigh of relief. "Yeah. Armour. Sure."

"Good. Thanks, Bassett. Now, all you boys, I want you to wear cowboy hats tomorrow because I've changed my mind. No baseball caps. Cowboy hats for the Kansas City Cowboys! McKim was right. Cowboy hats. Make them . . ." He started snapping his fingers again. "Make them?"

"Red?" Charley Bassett asked.

After all, we were supposed to be wearing our chocolate and maroon uniforms tomorrow.

I laughed, elbowed Bassett in his side, and said: "That's a good one, Charley." I was thinking: *Where in hell would we find red cowboy hats, you Eastern greenhorn?*

"Brown," Mr. Heim said. "Yeah, brown hats. No. Black. Yeah." A wicked grin masked his face. "Black."

"You payin' for these hats?" Fatty asked.

"Hell, no. You just come outfitted for tomorrow in black hats. If you don't have a black hat, you don't play. And don't get paid."

After Mr. Heim left, Charley Bassett, Pete Conway, Fatty Briody, and the rest of my teammates—except the poker players—came up to me, demanding to know where in hell they could

138

buy black cowboy hats. They cussed Mr. Heim as a miser. The poker players said we should form a union. Rowe pulled his .32 and told everyone to shut up, then he glared at me.

"This is your damned fault, boy. Cowboy hats. What a joke. But it's your town, so where the hell do we get those big lids?"

I had always wanted to own a cowboy hat, so I felt excited about buying my first—and a black one at that—but I had no clue as to where I would find one, other than atop some waddie's head at the Armour corrals.

"Alfred Cronkrite's," Cindy McKim said. "Do you know where it is?"

Whirling, I saw Cindy, beautiful as always, and, even better, her father nowhere to be found.

"Well," Dave Rowe demanded, "where is it?"

"Near the West Bottoms."

I could not take my eyes off Cindy McKim. Had I been able to focus on pop-ups the way I stared at her, I might have played longer in the National League. She smiled at me. I felt even happier.

So Cindy McKim led us to the street car, where we journeyed down to West Seventeenth Street and walked into the general store Mr. Cronkrite had opened five years or so back. We cleaned him out of black hats, and he said he would be happy as a loon when, before tomorrow's ball game, he would brag that he had outfitted the Kansas City Cowboys.

Of course, I'm not sure they were all cowboy hats. Jim Donnelly, you see, opted for something called a French Pocket, and it wasn't really black but navy blue. Most of the players grabbed men's crushers, on account that they cost only six bits each. Fatty grabbed an old Stetson, while Dave Rowe settled for a Fedora, saying: "At least I won't look like a complete idiot." Charley Bassett spent $3 on a stiff-brimmed Pine Ridge Sombrero, assuming, I figured, that it would make him look like the son of a Kansas lawman. Me? Well, I got a high-crowned hat with a silk ribbon band, fancy crease, and side dents. It reminded me of the one Dan Dugdale wore, but mine wasn't nearly so trampled and dusty, and it was black.

"Jesus-son-of-a-bitching-pig-shitting-asshole-damn-it-all-to-hell-bastard-loving-Christ," Dave Rowe said as he stood at the counter to pay Mr. Cronkrite. "I hope you bastards can see to catch or hit the damned ball tomorrow."

Cindy McKim grinned as I stepped toward the door. I started to take off my hat. "Leave it on," she said quickly. "I want to get used to it."

"I don't look like a cowboy?" I asked.

"I'm just used to seeing you in your new baseball cap. That's all." She offered me her elbow, and I led her onto the busy street, where Cindy suggested that we go find some cider at this place on Delaware Street. As Papa had tried to teach me to be a gentleman, I did not refuse.

We sat on stools at the counter, sipping the sweet cider—even though, in May, hot cider is usually not the preferred drink in muggy Kansas City.

"You're not talking much, Silver," Cindy said. Then she asked what I was thinking.

"Did your father find any good players on his trip to Topeka?" I asked, stopping myself from asking about any potential replacements he might have found in Leavenworth or St. Joseph.

She pushed away the empty mug of cider, and stared. It was not a pleasant stare. The smile was gone, the eyes had hardened and narrowed, and if I read her face correctly, the thought going through her mind had to be something along the lines of: *This boy's an idiot.* Which made me realize: I am an idiot. An insecure idiot.

"Well," I began again. "I mean. We've only won a single game. I'm thinking about the team. That's all. I know . . . Well . . . It's . . . um . . ."

"Why don't you try not thinking about baseball, Silver?" Still no smile.

"I just finished school," I blurted out. "I've been going to Mister Stokes's school. Where do you go?"

That made her relax. "Mother brings in a tutor for my brothers and sisters."

"Oh." Silence. Then I made myself ask another

141

question. "How many brothers and sisters do you have?"

The radiance had returned to Cindy's face. "That's how you make conversation, Silver. Is it that hard?"

I let out a sigh as Cindy answered. I ordered ore cider, adjusted the angle of my brand-spanking new cowboy hat, and we continued chatting and sipping for another half hour. Afterward, I walked her to the street car, and she got off with me, so we wandered the streets of Kansas City, aimlessly, until we found ourselves on my street, in front of my house.

"This . . . ," I began, gesturing at the shotgun house, ashamed of its appearance, its leaky roof, even though the bricks—mortared into place by Papa and myself—were solid.

"Is this where you live?" she asked, sounding excited, as if she was staring at a castle. Cindy McKim, I had to believe, lived in the best house in Kansas City's richest neighborhood.

"Well . . . we're moving . . . sometime soon," I explained.

"Can I meet your parents?" Cindy asked.

I did not have a chance to answer, for Mother had opened the door and stepped onto the porch.

She was not smiling, either.

CHAPTER TWELVE

"Girls and baseball do not mix."

I cocked my head and stared at Mother.

Papa had just left with Cindy McKim to catch a street car and make sure she got home. Apparently my parents decided I could not be trusted, and so Mother, still not smiling, had begun her lecture.

Oh, I guess the first meeting of Mother and this girl I fancied went well enough. After all, no insults had been traded, and Mother had given Cindy a courteous if stiff nod when I introduced her. Papa, on the other hand, practically danced with joy when he saw her. Of course, Mother put a quick end to that jig. She did serve coffee and slices of pound cake she had baked, muttered a few pleasantries, before glancing at our Seth Thomas clock and proclaiming: "Oh, dear, look at how late it is. Your parents must be worried sick over you, so, Papa, you must take her home. Besides, Silver, you have a baseball game tomorrow . . . and there shall be little rest for any of our darling Cowboys now that the schedule will begin in earnest."

Cindy could take a hint.

"They just don't mix," Mother now told me.

The Seth Thomas ticked loudly in what passed

for a parlor in the shotgun shack. I hated that damned clock.

"Didn't you and Papa go to a baseball game?" I gambled on this strategy. "Wasn't that the first time he courted you?"

"That's different," Mother snapped. "Your father is a kind person, a good provider, but he never showed the talent you have on a baseball diamond, Son. Your future belongs in baseball."

"Mister Stokes thinks otherwise," I said.

"Who?"

My head shook as a wry smile found its way across my face. Mother could tell you the starting nine for the Chicago White Stockings, but she could not remember the name of my school-master. Without answering her, I found another angle of attack.

"Cindy's the daughter of Mister McKim," I said. "You know . . . the vice president and treasurer of the Cowboys . . . the reason I'm on the team . . . for now."

Mother pressed the tips of her fingers together, a signal that never bode well for me. "And that is another reason girls and baseball do not mix. Especially this girl. Baseball is not just a game of manly skill, Son. It is a game of politics."

My head cocked the other way. "What?" I asked.

"Politics. Americus would be within his rights as a protective father to void your contract, outright release you, send you off to stacking bricks or slaughtering bovines with your father were you to . . . well . . . let's just say . . . well . . . what happens to you if Cindy decides you are not to her liking? Or what happens if Americus decides that he likes you fine enough as a ballist but not as a suitor for his daughter?"

"Americus?" I asked.

Her eyes rolled. "Americus McKim," she said, stressing every syllable. "The owner of the Kansas City Cowboys."

She had missed my meaning. He was Americus now. Not Mr. McKim.

"Baseball," I said, "and women do not mix."

"Exactly," Mother said.

I dismissed the unholy thought that Mother might be doing something immoral with Americus McKim to further my baseball career. Mother was quite naïve in some things, even if Mr. McKim flirted with her, she would remain oblivious to such acts. I could picture her sitting beside him in the stands at The Hole.

"Call me Americus, Missus King."

"And you must call me Samantha."

"May I tempt you with an ice-cream cake, Samantha?"

"Oh, thank you, Americus, but I must watch my figure."

"Yes. Must we all."

"You should turn in now, Silver," Mother told me. "Tomorrow will be an important game for you. You need rest. And for goodness sake, take that monstrosity you call a cowboy hat back to that store and demand a refund."

"That," I said, "I cannot do. It's one of Mister Heim's notions. We're all to wear black hats for the game tomorrow."

"That's ridiculous. You're not real cowboys."

"We're not real baseball players, either," I said, and pushed myself up from the table. "Not at one-and-six."

"Hush. Baseball is a long season. You shall improve. To bed," she demanded, and repeated: "It's an important game for you."

And it was, but not for me, though I had a fine view from my perch on the bench for those wild nine innings. No, the game was important for the Kansas City Cowboys as it set the tone for how our season, and our fans, would go for the next couple of months. Here, let Mr. James Whitfield tell the story. From one of Mother's scrapbooks, I have pulled out the article from the Kansas City *Times* and pasted it below.

COWBOYS GIVE GIANTS K.C. WELCOME
REAL COWBOY ESCORTS N.Y. BUS
TO LEAGUE PARK, WESTERN STYLE!
Gunshots outnumber batted balls
McKim lashes out at umpire

New York manager outraged
'Go Back To New York, crybabies'
Wildest Baseball Contest Ever
Our Gallant Heroes Fall, 7-to-2

"Truthful" Jim Mutrie's ballists from New York arrived at League Field under a mounted escort that had even these players formerly known as the Gothams cheering yesterday.

"Well, I've always wanted to see a real cowboy," said Buck Ewing, New York's powering catcher.

This resolute editor was unable to catch the name of the cowboy riding a wily black mustang steed. The cowhand, clad in a gray hat, fired rounds from his Colt revolving pistol as he galloped alongside the omnibus taking our visiting opponents from the Lindell Hotel. When the frightened omnibus driver set the brake to his conveyance in front of our new baseball facility, his face remained pale, and he refused to release his trembling grip on the brake lever. Perhaps he feared he was witnessing again the daring hold-up that Jesse James pulled at Kansas City's fairgrounds back in 1872 at our annual Exposition. Perhaps our steady city policemen thought the same as they chased our unnamed cowboy and former, we surmise, Pony Express rider. Or maybe our intrepid policemen merely wanted to cite that dashing young rider for violating our city firearms ordinance.

In any event, before I could ask the wild and woolly chap his name, he raked those silver spurs over his mustang's ribs, and like a thunderbolt dashed out of our city, away from the chasing policemen, waving their night sticks, and toward the East Bottoms.

A horse, a horse! My kingdom for a horse!
Withdraw, my lord; I'll help you to a horse.

"Kansas Citians," roared Truthful Jim, who had his Giants (don't call them Gothams anymore) off to a 6-2 record before being blasted by the Detroit Wolverines and Chicago White Stockings to drop them to a 7-and-6 win-loss record. "That is as fine a welcome as we have received and made that long train trip from Chicago worthwhile. And when your Cowboys come to see us in New York City, I promise to ride . . . how is it put . . . shotgun . . . for your coach, only I shall ride my big-wheeled velocipede!"

Then, to roars of citizens, Truthful Jim led his players into our stadium, and as men, women, and children paid their 50¢ to watch baseball, they continued stomping their approval. By our best guess, some twelve hundred pairs of cowboy boots practically stomped the stadium even deeper into the hole in the ground.

Yet smiles on the faces of our brethren from New York, New York, quickly disappeared when, in the bottom half of the first inning, third baseman Jim Donnelly sent a high ball tossed by the southpaw hurler Jim Devlin into deep center field, well over Danny Richardson's head. That hit scored Al "Cod" Myers, who had reached first base on an error, and by the time these Giants had the ball back into Devlin's left hand, Donnelly stood on third base. Moments later, Donnelly scored on a weak roller by Charley Bassett that allowed our noble shortstop to reach first base safely.

Thus, the Cowboys, newcomers to the National League, had a two-to-nothing lead. Above the din of stomping boots, came the mocking, singsong chant: "Gi-ants. Mid-gets. Gi-ants. Mid-gets. Goth-hams. Go home. Goth-hams. Go home."

Such taunts apparently are unheard of back East, as Truthful Jim stepped off the bench, yelling back at our fans, and even taking up his protest with the umpire. Tom York said he was powerless to do anything about yelling fans. Though presence of that bearded man with the black slouch hat, who, standing behind home plate, shot his pistol empty during the Kansas City offensive surge might have tempered umpire York's resolve.

Our hardy policemen, Kansas Citians should take note, escorted the black-hatted man out of League Park—but only after his pistol was empty.

Alas, New York's fine ballists did not stay small for long.

Buck Ewing, of course, saw to that, with a towering hit that cleared not only the center-field wall but also a phaeton on the hilltop, where a blonde girl in a blue dress and a dapper man in a flat-brimmed straw had parked to watch the contest and avoid paying the $1 it would have cost them to enter. Here, I thought our mustang-mounted cowboy could have earned his keep, for had he stayed nearby he could have galloped up the hill, roped the baseball with his fine lariat, and returned the ball to the playing field. Instead, however, the boy in the straw hat leaped from his buggy, and, after two feeble attempts, managed to snag the baseball, thoroughly dented by Buck's bat, which the young man dropped into sulking Dave Rowe's meaty hands.

With Danny Richardson already on second base, Buck's big hit tied the score at two runs apiece.

Dude Esterbrook gave the Giants the lead in the next inning, when his single scored Joe Gerhardt.

In the fifth inning, Mike Dorgan belted a ball that bounced off the wall in right field, then off the corner, then off Paul Radford's knee, and off Mox McQuery's fingers. Two more Giants née Gothams, making the score five-to-two, and McQuery ripped his big black Stetson hat (or whatever lid he happened to be wearing) off his head, dashed it to the ground, and pointed a finger in the general vicinity where Joseph Heim is known to sit and watch our contests. "I can't see with this foul hat on my head, Heim!"

After that, those black Western hats were retired, replaced by maroon caps.

But, alas, neither big black cowboy hats nor red with black-striped baseball caps seemed to make much of a difference for our National League ballists.

It was then 6-to-2 when The Mighty Buck tripled home Pete Gillespie, and scored on Roger Connor's wounded dove that landed just out of Mox McQuery's reach.

And in the ninth inning, the Giants tallied yet another run when Esterbrook singled home Roger Connor.

Yet our valiant Cowboys made things interesting in their last at-bat.

After Radford and Fatty Briody weakly grounded out, McQuery doubled, Myers walked, and Jim Donnelly reached first on a hit straight back to the Giants pitcher whose fingers refused to co-operate and come up with the baseball, although McQuery, playing wisely with two outs and down five runs, remained at the third bag.

This made the bases full, and brought the dashing Jim Whitney, who had pitched a fine game but for some sound knocks by some fine Giants, to home with a chance to cut Kansas City's deficit to one run on one swing of the bat.

Grasshopper Jim looped the first pitch from the crafty Devlin over second base, and it seemed certain that two runs would score and bring Charley Bassett to the plate. Yet somehow center fielder Richardson was running at the sound of the bat striking the ball. Catching the ball on the bound, Richardson ran—faster, we think, than that cowboy's mustang steed earlier in the afternoon—and let his forward momentum carry him to the bag at second. Yes, the play was close, but it appeared that Donnelly reached second a split second before the New York center fielder.

That valiant umpire, a veteran of many National League contests, however, ruled that Richardson had won the sprint, yelling that Donnelly was out and that the ball game was over.

Our city's fine malt and barley man, Americus McKim, did not agree with York's call.

Boots began stomping in the stands, shaking the nerves of York and the Giants. More pistols roared—but these two revolvers were fired by two policemen, who, like most of the Cowboy-cheering crowd, favored the home team. McKim hurled his black hat over the third-base fence and pointed a finger at York. Unsuitable language followed.

Truthful Jim came over from first base and began pointing back.

More unsuitable language left ladies at the ball park covering their ears or running for the exits.

And here it is to our relief that our six-shooter, mustang-riding escort was by now, in all likelihood, raising dust toward Lawrence, Kansas, and not in the vicinity with six chambers filled with leaden shot. Instead of bullets, only insults flew after the two constables had emptied their revolvers—words like "crybabies" and "cheaters" and "roughnecks" and "outrage". Cowboy boots stomped. But in the end, York's call stood, the Giants left victorious, the Cowboys went home with yet another loss.

And one wonders if Truthful Jim will have the nerve, and umpire Tom York the audacity, to show up for tomorrow's game at League Park.

They did. Both of them. Boots again stomped, although, as far as I knew, no mustang-riding waddie escorted the Giants to League Park on Wednesday. More policemen arrived at the game. Grasshopper Jim Whitney started pitching for us again, and the end result was the exact same as our Tuesday game. Giants 7, Cowboys 2. But this one had no last-inning controversy or almost heroics.

We did win the last game of the series, however, behind Pete Conway's stellar pitching, and Charley Bassett's eighth-inning double. Truthful Jim Mutrie did not say Bassett won that game, a 5-to-4 decision because of Conway or Bassett, however. As the New York manager explained to Mr. Whitfield: "We got jinxed. In the Lindell dining room, a man sat at the table next to us. And he was cross-eyed. I knew we didn't stand a Chinaman's chance as soon as I saw him."

CHAPTER THIRTEEN

The next day, we lost to the Boston Beaneaters, 8-to-7. Our crowd, once again, proved to be loud. Well, *loud* is an understatement, as is *obnoxious*. From my spot at the end of the bench, I could hear those vile curses above the pounding of boot heels on wooden floors, but our supporters did show some manners on that afternoon, as only one man fired his pistol, and it was only a two-shot Derringer. Two policemen arrested him immediately. They slapped manacles on him, chaining him to a fence rail, thus making him sit in the sun, while they watched the rest of the ball game.

After all, it was a close game.

This time, outfielder Ezra Sutton came bounding around third base on Pop Tate's hard-hit ball to Dave Rowe. Our manager and center fielder fired quickly to Fatty Briody, who swept the ball toward Sutton's head and whacked his target a good one. But Tom York ruled Sutton was safe, and that broke the tie in the top of the ninth inning.

"Jesus-son-of-a-bitching-pig-shitting-asshole-damn-it-all-to-hell-bastard-loving-Christ! How much are those Boston boys paying you to umpire, you chicken-livered bastard?"

No, that stream of profanity did not come

from Dave Rowe's mouth, but from Americus McKim's. Oh, Dave kicked up the dirt in the outfield, slapped his ball cap against his thigh, but said nary a word. After all, he must have felt worn out, for, although it was only May, it felt like August in The Hole.

The umpire turned to face Americus McKim. "Sir, I am paid by the National League, not the Boston Beaneaters."

"Then earn your damned salary, you blind son-of-a-bitch!"

Shaking his head, but smart enough to avoid any confrontation, Tom York stepped back into position, and told Stump Weidman to prepare to pitch to Myron Allen. Allen was called out on strikes, which led Mr. McKim and perhaps five hundred other men and women at League Park to think we had a chance to win.

We didn't.

Old Hoss Radbourn, long past thirty years old by then, struck out Stump, Fatty, and Mox to end the game. And those three Cowboys were swinging—more like hacking against a wily veteran like Radbourn—so Mr. McKim could not blame the umpire for any bad calls.

But, well, he did.

"If you could see, you mealy-mouthed horse's ass, what's a damned strike, my boys wouldn't have to swing at pitches over their damned heads!"

Empty lemonade cups and wrappers from ice-cream cakes pelted Mr. York as he chatted briefly with John Morrill, Boston's manager. He was cool, that umpire, for he turned the other cheek, refusing to do or say anything that might lead to a riot. Maybe that's why four policemen, including the two who had arrested the Derringer-shooter, stepped onto the field. They escorted Mr. York off the field, along with their prisoner.

When I decided it was safe to leave, I glanced up at the empty stadium. To my relief, Mother and Papa had gone. Well, once again I had barely moved off the bench, so there would be little to discuss. I changed my clothes, stuffed my gear in the grip, and hurried out of the stadium.

Most of my teammates had departed for the buckets-of-blood or cathouses. I practically ran to Delaware Street.

Fatty Briody kept telling me that most of the beer-jerkers at every grog shop on the National League circuit not only knew him by name, but would have a stein of foamy beer and a bourbon chaser ready for him as soon as he entered the saloon. That's pretty much how I felt as I sat at the counter and saw Mr. Bayersdörfer push a mug of cider in front of me. I didn't even have to ask.

"Have you been waiting long?" I asked Cindy McKim.

"No." The empty bowl of soup told me the truth

as she absently rubbed her thumb across the lip of her mug.

"You lost today, eh?" Mr. Bayersdörfer commented as he stood in front of me again. "But close game, right?"

"Yes, sir," I answered. "They beat us by one run."

"Miriam today make good soup," he said, changing the subject. "Chicken. Make feel better. You want?"

My stomach rumbled, but I shook my head. "No thank you, sir." I waited until he walked down the counter to wait on a priest who sat next to a railroad worker. This place brought everyone in, but I just cared about one, and she sat next to me.

"What's the matter?" I asked.

Cindy shrugged, and this was not like her at all. I found myself worthless in such a situation. Do I wait for her to tell me? Do I pry? Do I dare put my hand on her shoulder and whisper that everything would be all right?

With a sigh, she pushed away the cup, which, like the soup bowl, had been emptied. Her eyes were red, and that caused me to bite my bottom lip.

"I do not understand my father, Silver," she said.

"Oh." I let out a sigh, and my head bobbed. "He gets . . ."—I tried to find the correct word—"excited."

"Abominable," she said, and her voice rose. "His actions today were repugnant."

159

Guessing the meanings of such words, I tried to paint a softer portrait of her father, and put today's actions into context. "Well, he wants to win, and he was not alone today. Didn't you see the man with the Derringer, the one the constables had to arrest?"

I'm not sure she even heard me.

"He rarely touches intoxicating spirits," she said, and shook her head. "And he's in the beer business. So that's not what lights the fuse. He's a fine father at home, rarely raises his voice to my brothers or sisters or me. He goes to church. He gives to the poor. Yet, the moment the umpire yells for the game to begin, he turns into some . . . some . . . some ogre. No, it's even before that. As soon as he steps through the gates to League Park, he's . . . evil."

"People pay their money," I said, "and fifty cents is a lot of money for most of those people. So they think that gives them the right to cheer or boo or curse or anything. When Mother and Father and I attended the Onions games, we yelled, too."

"Did you or your parents ever yell 'Jesus-son-of-a-bitching-pig-shitting-asshole-damn-it-all-to-hell-bastard-loving-Christ?' "

The priest, who had paid his check and was heading out the door, stopped and turned, frowning. Mr. Bayersdörfer, who was bringing over a plate of cornbread, stopped, pivoted, and took the bread to the railroad worker.

"My goodness!" shouted a woman, and, covering her toddler's ears, pushed him to the far corner of the store.

I waited for the priest to leave before I answered. "Well . . . no . . . but . . ."

"And Father does not pay to go to any of your games," Cindy said. "He owns the team, after all."

"Which maybe gives him even more right to . . ." I shook my head, staring at the mug of cider without touching it.

"What does it mean?" Cindy asked.

Shrugging, I said: " 'Jesus-son-of-a-' " . . . but that was as far as I could get. "It's something Dave Rowe says. Your father just picked it up, is all. I've even heard a few other fans . . . sort of . . . adopt it, I guess."

"No, silly."

I stared into Cindy's blue eyes, and caught a glimpse of her smile.

"Not that foul phrase, Silver. I mean . . . the . . . it's an angry mob at those ball games."

"It's the West," I said.

"I went to Unions games, Silver," Cindy said, "and one or two last year. This is different."

"National League," I tried to explain. "You should have been in Saint Louis."

"That's Saint Louis," Cindy clarified, and I knew she had a point. St. Louis had never been civilized. God help any umpire who made a wrong call that went against the home team in that unruly town.

"They know baseball in Saint Louis," Cindy said, "but humility and sportsmanship escape them."

"Amen," I said.

Mr. Bayersdörfer, sensing all had returned to normal at our end of the counter, returned with another plate of cornbread. Cindy even thanked him as she picked up a piece to nibble.

"Sometimes," she said as she dabbed her mouth with a napkin, "I wish I were an orphan." She giggled. "Is that un-Christian?"

Not as much as saying Jesus-son-of-a-bitching-pig-shitting-asshole-damn-it-all-to-hell-bastard-loving-Christ. That's what ran through my mind. I did not, however, say it. What I said was: "I have similar thoughts . . . sometimes."

"Your father seems right pleasant," Cindy said.

"He is." I began to sip the cider. "Henpecked might be a better word."

She laughed again. "I guess I don't want to be an orphan. Mother is a saint."

"Mine's not," I said.

"No?"

"Oh, she means well. So does your father, I guess, in his own way. And I wouldn't be on the Cowboys' roster if not for Mother. She pushed me. Pushed me and pushed me. She even taught me how to pitch. Papa? He knows how to build a pier-and-beam foundation and how to mix mortar. He knows how to . . ." I stopped, deciding that describing his job at Armour might not be proper conversation while eating. "Well, he's a good man, a kind man, but he never was a sound ballist . . . even for a town team. So . . ."

I stopped, having realized I probably talked too much.

"What . . . ?" Cindy began, but waited for Mr. Bayersdörfer to refill her mug with cider. "What would you be if you weren't a professional baseball player?"

"Cowboy," I said without any hesitation.

"You are a Cowboy," she said.

"No." I laughed. "Not a Kansas City Cowboy. A real cowboy. Riding horses. Roping . . . I mean . . . lariating steers."

"Lariating?" she asked.

"Umm . . . yeah. Dug, he told me it wasn't a rope, but a lariat. So that would . . ." My shoulders slackened. "No. He might have said roping . . . yeah . . . he never said lariating. I just . . . well . . ."

"You are such a funny boy." Cindy laughed, wiped her eyes, and leaned over and kissed me. Not on the cheeks. But full on the lips. I held my breath, and prayed this moment would never end, but even when it did, I felt mighty fine, considering I had been riding the bench for five consecutive baseball games.

"You know how to cheer me up."

All I could do was stare. Cindy excused herself, and said she wanted to go pick up some lemon

163

cookies to take home to her parents. I kind of thought that maybe her parents were beginning to wonder about why she would need to rush off to Delaware Street to buy sweets or a gallon of cider or candies at Mr. Bayersdörfer's shop. I watched her hurry to the far side of the counter, where the Goldmans displayed their baked delicacies for the day, and watched as Miriam Bayersdörfer helped her select the cookies. My fingers traced my tingling lips.

"A wonder . . . eh?"

My eyes blinked and focused on Mr. Bayersdörfer, the fat, bald man with the Dundreary whiskers and fat nose.

"Sir?"

"A wonder . . ." His accent, though harsh and heavily European, I always understood. He handed me the check.

"Being in love," he said, and walked away. "Same way I feel . . . and Miriam and me . . . we are married . . . thirty-two years . . . come September."

We beat the Beaneaters on Saturday, 9-to-1, had Sunday off, so Mother made corn pone and sausages after church, and then took me to the empty lot where she made me work on pitching. I felt such practices worthless since all I needed was a hard behind to sit on the bench.

Papa then asked if he could borrow me to help

lay bricks for some work he was doing at the Robinson home.

"The Sabbath," Mother reminded him, as she often did.

"It's not work. It's fun. And it is good for his hands." Papa always said that since it was his only day off from the packing house, thus the only day he could lay bricks for extra money. "Builds muscles. Toughens hide."

"Very well," Mother said, accepting Papa's reasoning for getting around her Sunday-day-of-rest argument one more time. I didn't mind, either.

I ate-drank-breathed-sweated baseball six days a week, and for a couple of hours on Sunday after church and dinner. About the only time I didn't think about the game was when Papa had some small job to do, and these days I could only help him on the Sabbath. I used the trowel to apply just the right amount of mortar, then set the brick in place, over and over again. Mindless work, but in the months to come, this was the work—not throwing the ball or swinging the bat or anything else that my mother, or Dave Rowe, wanted to work on—that would lead me to a successful career on the baseball diamond.

We won Monday's contest, too, holding off the Beaneaters, 5-to-4, when Mox McQuery turned a double play, stepping on the bag at first, and throwing hard to Charley Bassett, who tagged out John Morrill himself to end the game.

"All right, gents," Dave Rowe barked. "Be at the station at eight-oh-five tonight. If you get left, you don't get paid."

"Hell, Skip," Fatty said. "We wouldn't think of missing this trip. We've won three of our last four games."

"That's right!" This came from Mr. Americus McKim as he made his way among the team members, shaking hands, patting backs, bragging that we had found our way. He was certain we'd return from our trip east with a two-game lead in the National League standings.

Staring at the stands, I saw my mother and father—smiling at the victory, even though I had never left the bench—but no Cindy McKim. So when Mr. McKim practically knocked me to my knees with that slap on my back, I turned to him.

"Are you going on the trip with us, sir?"

He laughed, saying: "I got a telegram from the president of the National League begging me to stay put. Nick Young doesn't seem to like our Western hospitality in Kansas City." Then, addressing Rowe: "Do you know what we were called, Dave?"

"No," Rowe answered curtly.

"Hooligans," Mr. McKim answered. "Hooligans. Jesus-son-of-a-bitching-pig-shitting-asshole-damn-it-all-to-hell-bastard-loving-Christ, don't that beat all!"

"Yeah." Rowe drew the self-cocker from his back pocket and dropped it inside his satchel. "Eight-oh-five, boys. Even you, King."

My mouth fell open, and I spun, eyes hopeful, at our manager.

"With luck, I can pawn you off on those turds in Philadelphia." Rowe picked up his grip, and walked toward the steps.

Fatty Briody, however, came and put his arm around my shoulder. "Don't let that boy get you down, kid. This is gonna be your first road trip, ain't it?"

I sighed. "I was at Saint Louis. Remember?"

The fat catcher laughed. "That don't count, kid. That ain't even out of this state. Denver didn't mean nothin', neither, as we was just barnstormin'. You gonna see it all, Silver, and I'm gonna make sure you do. I'll see you get either the cure or the clap, I guarantee you, kid."

I wasn't sure I wanted the cure, and I knew the latter would not please Mother or Cindy, or me.

"Hell's bells." Fatty laughed. "This is why I play the damned game. We ain't back home for almost a whole damned month."

A month on the road . . . a month with Dave Rowe riding my bench-hardened arse, and maybe even leaving me with the Phillies for the rest of my career . . . and a month without Cindy McKim.

CHAPTER FOURTEEN

"Kid," Fatty Briody said, nudging me awake. Yawning, I sat up in my seat and stared out at the Missouri countryside as the sun broke over the trees and hills. Or maybe it was Iowa. We certainly had not reached Philadelphia. The pudgy, kind-hearted catcher handed me a cup of steaming black brew.

"Thanks." I blew on the coffee, and, after testing it and yawning again, saw Charley Bassett and Mox McQuery sitting across from me. My grip rested on Mox's lap.

"We borrowed yours," Mox said. "It's the flattest."

"All right." Not fully awake, I tried another sip of coffee. Black, strong, but surprisingly sweet, only not from sugar. Mox pitched a flask at Fatty, who unscrewed the lid, took a morning bracer, and held the pewter container toward me.

"Sweet enough for you, kid, or do you need another cube o' sugar?"

The three of them laughed. I shook my head, and Fatty handed the flask to Charley Bassett.

"It's a long way to Philadelphia, kid," Fatty said, "and I didn't bring no book to read."

"Like you can read," Mox McQuery said.

"So we figured to pass the time with cards," Fatty said. "You ever played poker, kid?"

"No," I answered sleepily.

Mox McQuery and Charley Bassett grinned with eager anticipation.

"That's what I thought, kid. Don't worry. After we clean you out, your marker will be good."

I laid down my cards on my grip. Mox McQuery groaned and tossed his cards atop the pile of greenbacks and silver in disgust.

Smiling, I slid the pot off the case and into my hat, which I kept between my legs.

"You took one card," Charley Bassett said. "If you don't mind my asking, which one did you get?"

"The six of diamonds," I answered.

"Christ, boy." Mox McQuery emptied the flask. "You don't draw to an inside straight, Silver. The odds are against it."

I frowned. "Does that mean I lost?"

Fatty, Bassett, and even Mox laughed.

By then, Cod Myers and Jim Donnelly, sitting across the aisle, had joined in our game. Our card-playing Cowboys and some other ball players, including Dave Rowe and Stump Wiedman, had another game going on at the far end of the rocking coach.

Cod Myers took the cards, and began shuffling.

I knew he was no amateur from the way his fingers moved over those paste cards.

"Let's see if five-card stud can change my luck," Myers said.

Getting the five of spades in the hole and eight of clubs up, I folded on the first bet.

"I can't get my money back, Silver, when you pass that quickly," Jim Donnelly said.

"Yeah," Mox McQuery agreed, "and the bet was only a quarter."

"Five cards," I said. "I've seen forty percent of my hand, and everyone's up card is higher than that lousy eight."

Fatty whistled. "You done all that cipherin' in your head?" Grinning, he nudged me, but Mox McQuery did not seem amused.

"But you could pair up," the first baseman said.

"So could any one of you," I answered.

McQuery cursed underneath his breath, shook his head, and looked at his hole card as if it might have changed.

Charley Bassett laughed. "You sure you never played poker, kid?"

I grinned across my hard-shelled suitcase at him.

"How 'bout you, Bassett?" Fatty Briody opened the new flask a porter had brought him. "Where'd you learn to play poker?"

"Brown University." Immediately Bassett realized he had answered too quickly. And too honestly.

"Brown . . . University?" Fatty said.

Shortstops, I had learned, have to think quickly when they're in the field, and Charley Bassett was a good shortstop.

"That's right," he said. "It's a saloon in Dodge City. Right across from the . . ."

"Long Branch?" I fed him.

"You've been there, kid?" Bassett asked.

"No." I shook my head.

"Don't you worry, kid," Fatty said as he passed the flask across the aisle to Jim Donnelly. "Wait till I show you Joe Burns's saloon on Rose Street."

"I've been inside buckets of blood worse than this place," Charley Bassett said. He looked uncomfortable as he squeezed between Fatty and me at the long, crowded bar at 804 Rose Street in Philadelphia.

The beer-jerker stepped up to us, dabbing his busted lip with a beer-soaked bar towel. His right eye was beginning to swell shut, and one of his incisors resembled a fang now more than a tooth. Behind us, two burly men dragged an unconscious man out through the doorway.

Charley grinned at the bartender.

"What'll it be?" the beer-jerker said in a thick Irish brogue.

"Draw us three beers, Paddy," Fatty answered, "and top mine off with a wee shot of Irish, only not too wee."

As the banged-up barkeep moved toward the taps, Charley Bassett turned to Fatty and whispered: "But I've never been back to *those* places."

"Don't worry, Kansas," Fatty said. "Between what you and the kid took us for on the trains, you've got more than enough coin to cover any doctor's bills. Besides, ballists and thieves are two peas in a pod. We stick together." He nudged the tall man next to him. "Ain't that right, pickpocket?"

The pickpocket glowered. "Bugger off."

Quickly I patted my pockets for my change purse and Illinois key-wind watch.

We made it out of Joe Burns's saloon, fully roostered, but alive—and with our wallets and other valuables. We even had struck up a pleasant conversation with two of the thieves, though not the one who had told us to bugger off. The two wished us luck in the game the next afternoon.

Which we needed.

Truthfully, I don't remember much about those four games we played in Philadelphia against a team that seemed to be officially named the Quakers but that everyone called the Phillies. As for the "Quaker City" itself?

The Liberty Bell . . . Independence Hall . . . Carpenters' Hall . . . Christ Church . . . Betsy Ross's house? I saw none of those historic sites, merely the miserable room I shared with Fatty Briody and its ticky mattress on Arch and Seventeenth, Jim Burns's grog shop on Rowe Street, the train station, and, of course, Montgomery, Ridge, and Columbia Avenues and 24th and 25th Streets, which surrounded Recreation Park.

That's what I learned on my first cross-country road trip with the Kansas City Cowboys. You saw hotels, a lot of cheap cafés, saloons, and train stations, and baseball diamonds. We won one game in Philadelphia, a 15-to-1 rout, lost the other three, boarded the B&P, and made a relatively quick trip to the station at Sixth and B Streets. I did not see much of anything in Washington City, either, except for the hotel, where I made an embarrassing mistake.

After checking into the nice, multi-storied stone building—our nation's capital certainly offers better hotels than Philadelphia—I followed Fatty and our bellman across the lobby. I stopped when the man hauling our grips paused before being joined by another dude, who motioned us inside a tiny cubicle.

To my amazement, Fatty stepped right inside, turned, and, backing up against the paneled wall, said to me: "C'mon, kid."

"Fatty," I said, and, lowering my voice into a whisper even though the two hotel employees could certainly hear me, added: "There's not even a bed in that room."

Behind me, Pete Conway, Grasshopper Jim

173

Whitney, the bellman with their luggage, and a lady in a blue dress carrying a parasol laughed out loud. The lady turned, shook her head, and gave me a pathetic look before she moved on toward the dining room. Even the two men next to the door grinned. Blood rushed to my head, and I felt my face flush.

Fatty chuckled. "Kid," he said, "this is an elevator."

I almost got to play in our one game at Swamp-doodle Grounds.

After we took a 2-to-1 lead in the top of the ninth, Dave Rowe yelled at me to get ready to pitch, that if the Senators tied the score in their last at-bat, then I'd have to come in to relieve Grasshopper Jim. I leaped off the bench and began doing my stretches to loosen up.

"What the hell are you doing?" Rowe said as he pulled his cap low on his head.

"Loosening my muscles," I answered, somewhat embarrassed.

"Jesus-son-of-a-bitching-pig-shitting . . ." Rowe marched off to center field, adding several new oaths to his usual string of blasphemy.

It didn't matter, and I think Dave Rowe knew the Senators had no chance to tie the score. Grasshopper Jim struck out Paul Hines and Ed Crane, and then got Barney Gilligan to ground out to Cod Myers at second base to end the game.

The Senators were even worse than we were. They had won four games out of twenty. We had won six and lost twelve.

We packed our gear, went to the depot, and caught a train heading for New York City.

Fatty Briody picked up the two cards Charley Bassett had dealt him, cursed, and tossed his hand onto the deadwood.

I drew three.

"Dealer's pat," Charley Bassett said, and craned his neck. "Your bet, Mox."

McQuery shrugged. "Check."

Our two card-playing Cowboys had joined us on the train trip to New York. The red-headed Irishman bet $1, and the pockmarked, dark-haired one smoothed his mustache, stared at the redhead, and finally chipped a coin onto the pile.

"Well, what do you want to see when we get to New York?" Fatty asked.

Sliding my bottle of beer between my legs, I scratched my bottom lip with my left thumb, studying Charley Bassett, then the redhead, then the dark-haired one, and then I saw the look on Mox McQuery's face.

"Pass," I said, and tossed in my hand, looking at Fatty. "I'd really like to see that Statue of Liberty they're putting up."

"No foolin'?"

"Yeah. I've only seen the woodcut in *Frank Leslie's Illustrated Newspaper* back when the statue was still in Paris."

The rest of the poker players laughed at my naiveté.

"Fatty ain't thinkin' 'bout bein' no tourist," one of the poker-playing Cowboys said.

"Yeah, kid," Fatty said. "Hell, I was there when they unloaded that gal's head last June. But let me tell you this . . . she ain't nothin' to look at, kid. I mean, she's frownin' somethin' harder than even Dave Rowe on his worst day. Cold, she is. Like . . . stone. You want to see a girl, a good-lookin' one, I'll take you over to Five Points, kid. You ask Charley, here. He'll tell you that I know where to find the chirpies."

Charley Bassett was staring at Mox McQuery probably as stiffly as the Statue of Liberty's head.

"You checked," Bassett said.

"That's right," our first baseman answered. "And now I've raised."

Fatty Briody turned away from me, wetting his lips. "That ain't friendly, Mox," he said.

"This ain't baseball, boys," McQuery said. "It's poker."

The card players tossed in their cards, and, swearing, Charley Bassett called the raise.

McQuery laid down a straight.

Bassett shook his head, and dropped his cards on my grip. "Yours is higher," he said.

McQuery leaned his head back and laughed like a coyote, but as he started to rake in the money, I opened my big mouth.

"Charley," I said, "you don't have a straight. That's a flush."

Fatty Briody leaned over. "Sumbitch," he said, "and a jack high straight flush at that."

Charley's eyes lit up, but Mox McQuery hurriedly tried to slide the cash and coin into his lap. "He called it," McQuery said. "You got to call your hand right. He called a straight. So I win."

"No," I said, and the card players excused themselves, explaining that they were going to the smoking car, but thanked us for the friendly game. Only it wasn't so friendly any more.

"The hell do you know about poker, boy?" Mox McQuery snapped. "You never played a hand till you got on the train in Kansas City."

So I reached into my other satchel and pulled out the book that I had purchased at a store on Arch Street in Philadelphia. Maybe I had not seen Betsy Ross's home, and probably I would not get to see the Statue of Liberty as she was being erected, but I had seen Salzer's Books & Sundries.

Fatty picked up the book, looked at the cover and read slowly: *"The American Hoyle; or Gentleman's Hand-Book of Games."* He looked at me, and I took the book, opened it to the entry on poker, found my place, and read: " 'Thirty-Two: Upon a show of hands, a player who miscalls his hand, does not lose the pool for that reason, for every hand shows for itself.' "

"Sumbitch, kid." Fatty opened his flask and drank. "You learn poker . . . from books? How'd you learn to pitch?"

"He hasn't!" McQuery snapped, and I figured I had a new enemy as a teammate.

Fatty chuckled, nodded at Charley Bassett, and said: "Reckon the kid's right, Kansas. Take your winnings." He handed the flask toward McQuery, who snatched it. Then Fatty turned to me: "What's it say 'bout checkin' and then raisin'?"

"Nothing," I said, "but it's not the latest version of the book."

McQuery slammed the flask on my luggage. "So . . . maybe that ain't the rule now. Maybe . . ."

"Shut up, Mox." Fatty grabbed his flask. "Poker ain't like baseball. They ain't changin' the rules every year to help all them Eastern teams."

Now McQuery pointed a finger in my face, and, as a long-time first baseman, he had cruel-looking fingers. "You'd done passed, boy. Wasn't none of your affair. I ought to thrash you like a reaper."

"Careful, Mox," Fatty said. "You'll never get

to become no copper if you get arrested for whuppin' up on a kid."

"Actually," I said, thinking back to Dan Dugdale's stories, "a lot of Western lawmen once rode outside the . . ." Mox McQuery's face and crooked fingers silenced me. He was dead serious. He really wanted to kick my arse.

McQuery rose, dumping my grip onto Fatty's and my lap, pushed the passing conductor out of the way—without any apology—and moved like a charging bear to the door and through it, making his way to the smoking car.

"For the son of a Dodge City lawman," Fatty said, staring at Charley Bassett, who was picking up the scattered coins Mox McQuery's tirade had left on the seat and on the floor, "you sure don't know how to read a poker hand."

"Sorry."

I looked at the conductor, smiled meekly, and said: "Mox didn't . . . um . . . see you."

"He didn't see any of Dupee Shaw's fast balls today, neither," Fatty said. "That's what got him into such a foul temper. Don't worry, boys, there's more to the National League than poker. But I think I'd best gather up these paste cards for a spell."

I obliged him, realizing I had learned an important lesson. Poker and baseball do not mix. After that, I never played cards again—at least, not with my teammates. But Fatty Briody was right. There was more to do on the road than play poker on a train. I found the bottle of beer between my legs and took a sip.

"Wait till I show you two boys Five Points," Fatty said, and repeated his mantra: "Cure or the clap. I'll make sure you get one or t'uther." Then, leaning back in his seat, he took my book of poker rules, and began reading.

Truthful Jim Mutrie, despite his boast in Kansas City, did not greet us at Pennsylvania Station and escort us to our hotel with his big-wheeled bicycle.

I did not see the Statue of Liberty, but I was learning. I did not hesitate stepping into the elevator at our hotel, and by the end of our three-game series, I no longer sweated or thought I might vomit when the contraption began its ascent or descent. And I knew better than to take off with Fatty Briody and Charley Bassett to some brothel in Five Points. I remained faithful to Cindy McKim.

But I did drink beer. A lot of it, and the saloon at the hotel was a good place to do it.

"Are you of age?" the barman asked on my first night in New York.

"Hell, yeah," said Stump Wiedman, who beckoned me down the long mahogany bar. "He's older than me, Myrt."

That's all it took. Myrt drew me a foamy beer,

and I spent that night drinking with a few of my fellow ballists. Stump and Cod Myers on the first night. Pete Conway and Grasshopper Jim on the second. And Fatty Briody and Charley Bassett on the train to Boston. And, to tell the truth, I don't know who I got drunk with in Boston.

The Giants swept us, by the way, and the Beaneaters took two of three, and, honestly, they should not have lost the game on the 7th of June, 3 to 2.

So we boarded yet another train after the Tuesday loss and rode to Chicago.

I drank on the long train trip west, too.

I probably would have become just like Fatty Briody, Mox McQuery, or most of my teammates: a boozing, brawling ballist if not for a player I met in Chicago.

His name was Mike Kelly.

CHAPTER FIFTEEN

You've heard of him, I know. Even if you never picked up a copy of the *Sporting News* or *New York Clipper.* Join me in the chorus, and don't fret if you cannot carry a tune:

Slide, Kelly, slide!
Your running's a disgrace!
Slide, Kelly, slide!
Stay there, hold your base!
If someone doesn't steal you,
And your batting doesn't fail you,
They'll take you to Australia.
Slide, Kelly, slide!

We won the first game when Charley Bassett scored on Pete Conway's bloop single for a one-run victory, but lost the next day, 8-to-2, in a contest in which I finally stepped onto the diamond during a game to play ball.

Of course, the game was pretty much over by then—we trailed by six runs in the ninth inning—but as Stump Wiedman had just been hit in the groin by Cap Anson's line drive, Grasshopper Jim was drunk, and Dave Rowe wanted to save Pete Conway for the contest the next day, he reluctantly told me to take the mound as Cod

Myers and Mox McQuery carried Stump from the pitcher's lines to the side of the bench.

"And don't waste time with that loosening-your-muscles horseshit," Dave Rowe grumbled before he walked to the umpire to inform him of the substitution.

Two games I had played in, and only because the pitcher had been drilled with a hit ball.

Fatty trotted up to me before I made my first pitch, pushed back his cap, and spit tobacco juice into the West Side Park dirt.

"Kid," he said, "you gotta show Dave your stuff. Don't mess 'round. Just get these blokes out." He shifted the quid to his other cheek. "This is Chicago, kid. Lots of folks read the Chicago newspapers. Fire 'em in to me."

I glanced at his hands.

With a smile, he spit out more juice. "Don't worry 'bout my hands. I been doin' this a long time."

"You want to go get the mitt Dug gave you?"

"Hell no, kid. Have everyone call me a girlie? That's bullshit. I'll catch whatever you throw me."

And he did, though even the umpire and Abner Dalrymple grimaced at the sound my first pitch made on contact with Fatty's meaty hands.

Dalrymple struck out, yet Fatty somehow managed to hold onto the baseball.

I struck out George Gore, too, on three consecutive pitches, and that brought King Kelly to the plate, with Tom Burns on second base and Anson on first. Not that the White Stockings needed any more runs in the bottom of the eighth inning, but professional ballists do not quit coring runs on purpose. There was no mercy in baseball. Especially in a city like Chicago.

Now I had seen Mike "King" Kelly the previous year, when Mother had taken me to St. Louis to see Chicago play the Browns in one of the United States Championship contests. And I had watched from the bench when Albert Goodwill Spalding's White Stockings came to Kansas City for our season opener. Chicago, of course, won those two games against us, and likely would have won three, but our first game had been rained out. Like most baseball enthusiasts in America, I had read about King Kelly, had worshiped him, and envied him. And now he stepped over the batsman's line, and hefted that Spalding No. 3 bat.

He laid the top of that thirty-nine-inch long, handsome piece of basswood, shining with orange shellac on his shoulder, spit tobacco juice over home base, and put his hands over the handle that looked too thick for even my big hams to get around.

"Low," he said in a heavy Irish brogue as he bent his knees and stared at me with such intense focus that I felt beads of sweat pop out on my forehead. My hands suddenly felt clammy. My mouth turned to sand.

Mike "King" Kelly, the man Frank Harding would write a poem about a few years later, and, in 1893, George G. Gaskin would turn into a popular song: "Slide, Kelly, Slide".

Five-foot-ten, a hundred and seventy pounds, handsome as any ballist around, with a well-groomed mustache and piercing blue eyes. Back in '78, when he was but twenty years old, he had joined the Cincinnati Red Stockings before moving to Chicago in 1880.

The voices of women, yelling encouragement at their favorite ballist, came from the stands. Never before had I heard a woman, except Mother, at a baseball game—and usually I was sitting next to her. Sure, they came to many ball games, but to my understanding ladies were supposed to be quiet.

"Play," the umpire barked, and Fatty Briody moved his thick hands toward the inside of home base.

I went into motion, and, to my amazement, saw King Kelly watch the ball slide past the corner of the plate right above his knee. Even more amazing to me, was the fact that Fatty Briody didn't even have to move his hands, although he dropped the ball on the plate, rose from his squat, and shook his stinging hands, all the while cursing.

"Strike!" the umpire called.

The King stepped out of the box, smiled at Fatty as my catcher picked up the ball to throw back to me. After Fatty settled back into his position, Kelly looked at the umpire and said: "I imagine, Mister Coffelt, that you won't allow me to change where I'd like my pitches."

"You know the rules, Mike," the umpire said.

"Aye, Kerry. That I do." He stepped back toward home base, and his eyes, his focus, grew even more intense.

Fatty set up in the same spot, and braced himself for another hard pitch. Yet something about Mike Kelly made me think: *Not so hard this time. He has seen your fast ball. Slow this one down.*

Actually, I took a lot off that pitch, more than I expected, more than Fatty was prepared for, but I certainly fooled King Kelly.

He swung so hard, and so early, that he spun around and fell to his knees.

The crowd gasped.

"That's strike two," the umpire said.

Kelly brushed off his pants, checked his bat, spit tobacco juice into his hands, and looked at the umpire. "I don't recall seeing this bloody kid before, Kerry. Do you?"

"Fresh fish," the umpire said.

That was King Kelly, to be sure. As Fred Pfeffer would tell me at Tom Cobb's saloon later that night. "It's King's way, son. He plays smart, you see, plays the umpire as wisely as he plays the opposing nine. Makes a friend of him, he does, engages his confidence, figures a way to get the best of those decisions. You won't find a smarter ballist than King Kelly, sonny, and that's the God's honest truth."

Two strikes. No balls. Fatty moved his thick hands toward the far side of the plate, and I sent a fast ball out of the reach of King Kelly's giant bat. King Kelly, of course, was too smart to chase a ball that far out of the strike zone.

He tapped the heels of his shoes with his thick bat, one foot at a time, and settled in for another pitch. Which I blew past him, just below the belt, dead center. He cut loose with a mighty swing, but couldn't catch up to my pitch that knocked Fatty Briody onto his hindquarters, who managed somehow not to drop the ball.

"The striker," the umpire said, "is out."

As the Chicago fans groaned, and maybe even cried, Mike Kelly stepped away from home base, spit tobacco juice, and shot me a glance as he walked back toward the bench. In that glance he winked at me, shook his head, and then tossed his bat to Cap Anson before fetching his glove and trotting off to center field.

I moved to our bench, where Fatty, McQuery, and Myers all slapped me on the back. We prepared for our last at-bat.

"C'mon," Jim Lillie said. "We're still in this game."

We weren't. Paul Radford and Fatty Briody grounded into outs on the first pitches in the ninth inning, and McQuery popped up to Kelly in center to end the game.

"We'll get 'em tomorrow, boys," Charley Bassett said.

"Like hell," Dave Rowe mumbled as he shook his head and opened a bottle of beer.

" 'Cause we don't play tomorrow, Kansas," Fatty told him, dipping his stinging hands in a bucket of water. "Tonight's Saturday. What say you and me go find us some chirpies?"

"I don't know," Charley whined.

"C'mon. How 'bout you, kid? You pitched fine, boy. Time to celebrate with some gal you'll fancy."

"Didn't pitch that fine," Dave Rowe said, and finished off his beer in about one swallow. "We lost, didn't we?"

"Not because of the kid, Skip." Fatty pulled his red hands from the water, and held them out for our manager's inspection. "Time you laid off him, too, Skip. And it's time you let him do some hurlin'."

"Who the hell made you manager, you fat slob?"

"Hey, Dave!"

Rowe turned toward Mox McQuery, who held up a bottle of gin. Our surly manager with the sour face tossed his empty bottle toward the fence, and headed for the liquor McQuery had offered him.

As Dave Rowe had turned, McQuery gave me a wink.

Another thing I learned about most baseball players: teammates have short memories. McQuery had forgotten all about that poker argument. I decided he would make a mighty fine peace officer when his days on the baseball diamond had ended.

So we found our way back to our hotel. Naturally, Fatty Briody, Charley Bassett, and a few others made their way to some dance hall or brothel; Dave Rowe headed out to piss somebody else off; some players went to supper; Stump Weidman stayed in bed; a few went to the hotel saloon. I found my way to Tom Cobb's saloon.

Fatty Briody had once told me that beer was an acquired taste. I had acquired it early.

I bought a beer for Fred Pfeffer, and he bought one for me. Unlike that dreary grog shop in Philadelphia, Tom Cobb's place was pleasant, and full of baseball players, professionals and amateurs alike.

After my sixth pail of lager, a hand slapped my back, and I turned to stare into those blue eyes of King Kelly.

"Tell me you're from County Cork," he said, putting his right foot on the brass rail and tapping on the bar with a coin. "Another pail for this thrower of flame, Tommy, and three for me."

"I'm from Kansas City," I said softly.

"But you're Irish, right, laddie?"

"Missouri," I said.

"No matter. You're a King, and I'm the King." The beer arrived. We drank. Then we drank some more. I forget how many. In fact, I don't remember much of anything until I found myself in a hack well past three in the morning, sitting next to Mike "King" Kelly, trying to sing a song, even if he was singing in Gaelic. Suddenly, King Kelly leaned out of the conveyance, and began banging on the roof. "Mack!" he called out to the driver. I reached over quickly, getting my fingers inside his belt—for the ballist still wore his baseball pants—to keep him from falling onto one of Chicago's paved streets. "Stop this bloody torture chamber!" he yelled.

"Whoa!" called out the driver, and the hack pulled up alongside a curb.

Out jumped King Kelly, and I followed, watching him as he weaved around the rear of the cab, to the sidewalk, against the shuttered brick building, then stumbled back to the rear wheel of the wagon. He loosened his belt, unbuttoned his britches, and began urinating on the wheel and the street.

"I have . . . to . . ." He gripped the top of the wheel, finished his business, and began working on buttons and belt, though he couldn't seem to figure out which he should do first—and, even drunk as I was, I had no intention of helping him.

"King!" called out the driver.

"Just a minute," I said, and whispered to the speedy, daring White Stockings outfielder: "Hurry, King. Hurry."

"I always hurry," he said, managing to buckle his belt and get most of the buttons done up. He turned, fell back against the cab, and grinned. "And sometimes . . . I cheat."

"King!" the driver called out again.

"We're coming." Turning to open the door, I saw the policeman and drew a sharp breath.

It was then I remembered what the concierge—whatever he was supposed to be—had told me at the hotel: "Coppers have been tetchy, you see, since that Haymarket riot in May." He had gone on about those *damned anarchists* and told me to be careful. I knew even I might be bad-tempered after seeing a bomb and a gun battle leave eight policemen dead and fifty-nine wounded.

"Mike," I said, trying to rouse him, but I stepped away as the policeman approached us. I smiled, letting him see the palms of my empty giant hands.

He was a big man with a handlebar mustache, wearing the brass buttoned blouse and the high pith helmet. His shoes clicked on the sidewalk, and his left hand clutched the handle of his nightstick.

"What's the trouble?" he asked.

That Irish accent made me feel a little better.

"Oh." I waved toward Mike Kelly, who had turned back to grip the wheel again. I feared he might vomit, or pass out. "The wheel seemed to be . . . um . . . unstable," I ventured. I looked up at the top of the coach, but saw only the dark night. *Criminy,* I thought, *I might pass out or vomit myself.* "Driver asked us to check it out."

That's when Mike King Kelly turned around and fell against the coach again. At least he kept his feet.

The policeman walked up to me, but kept his eyes on Kelly. After peering through the open door of the coach to make sure no anarchist remained inside, he stepped to the rear wheel. At length, his hand left the nightstick, and he turned to me.

"Aye, yes, I see your problem, lad. It's your wheel. It seems to have sprung a leak."

He moved back to me, gave the cab driver a mean stare, and stood inches from my face. "That's King Kelly, isn't it?" he asked.

"Yes, sir."

"You know that miser of an owner he has . . . . Mister I-Must-Be-God Spalding . . . held out two hundred and fifty dollars of King's pay this year. He doesn't get it back if he keeps on drinking. Do you know that?"

My head shook.

"Don't you play with him, lad?" the peace officer demanded.

"Against him."

"Against him?" The policeman stepped back,

which allowed me to breathe again, for his breath stank of tobacco and rotten food.

"I'm from Kansas City," I said. "With the Cowboys."

Now he smiled. "And what are you doing with the enemy on a night like this?"

I shrugged. "He's not an enemy. Only an opponent."

"Now, that is an attitude I like. Get him home, lad. Home and to bed. Maybe he'll make Mass, though I doubt it. As long as he's ready for the Monday game, right?"

My head bobbed, and I moved fast, practically shoving Kelly onto the floor of the coach. I turned back toward the Irish peace officer.

"Thank you, sir," I said.

"Don't thank me, lad. Just get King Kelly home before I change my mind."

I wet my lips. "I don't know where he lives."

"Get him somewhere."

Which proved to be a Catholic church, just off Taylor Street, not far from West Side Park. It was the cabbie's suggestion.

By the time I made it back to the team's hotel, the sky was turning light gray in the east, and, somehow, I managed to find enough money in my pockets to pay the hack. I even felt sober, relatively speaking. When I reached my room, I found Fatty Briody snoring. The room smelled sour, so I moved to the window, forced it open, and sat in the chair, letting the wind—cool for June—waft life back into the room and myself.

I had struck out King Kelly, and, in return, he had taught me a lesson. I could go through my baseball career—however brief it might turn out to be—like King Kelly or Fatty Briody, as a drunkard. Or I could stop, practically before I had even started, right now.

Which is what I did. Since that night in Chicago, I have never consumed more than one glass of wine or a bottle of beer—and never any ardent spirits— with supper. And even those occasions prove rare.

No one ever wrote a poem about me. People never sang a song about me. Emery & Hughes would not ask me to pen my autobiography in 1888, or any other time. Few people remember me. But as I write this in 1903, on a beautiful October after-noon before the fourth game of the first "World's Championship Series" between the National League and the new American League, I know this.

Mike "King" Kelly, who the world remembers as one of the greatest ballists ever to steal a base, chase down a fly ball, or hit a mammoth home run, has been dead for nine years. He left behind a widow and bar tabs across Boston, where he had been sold to the Beaneaters after the 1886 season and where he would spend most, but not all, of his final years in professional baseball. He was only thirty-six years old when he drank himself to death.

CHAPTER SIXTEEN

A herd of Texas longhorn cattle, fifty yards across, two miles long, moves across the Flint Hills of Kansas on a miserably hot August morning. You can't see most of the cattle, however, and certainly not much of that rolling countryside. All you can see is the dust, thick and choking, like smoke.

In my imagination I could see, though, everything, clearly. I even saw myself as one of the cowboys, riding on the western flank—or maybe the swing position. . . . I never could get those two straight in my mind. Swing? Flank? Which one was which? Certainly not point or drag—those positions I understood. Yet I found no Dan Dugdale here to sort out such details about driving a herd of cattle from Texas to some Kansas end of trail. While I could certainly point out second base or shortstop on a baseball diamond, despite all my interest in cowboying, *swing* and *flank* still confused me.

"Boy," a voice said as someone sat down in the seat across from me. "What the Sam Hill are you staring at?"

That vivid image of me working cattle disappeared, replaced by the reflection of a teen-ager pressing his head against the window in a Wabash, St. Louis & Pacific passenger car. As the locomotive rolled through midnight's blackness somewhere between Chicago and St. Louis, the glass felt cold against my forehead, and I shifted my head from the window to the hard back of my seat, yawned, and answered: "Nothing. I'm not looking at anything."

Then I realized who had taken a seat across from me.

Dave Rowe, our hard-rock manager, stared in silence at me, smoothing his light-colored mustache with tobacco-stained fingers.

"Nothing." I made myself repeat.

"Uhn-huh." Rowe looked across the aisle, where Charley Bassett and Grasshopper Jim Whitney were sleeping. No one else in the car was awake.

My neck ached, probably from daydreaming about being a real cowboy, instead of a baseball Cowboy who had not pitched in months. I made the mistake of rubbing the back of my neck, grimacing while I kneaded the joints, and that gave Dave Rowe an opening to resume our—well, for the two of us—conversation.

"It's a grind, ain't it?" Rowe said.

Releasing my neck, I blinked. "Huh?"

"Baseball. A hundred and twenty-six games. End of April to early October. A grind. Wears a body down."

My stomach knotted. This was Dave Rowe, our pistol-packing manager, and the man who had sworn—and pretty much lived up to his word—

that I would never set foot in a ball game as long as he told the umpire who started. Yet Rowe was speaking civilly, and had not uttered one bit of blasphemy.

Sure, baseball had been a grind. Spring had blended into summer. Games—most of those losses—got all mixed up. Did Fatty make that error that cost us the game in Detroit? Or had George Baker been catching that one before he busted his hand? Train trips and hotels were forgotten. We kept losing. I kept sitting on the bench.

"I guess so," I said. I could think of no fitting response, yet a fierce edge—as though I sat on a dozen shattered bats—replaced that weariness and outright boredom I had been feeling. Dave Rowe, I told myself, must have decided to set me up, see what I would say, just to give him an opening to jump down my throat, embarrass me, or—given the nature of a man like our outfielder and manager—whip out his .32 and put me out of my misery.

He hooked a thumb in the direction of the snoozing ballists. "Shorty's knees are worn out. Stump's got nothing in his arm except gumption, and Jim Lillie twisted his testicles in Detroit. Ain't sure if he done that against the Wolverines or some hussy. Yep. It's a grind, baseball. Wears on a fellow. And we got a lot of games left before this charade of a season and travesty of a team are over."

No longer could I wait for Dave Rowe's ambuscade. That's something else Dan Dugdale had told me about cowboying. "Cattle are stupid. Even dumber than cowboys. You get suspicious of one, think that old mossyhorn's figuring out a way to gore you, just pop him on his hindquarters with a lariat. Let him know you ain't dumber than he is."

Straightening in my seat, I stared into Dave Rowe's cold eyes and told him: "Sitting on a bench from May to August is a grind, too." I tried to mock his accent. "Wears on a fellow."

He stopped fooling with his mustache, and studied me the longest while. At length, he pushed himself to his feet, keeping, to my relief, one hand on my seat while his right hand gripped the back of the seat across the aisle. That meant he couldn't draw that Smith & Wesson without risking losing his balance. The WSL&P's engineer had to be making up for lost time, for our train rocked and rolled down the iron rails faster than Shorty Radford could steal second base.

"I warrant it is, boy," Rowe said. "Maybe we'll see if we can't rectify that a little once we reach Saint Louis."

He nodded at me, a farewell or a goodnight, before he turned to make his way across the car and to the smoking car.

My mouth dropped open.

As soon as the door to our car closed, Charley Bassett sat up. He had been feigning sleep.

"Jesus, Mary, Joseph, and Cap Anson," he said.

"Rowe must be on his way to Bedlam. You smell rye on his breath?"

"No."

"Opium?"

I shook the cobwebs out of my brain.

"Rowe," Charley said, "acted practically . . . human."

"Yeah." It hit me then, what Dave Rowe had suggested. That I might actually get a chance to play baseball again when we took on the Maroons. I said as much to Charley.

"Makes sense," Charley said. "I mean, you beat Saint Louis back in May. And not just with your hurling. You hit that ball plumb over the fence. Rowe's only hit three long balls, and I haven't hit a one."

My head nodded in befuddled acknowledgment. Maybe I would get to play baseball. Like Charley Bassett said, it made sense.

The Kansas City Cowboys rode into St. Louis on August 19th riding a seven-game losing streak. We had been on the road since July 22nd, and during that time we had been swept in a three-game series at Chicago and Philadelphia, losing by a combined fifty runs. That misery had been eased, though, when we won three from the Washington Senators—the one team in the National League that made us look great. Yet the New York Giants ended that winning streak with

14-to-4 and 5-to-4 victories, before we pulled out the last game of the series, 4-to-3. We lost in Boston, 4-to-1, came back to beat the Beaneaters, 6-to-5, and then proceeded to embark on our latest run of misfortune—or just bad baseball. Anyway, we arrived in St. Louis with a record of nineteen victories and fifty-nine losses.

The Maroons hammered us, 10-to-2, on a vilely hot and humid Friday afternoon.

"Don't fret none, boys," Fatty Briody said as we packed up our gear after the loss. "It's a hard thing to win the first game on the road."

"Fatty," Mox McQuery said, "we've been on the road for thirty days."

"That ain't nothin'." Briody's sweat reeked like bacon and beer. "When I was playin' team ball in Lansingburgh, we didn't have no ball park to play at. Spent that whole summer movin' from town to town. Schaghticoke. Clifton Park. Guilderland." He snorted and spit tobacco juice between his shoes. "Dutchmen. Hell. Them Lutherans didn't know nothin' about baseball. Schenectady. Albany. Even as far away as Poughkeepsie and Londonderry Township."

"Shut your trap, Fatty," Dave Rowe said. "Let's get back to the hotel and find some whores. Remember, I do my drinking at Dunn's grog shop on the river. And I do my whoring at Sue's. Don't let me see you bastards there."

So we left the Union Grounds, dodging the

occasional beer bottle—empty, of course—hurled in our general direction, boarded an omnibus, and finally disembarked at the hotel. Although I did not partake in any horizontal refreshments, that did not help us in Saturday's double-header.

Not much had changed during the long, tortuous season. Playing at home or playing on the road, we lost games. I sat the bench. I might drink one beer with the boys when we did win, which proved rare, for I still remembered Mike King Kelly and that awful night in Chicago.

I remembered Cindy McKim, too. I would find a letter waiting for me at every hotel during that miserable month of travel. The boys mocked me as a hen-pecked teen, but I didn't mind. No one wrote them on the road, not their wives, not their concubines. Mother still resented Cindy, but when we were playing in Kansas City, I would find a way to meet her, sneaking off to find some apple cider or ice cream.

St. Louis was the last leg of our long trip.

We arrived home in Kansas City early Sunday morning, our most recent losses now numbering ten consecutive games. And despite Dave Rowe's comment that night on the train, I had yet to leave the bench. It didn't matter that much to me. We were home now, and I could not wait to see Cindy.

After that ten-hour train trip from St. Louis to Kansas City, I found myself excused from attending church, and, since Papa had no brick-laying jobs that afternoon, I had the afternoon and evening free. Telling my parents that some of the Cowboys had elected to practice anyway, I grabbed a bag of baseballs and my bat and made my way toward The Hole—but discretely changed directions.

Cindy McKim waited for me at Barrett & Barrett's. Since Mother had become prone to pass by on the off chance—actually, a really good chance—of finding me there with Cindy, we had been forced to find a new place for apple cider. The Barretts favored a style called "York State". We actually liked Bayersdörfer's better, but liked keeping company with each other, and not Mother, more.

That Sunday afternoon changed the direction of our season, and my life. After leaving the Barrett place, we stopped by the window at Charles Pringle's shop on Main Street. Mr. Pringle, who always sat behind our bench at The Hole, supplied Kansas City with "The Van Orden Shoulder & Skirt Supporting Corsets," and something about that display in the window came over me.

"What are you thinking?" Cindy asked.

"That I want to kiss you." Now, you've read enough of this account by now to know that I do not say such things, ever. Yet those words came right out of my mouth, and the next thing I knew Cindy was in my arms and I tasted the strawberries of her lips and breathed in the fragrance of summer all over her. It was a long kiss, and the only way we separated came from a genteel woman's comment, as she passed by us with her husband.

"I tell you, Bill, the police should run Pringle out of this town on a rail. I'm sick of seeing such licentious displays on *Main* Street!"

"Yes'm, Martha," Bill said, but as he hurried his wife past, he kept glancing back at Cindy and me . . . or maybe the unmentionables in the window.

Cindy laughed, took my massive hand in her dainty one, and led us away from that impious store and into the much more refined Palace Drug Store, where we splurged on ice cream and soda. Things might have continued on a more pious path had we not met Fatty Briody when we stepped back onto Main.

His breath reeked of rye, almost rendering me intoxicated. He wrapped those massive arms around our shoulders and nearly carried us downtown, saying: "You kids gotta see this. You just gotta see this. Ain't never seen nothin' like it before. You ain't. I have. It's absolutely fantastic. Saw it last night with Hofmann. Gotta see it to believe it."

Hofmann, a liquor wholesaler next to the Palace Restaurant on 12th Street, came to our games, and usually escorted Stump, Fatty, and Mox—our most serious drinkers and gamblers—to The Turf

Exchange on Delaware Street, a pool hall and gambling den notorious for running the gambling concessions at The Hole, which our team officials, the National League brass and our city police conveniently overlooked. Even Dave Rowe occasionally showed up at The Turf Exchange, forgetting his rule that players and the manager should not drink in the same establishment.

When I saw The Turf Exchange and the crowd outside the door, I tried to pull away from Fatty but had as much chance as a prairie dog escaping a hawk's talons. "Fatty . . . ," I begged.

"Hush, kid," he said, and squeezed me tighter. "It ain't what you think."

It wasn't, and, most certainly, I found it more stimulating than any Van Orden Shoulder & Skirt Supporting Corset.

"First seen that done by a couple of Italian wenches," Fatty said as he staggered out of The Turf Exchange two hours later. "Couldn't been no more'n ten or twelve. Had to sneak in, which wasn't hard to do." He fell against the brick wall, and grinned. "Morlacchi and Baretta. That was their names. God, they was debauched. But tonight . . ."

". . . was wonderful," Cindy cut him off.

Have you ever seen the can-can? Done by a line of eight buxomly, leggy lasses? Hell, Cindy and I had not even sipped any of Fatty's rye, and we were stunned by it all. I imagine Leopoldina Baretta and Giuseppina Morlacchi must have made that high-leg-kicking dance seem much more refined, more fitting for our Walnut Street Theatre & Coliseum, than watching a bunch of, well, soiled doves show their moves at The Turf Exchange.

"I think I can do that," Cindy said. Let me make it clear that she and I were sober. Lifting the hems of her skirt, she did it. Kick . . . laugh . . . kick . . . laugh, revealing the whiteness of her limbs and a glimpse here and there of bloomers—which the Exchange's can-canners had not been wearing.

I held my breath. Fatty laughed. And Cindy danced herself right into my arms. I wanted to kiss her, but did not—not in front of Fatty Briody.

Fatty said: "Can you do that, Silver?"

I tried.

It wasn't exactly the way the prostitutes had been doing it. Certainly not like Cindy McKim, and I don't think either *signoras*, Morlacchi or Baretta, would have recognized it as the can-can.

First I twisted on my left leg, then lightly sprinted to my right, back again, flip-flopping on my toes and bouncing more like a rubber ball than a dancer. Finally, I just stopped and swung my right arm hard, because, being a pitcher, that's sort of what I did. I didn't mean to punch Fatty Briody in the chest, but it happened, and he staggered away from the wall, laughing, and then, suddenly, he was lying on the boardwalk.

CHAPTER SEVENTEEN

"Criminy."

I lifted Fatty's head. He blinked.

Kneeling next to that kind, fat ballist, Cindy McKim asked: "Are you all right, Mister Briody?"

People kept walking by, some from The Turf Exchange escorting the can-can dancers out for the evening. No one stopped, but most stared as they stepped around us or over Fatty's spread-eagled legs.

"Nobody calls me *mister,* honey," Fatty said. He pushed himself up as a gambler in a bowler passed by, smirking.

"Wipe that off your face, boy, or I'll mop up this street with your face," Fatty snapped as the man picked up his pace, disappearing into the darkness. Then, looking at me, he said: "You ought to pitch like that, kid." He shook the cobwebs out of his head, laughing, before he continued: "Hell of a delivery. Damned near busted my ribs."

Knowing him to be a prankster, and feeling relief that I had not really hurt him, I lightly offered: "I have a bag of baseballs with me."

Which I did. I'd been carrying them with me all night. The bat, I had left underneath a rose-bush two streets from home. Had I any brains,

I would have left the bag of baseballs there as company for the bat, but as Dave Rowe constantly reminded anyone slinging ink for a newspaper or *The Sporting News* or playing baseball for the Cowboys or another National League team: "Pitchers are stupid."

Fatty sat up, then stood up, and said: "Fetch one, kid."

He stepped across the street, pacing the fifty feet and squatted in front of Hofmann's office.

By that time, everyone had departed The Turf Exchange, and the street and boardwalks had emptied except for the three of us.

"How many balls you got?" Fatty asked. "And don't tell me two."

I cringed. Fatty laughed. Feeling the heat on my face, I chanced a glance at Cindy. The yellow light from a street lamp shined down on her, revealing that wonderful face and a devilishly cute smile.

"Three," she answered, reaching into the bag and tossing me the first baseball.

Feeling like a fool, but not wanting this evening with Cindy to end, I took the ball in my left hand and with my shoes drew makeshift pitcher's lines in the street. I twisted on my left leg, bounced to my right, back and forth, and, recreating my version of the can-can, I finally slung the ball to the shady figure across the street. I lost sight of the ball in the darkness, but I heard almost immediately the solid slap of the catch, followed by Fatty's curses. A window rose a block away, and a German accent shouted: "*Halt die Klappe!*"

"Are you all right, Mister . . . Fatty?" Cindy asked.

"Yeah. Give the kid another ball."

The next one produced another string of curses from Fatty, but no German response.

"Last one, kid!" Fatty called out.

Cindy underhanded the baseball to me, and once again I did my silly little dance and cut loose with the ball. There was no loud slap of flesh, no curses from Fatty, just what sounded like the splintering of wood. I could barely make out Fatty as he waddled to the far boardwalk. After exchanging glances with Cindy, we hurried across the street.

"Lost the ball in the dark," Fatty said.

We found it . . . well, not quite. What we saw was the hole the baseball had left in the door to Hofmann's office, and I don't need to tell you that a door that led to a liquor wholesaler's office in this part of town was the heaviest, sturdiest, toughest anyone would find in Kansas City.

"Let's get out of here!" Fatty yelled, and we followed him like proverbial schoolchildren who had just broken a window of a neighbor's house while playing ball.

A few blocks down the street, Fatty entered a dram shop, while Cindy and I boarded a Corrigan Company street car. I helped Cindy on, and she leaned her head against my shoulder and ran her fingers through my silver hair. The night, for August, had turned cool, but we felt warm. Hot. We kissed softly, then hungrily as we had the street car to ourselves, except for the thin cadaver of a driver, and he and his mules minded their own business.

Which you, dear reader, should also be so inclined.

That Monday afternoon, we played the New York Giants in our first game at The Hole in better than a month. Fatty begged Dave Rowe to let me pitch, told him that I had this move that would confuse even the best ballists—which filled the Giants' roster. New York came to Kansas City with fifty-eight wins, twenty-eight losses, and two ties.

Rowe looked hung over. He spit, wiped his mouth, and said: "Show me, boy."

"Fatty . . . ," I pleaded.

"No," he snapped. "You do it, kid. Show Skip. Just like you done last night."

Reluctantly, I did, and Fatty was prepared, sporting that monstrous glove Dan Dugdale had given him. The leather still popped, but Fatty didn't curse. "That's heat, Skip!" he beamed.

Rolling his eyes, Dave Rowe turned toward Grasshopper Jim, only, at that point, Mr. Joseph Heim came up to us, followed by a small Negro boy who could not have been older than eight years.

"Rowe," Mr. Heim said, "meet Leviticus."

Dave Rowe glared at the boy, before turning to give our team president a murderous look.

"He's our mascot." Mr. Heim stood straighter, as if he had just ended poverty and hunger.

"Our what?" Rowe asked.

"Mascot. Grin for Dave Rowe, Leviticus."

Puffing out his chest, the black kid grinned.

Dave Rowe did not. His cold eyes flashed with hatred as he stared harder at Mr. Heim.

"Don't you see," Mr. Heim said, "this nut-colored son-of-ham has a double row of teeth. Parents swear it'll bring us luck." He patted the boy's back like he was tapping a keg of beer. "We could use some luck."

That caused Dave Rowe to start with "Jesus" and end with "Christ", and in between include every bit of profanity Leviticus, no doubt, had ever heard. But the boy kept smiling. The poor child must have been deaf.

"Hell," Rowe said. "A darky mascot and a fool pitcher. All right. You're starting, King, and you . . ." He spit tobacco juice between the boy's bare feet, but apparently could not think of anything else to say, except a few more curses.

I don't know what sickened me more, Dave Rowe, Mr. Heim, the abuse of that little boy, or the fact that I would take to the field and pitch with a movement that would lead to hoots from everyone at this baseball game.

We won the coin toss, and elected to be the home team, so I jogged out to the pitcher's spot and, feeling nauseated, watched as third baseman Dude Esterbrook came up to bat.

After Esterbrook called out—"Low!"—I shunned the fancy footwork and fired a fast ball that the umpire called a ball.

"You show a rank lack of judgment!" Mr. McKim shouted, which reminded me that Cindy would likely be in those stands, too. So would Mother, but Papa was working at the packing house. Mr. McKim directed that shout at the umpire, but Fatty Briody, my catcher, seemed to think he was yelling at me.

He stepped out and threw the ball back to me. "Like you done the other night, kid," he told me.

When my next pitch missed inside, Fatty rose and threw the ball back to me so hard it almost broke my hand. "If you don't pitch the way I tell you, bucko, I'm gonna mop up every bit of dirt on the field with your face. And if you ain't noticed, we gots lots and lots of dirt here."

"Come on, Silver!" That was Cindy's voice.

I shook some feeling back into my right hand, and when Esterbrook was ready, I began. The crowd laughed so hard the stadium appeared to shake when I twisted off my left leg and danced to my right. They roared with delight as I bounced this way and that. Dude Esterbook was laughing so hard that he had doubled over right when I fired a fast ball dead center, just above the knees, that knocked Fatty down.

"Strike!" the umpire yelled.

Two pitches later, Dude Esterbrook carried his bat to the bench.

"The hell happened to you, Dude?" the Giants' left fielder Pete Gillespie asked.

"Hell's fire, Pete," Esterbrook said, "I was laughing so hard I couldn't see straight."

Pete Gillespie did not laugh after he too struck out.

Roger Connor, the Giants' first baseman, did manage to hit my fifth pitch, but Mox McQuery took only a few steps to his left to catch the little pop-up for the third out.

A couple of cowboys—actual working, riding, *cowboys*—stood, drew their pistols—actual, working, firing *pistols*—and shot off a couple of rounds into the air. They were promptly arrested by policemen and handcuffed to the balustrade so they could watch the rest of the ball game. So could the coppers.

Half of the seats in the stands at The Hole had remained empty when our ball game had started, but somehow word of my antics must have gotten out. By the fourth inning, the stands were nearly full and that laughter, whenever I began my can-can inspired delivery, had grown. Because of the heckles, jeers, and applause, no longer could I hear Cindy McKim's voice if she was encouraging me. I couldn't even see her because, when I stepped inside the pitcher's lines, every-one stood. And laughed. Even the Giants chuckled among themselves, and at us . . . but mostly at Dave Rowe.

"Hey, Rowe, never knew you to be a baseball genius!"

"Rowe, did you teach that hurler how to dance?"

"Rowe, is Silver as good in the hay as he is at pitching?"

"Rowe, maybe you should try them moves when you bat next. You ain't had a hit all game!"

By the seventh inning, the laughing and jeering had ended. When I stepped up, got ready to pitch, it felt more like a church before the preacher started his sermon in The Hole.

We led 7-to-nothing. The New York Giants had failed to get a hit, and only four balls had gotten past the infield—all easy pop-ups—two to Rowe in center field, and one each to Shorty Radford in right and Jim Lillie in left.

But I did not finish with a no-hitter. This was in August in Kansas City, and The Hole had turned into a sweat lodge. I had not pitched in a real baseball game in months, so my stamina did not come close to the strength and endurance Grasshopper Jim, Stump Wiedman, and Pete Conway had developed.

In the eighth inning, shortstop John Ward and

pitcher Jim Devlin walked, and Dude Esterbrook managed a single that just got underneath Charley Bassett's fingers, allowing Ward to score. Pete Gillespie, however, struck out to end the inning. He broke his Spalding No. AA over his knees, threw the pieces of the bat at me, and had to be restrained by umpire Kerry Coffelt and Giants catcher Buck Ewing.

I wasn't sure I could even finish the game after we were shut down by the masterful Jim Devlin in the top of the ninth, but then I heard Cindy McKim shout: "You can-can do it, Silver!"

That brought up a chorus that waved its way across The Hole.

"Who can do it?"
"Silver can-can."
"Who will do it?"
"Silver can-can!"
"Can Silver win?"
"Yes, he can-can!"

My face flushed, I lost my composure, and gave up a single to Roger Connor and a double to catcher Buck Ewing.

"Come on, Silver King!" Cindy yelled. "I love you, Silver!"

Joe Gerhardt and Danny Richardson went down swinging, and Mike Dorgan grounded out to Charley Bassett.

We won, 7-to-1, and Fatty Briody flung his

massive pillow of a baseball glove into the air, raced forward, and almost crushed me to death in his vise-like bear hug.

"Did you see 'em, Skip?" Fatty badgered Rowe. "Did you see that? He was somethin', wasn't he, Skip?" Then Fatty anointed my sweaty head with Heim beer.

"He was something," Dave Rowe agreed. "Made a mockery of baseball with that sissy stuff. Hell, this darky boy with his silly teeth played more of a part in our win than this punk."

"Absolutely!" Mr. Joseph Heim agreed, patting Leviticus's head, but he stopped Charley Bassett when our shortstop started to pour beer on me. "You can pour anything made by Adolphus Busch or the Main Street Brewery over anyone's head, Charley. But my beer is to be drunk."

Taking Leviticus's hand, Mr. Joseph Heim slipped the kid a Morgan dollar, and led him away.

"How you feel, Silver?" Charley asked, after sipping some of Mr. Heim's beer.

"Tired," I answered with all honesty.

"But you can pitch tomorrow, can't you?" Fatty asked.

I tried to grin, but my muscles would not co-operate.

"Maybe that little Negro did bring us luck," Mox McQuery said.

"Maybe," Grasshopper Jim agreed.

"Best hope so," Dave Rowe said. "Because you're pitching on the morrow, Jim."

That announcement didn't bother me. I had nothing to prove to Dave, Fatty, or the National League. Besides, my arm and shoulder ached so much—as did my legs and ankles—I wanted a day to recover.

I've never figured out how those dancing girls can do the can-can and keep right on smiling. Hell, they didn't even break a sweat.

Luck is funny when it comes to baseball. And girls. And mothers.

Grasshopper Jim pitched a fine game on Tuesday, but we lost 6-to-2. Pete Conway did not pitch well at all on Wednesday, and we lost 12-to-7. Mr. Joseph Heim fired Leviticus, our mascot. The poor boy, and his parents, were escorted out of the park by city police. That's the kind of boss Joseph Heim could be. Fatty, bless his heart, took up a collection among our players and the Giants, and elected me to see to it that the boy and his parents got the money. "You're the only one amongst us who wouldn't keep this for hisself," Fatty told me. I didn't tell anyone that I saw Fatty stick a couple of greenbacks into his pocket before handing over the collection of cash and coin to me. It took me two days to find the family, but I did—and more

216

than made up for the money Fatty had—ahem—borrowed.

I did not see Cindy after my second victory in the National League, and I did not sneak out of the house to visit her. Mother was waiting for me outside the gates of The Hole—another reason it took me those two days to find our fired mascot. My mother did not grab me by the ear, and she certainly did not congratulate me on my great victory, but she did give me the coldest stare I had ever experienced in my life—and Mother had given me plenty of frigid stares.

"You!" She pointed a finger at me.

I thought I understood. "It was Fatty Briody's idea," I tried to explain.

"I am not referring to that ridiculous pitching movement, a can-can . . ."

"Then . . . ?" My eyebrows knotted. I had no clue what she meant.

" 'I *love* you, Silver.' " She said it with such mocking distaste, I stopped as if she had hit me with a bat. Even one of Dave Rowe's Jesus-son-of-a-bitching-pig-shitting-asshole-damn-it-all-to-hell-bastard-loving-Christ had never sounded so malevolent, so vile.

My cold stare might have matched Mother's.

"You must stay away from that . . . that . . . concubine!"

That's when I pulled away from Mother.

"She's not a concubine," I snapped. "She's

217

a sweet girl. You heard her at the game today, Mother. 'I love you.' Well, maybe you ought to know something else. I love her, too!"

She made as if to slap me, but I leaped back.

"Charles Frederick Koenig!" Mother screamed. My real name never got mentioned, even at the peak of Mother's wrath.

My anger, though, matched Mother's.

"All you ever wanted from me was to play baseball. And maybe that's all I wanted for a while, too. But what I really wanted was to be a cowboy. A real cowboy. Not a Kansas City Cowboy. I never got a horse or pony. I begged for one every Christmas, every birthday. What did I get? Spalding bats, even when I could barely lift one. Eureka balls. Web belts, shoe plates, and Guth's improved supporters!"

"Silver!" The mention of a chamois-skinned men's supporter did not have the same effect on Mother as seeing a Van Orden Shoulder & Skirt Supporting Corset had had on me.

"This was all for you, Mother. Always. The only thing you ever wanted was a son who could play baseball . . . because you never could. Well, here's all I want now. Not to be a cowboy. Not to have a pony or a horse or a friend like Dug Dugdale. I want Cindy McKim. And I aim to have her."

CHAPTER EIGHTEEN

My eyes opened but would not focus. Felt like Mike "King" Kelly was tearing at the inside of my skull with his massive bats. Sand from The Hole coated my tongue, lips, and throat. My stomach roiled, and every muscle in my body ached. I had not had one drink, not even a beer, and barely a glass of water, the previous night, but I did not know where I was. Slowly, an apparition appeared in front of me, standing over me. It spoke.

"Did you sleep here all night, Mister King?"

I tried to sit up, but could not make myself rise, could only groan. The apparition leaned down, and I felt strong hands, big hands—hands that made mine feel small like Cindy McKim's—grip my arms. I felt myself being lifted as if out of a dark, hard coffin. My knees bent. My legs touched the ground. My butt still sat on something solid.

"Rest here for a minute, sir," the voice told me.

Running my tongue over my chapped lips, I slowly remembered the argument with Mother, and then wandering the streets for half the night.

The apparition had returned, was handing me a ladle of water. I drank. The water revived me, and I said: "Thanks."

"You sleep here all night, Mister King?" I was asked again by the giant.

He was a black man, bigger than me, and wore tall, scuffed boots, duck trousers, a collarless muslin shirt, and a massive cowboy hat I had never seen the likes of, not even at Alfred Cronkrite's store in the West Bottoms. He was a young man in his twenties, he seemed oddly familiar.

"Want some more water, sir?"

"Yeah. Thanks."

Three ladles later, I recognized the home bench at The Hole, but I still hadn't placed the black man.

"You know me?" I asked him.

"Seen you play," he said. "You pitch fine. Real fine."

I laughed. "Means you've been to two games," I told him. "One in Saint Louis. Unless you were in Denver early this spring."

I blinked, and, grinning, he took the ladle. "I was here Monday," he informed me. "Never seen such moves or hard throwin'."

"It was a joke," I told him.

"Them Giants wasn't laughin' by the end. And I saw you and Dan playin' catch that time near the Armour pens."

Then I remembered him. He was one of the cowboys sitting on the top rail of the pen when Dan Dugdale had roped Molly.

The black man said: "My name's . . ."

"Hackett!" was shouted out some distance from us.

Our heads turned to find Mr. Joseph Heim walking toward us. Behind him came Cindy's father, Americus McKim, and *Times* sports scribe James Whitfield.

Setting the ladle on the bench, the black cowboy stood, turned, and grinned the most sickeningly sweet grin anyone had ever mustered. He also thickened his accent like some actor in blackface doing a minstrel show at the Gillis Opera House.

"This is him," Mr. Joseph Heim announced to Mr. McKim and Mr. Whitfield, stopping a respectful distance from myself and Hackett. "Our new mascot."

"What does he have?" James Whitfield asked. "*Three* sets of teeth?"

"Jes' dis one," Hackett said as he rubbed a big index finger across his uppers, which were straighter than mine. And, unlike, Mr. Whitfield, Hackett had all of his.

"Well . . . ," Mr. McKim began, staring at me, which caused my stomach to roil again. Did he know about Cindy and me? "What do you do?" he then asked, turning toward Hackett.

"I's the seventh chil' of a seventh daughter," Hackett said.

Mr. Joseph Heim's hands clapped. "That's good luck. Great luck. And he's an honest-to-God cowboy. Trailed longhorns from Texas all the way up to Montana. Ain't that right, Hackett?"

Hackett grinned.

"He's our new mascot, Mert Hackett," Mr. Joseph Heim stated proudly. "What do you think?"

"God help us," Mr. McKim said.

"Listen," Mr. Joseph Heim said. "The Giants bring that thirty-eight-pound bulldog with them wherever they go. He's their mascot. How many games have they won? More than us. Boston hired itself a mascot, some old white-washer or something like that, stays on the Beaneaters' bench, and they aren't a bad team. Whitfield here told me that Boston's mascot is the seventh child of a seventh daughter. Well, Hackett is, too. We need a mascot. And you tell these gents what you told me, Hackett."

Hackett said boastfully: "I says . . . 'I'll fight that dog 'em Giants brings to this park, any time. I'll whup'm, certain sure, and then we'll whup 'em Yankee boys.'"

Whitfield did not respond to that, instead he turned his attention to me. "You're here early."

"Double-header," I reminded him.

He pulled the pencil from atop its perch on his right ear, and fetched a notebook from his coat pocket. "You pitching, Silver?"

"That's up to Dave," I said.

"You look like shit," Whitfield said.

"He won't look that way for long," Mert Hackett said. "You waits. Waits to see how I fix'm up. Seventh chil' of a seventh daughter. That's luck. Best luck of any kind."

"And a real cowboy," Mr. Joseph Heim added.

The owners of our baseball team walked away, and Mert Hackett and I watched them go. When they had disappeared, I turned to study the big man, who looked at me and grinned.

"What game are you playing?" I asked him.

"Ain't playin' no game," Hackett said, and stretched out his long legs. "But sure wish I was."

"They're playing you for a fool," I said.

He chuckled. "As a cowboy, I earned a dollar a day. These days, I make that much slamming hammers into steers' heads, and that's a bloody job that most cowboys wouldn't ever dream of doing. That beer man . . . Mister Heim . . . he says he'll pay me five whole dollars for ever' victory I win for y'all." Mr. Heim had paid Leviticus only one dollar. "I get to sit on the bench with you boys, and watch some real, honest-to-goodness National League baseball . . . for free. Now, Mister King, you tell me who's playin' who for a fool."

"Jesus . . . ," Dave Rowe stopped his usual string of curses. He shook his head at Mert Hackett and Mr. Joseph Heim. "A damned rabbit's foot is cheaper, you know. You want to find a good-luck mascot for us, Heim, how about a redhead with green eyes and a bottle of gin? What is it with you and darkies anyway?"

Beside me, Mert Hackett just grinned, but I could see his right fist clench into a ball so tightly that his hand shook. His arms bulged with muscles, and it had to take a lot of strength, mentally and physically, and a great deal of fortitude to slaughter pigs, cattle, and sheep six days a week.

"Seventh child of a . . . ," Mr. Joseph Heim began to remind him, but Rowe cut him off.

"I know. I know."

As we all watched Fatty Briody marching toward us, Rowe bit off a mouthful of chewing tobacco, shoved the rest into his pocket, and said: "All right. Let's see how good your luck is, boy. King."

I blinked, my name slow to register as I stared at the manager.

"You're starting. Both games." He spun, tipping his ball cap at Fatty who was less than two feet away now, and said: "That suit you?"

Fatty Briody could only grin.

Now, lest you think of me as some superhuman specimen, let me explain that our opponent that afternoon was the team from Washington, and the Senators played bad baseball. Really bad. Yet in that first game, they had a rookie hurler, a kid nobody had ever heard of, and he pitched tough. Really tough. Six-foot-one, but rail thin, and not more than twenty-three or twenty-four years old. Yet he threw with exceptional speed, mixed up his pitches, and kept us off balance when we came to bat. He did not have to do some silly dance to strike people out.

Again, our crowd filled maybe a quarter of the stands at the start of that game, but word soon spread that Silver King was *can-canning* things again, and with the score tied at 2 in the sixth inning, people began filling The Hole.

I came in, my shoulder hurting as though Papa had forced me to fill my hod with fifty pounds of bricks and mortar all day. Mert Hackett jumped up and moved behind me, then worked his massive hands on my shoulders, kneading and crushing, and dumping ladles of water over my arm and my sweat-soaked head.

The kid pitching for Washington struck out Cod Myers and Jim Donnelly before Charley Bassett and Jim Lillie walked.

"See," Mert Hackett whispered. "He's tirin', too. You just watch yourself. . . ."

"Hell!" Dave Rowe yelled from the plate. "What the hell!"

Cod had tried to steal third base, but catcher Barney Gilligan easily nailed him.

"You dumb son-of-a-bitch!" Rowe roared. "I could have driven you both in. Dumb bastards!"

"Rowe's testy," Mert whispered. "But you watch Gilligan. He bats first, and he's mean. He's also figured you out, King. Was I you, I'd shun that can-can nonsense and just fire inside. Fool looks like a baby tryin' to hit an inside pitch."

His hands pulled me off the bench, and I

225

gathered my thoughts, pulled a fingerless glove over my aching catching hand, and returned to the field.

Barney Gilligan seemed small for a catcher, and old for one, too, but he had been playing this game for a long time, mostly with the Providence Grays back when the Grays were tops. Why, he had caught Old Hoss Radbourn and Pud Galvin back in the day. And he swung three No. 4 Spaldings before he came to bat, picking the bat he liked best.

Fatty Briody grinned, settled into his crouch, and the umpire got set. I tried to drown out the cheers, while at the same time trying to hear Cindy's voice. One thing I did not do was look into the stands, fearing I would see Mother.

"High!" Gilligan called.

With a nod, I fired a fast ball, but without the can-can tomfoolery. I did something else, something I don't think I even realized. Instead of coming up over my head, I threw the ball from my side—perhaps because I could not lift my arm all the way over my head. I don't know. I didn't even remember doing it. The ball did not catch the inside part of the plate. It went outside, and Gilligan did not swing.

"Strike!" the umpire yelled.

"He can't do that," Barney Gilligan cried.

"Do what?" the umpire asked.

"Throw from third base!"

Fatty Briody had stepped out in front of Gilligan and the umpire and started to yell at me for forgetting to do that stupid move, yet he stopped, spit tobacco juice into the dirt, and returned to his position. I had just thrown a strike to one of the hottest hitters for one of the worst teams in all of baseball.

Gilligan swung at the next pitch, which I also delivered side-armed. He missed badly.

Fatty stared at me the longest while, but said nothing. I took the ball, and found my place. But I glanced back toward the bench, and found Mert Hackett. Yawning, he raised his right arm over his head, and brought it down. He grinned at me, and mouthed: "Inside."

It hurt like hell, but I made myself throw a fast ball, high, overhanded, and inside. Mert Hackett had been right. Barney Gilligan looked like a five-year-old swinging that big bat at an inside pitch. He fell out of the batsman's lines and onto his knees near the Washington bench. Yet ever the good sport, he merely ignored the catcalls and laughter from the grandstands, tossed his bat up with his right hand, caught it with his left, and strode calmly back to the bench.

Phil Baker walked, and again I turned back toward our bench while Jimmy Knowles, playing second base, came to bat.

This time I saw Mert Hackett raise his left leg slightly, then his right, then his left, at what I took to be a sign for me to go back to the can-can routine. Which I felt ridiculous doing, but, still, I followed Mert Hackett's instructions. Don't ask me why. Perhaps he had put me into a trance.

I shook off any thought, and told myself aloud but in a whisper: "You're thinking like Mister Heim, Silver. Just pitch."

The crowd erupted as I returned to the can-can. Jimmy Knowles grounded into a double-play turned deftly by Charley Bassett, Cod Myers, and Mox McQuery.

Dave Rowe rocked the Senators' kid's first pitch for a triple, scored on Shorty Radford's infield single, and we went on to post a 5-to-2 victory.

To be honest, I don't remember a thing about the second game I pitched. I blame that on heat stroke. We won, I was told, 7-to-0.

After the game, a double-header sweep, we invited the Senators' players over to our bench to share a keg of Heim lager—just as though we were playing team ball in Denver or somewhere. The kid who had lost to me in the first game came up and said: "How do you pitch that way?"

I shrugged. "I don't know."

"Wish I could do it, but I'm not much for dancing."

I held out my hand, and we shook. "My advice doesn't amount to much," I said, "but if I were you, I wouldn't change anything about the way you pitch."

He beamed as if I were Cap Anson or Mr. Spalding himself.

"You think so?"

"I know so."

"Thanks . . . umm . . ."

"Call me Silver."

"Thanks, Silver." We shook again.

"My name's Mack," the kid said. Kid? He was a few years older than me. "Connie Mack."

That night, Fatty Briody told me in no uncertain terms that I would not sleep on the bench at The Hole again. He took me to his place in a flea-bag hotel off Delaware. He didn't even go out drinking.

Connie Mack came back to pitch the next day. I watched from the bench, while Mert Hackett worked my arm back into some semblance of shape. The Senators won, 5-to-2, and, no, Connie Mack did not win that game doing can-can routines or side-arm deliveries.

"Can you pitch tomorrow, King?"

I looked up to find Dave Rowe staring down at me. Dave Rowe had just asked if I could pitch, and he had called me by my name, not "boy".

"Sure, he can, Mister Rowe," Mert Hackett answered. "I gots his arm all fixed up. Ain't that right, Mister King?"

"I didn't ask you," Rowe snapped, adding a vile word.

"I can pitch," I told him, though I wasn't sure I could.

"Good," Rowe said. "Because when you lose, maybe I *can-can* your sorry ass." He must have been waiting to try that *can-can* shit out. "And get rid of this stupid mascot, too."

But we won, 8-to-1, our third victory in four games, and our fourth in seven. I know that's not quite the same as fourteen-game winning streaks, but for the Kansas City Cowboys it appeared phenomenal.

And when Mr. Joseph Heim paid Mert Hackett another $5 gold piece, Dave Rowe went crazy mad.

Tomorrow was the 1st of September, and the Philadelphia Phillies were coming to play us.

"Grasshopper," Dave Rowe said, "you're pitching. Every damned game of the series."

"Skip," Fatty said, "you can't. I mean, use Grasshopper in one game, but you can't stop this kid. He's on fire. Nobody can hit him. Not even you, Skip."

That's when something else happened that changed my life, and changed the Kansas City Cowboys' season.

Dave Rowe pulled out his Smith & Wesson and shot Fatty Briody in the gut.

CHAPTER NINETEEN

The clipping pasted below shows you exactly how James Whitfield recorded that horrific incident in the Kansas City *Times*.

Our valiant Cowboys bounced back to pound the Senators from the Great Capital City, 8-to-1, yesterday afternoon as rookie Silver King dominated the boys from back East with his Western dancing-pitching—or should we call that Western pitching-dancing?

Yet by the fall of evening, the Kansas City ballists were saddened, disheartened, and numbed by the loss of the great, boastful, friendly, and all-loving catcher, Charles Briody—affectionately called "Fatty" by teammates and opponents alike.

It seems that one of Silver King's hard-hurled pitches—we could not ascertain whether it was his "Can-Can" delivery or this new and quite unique side-armed throw—got past that sofa cushion Briody wears when catching the local rookie and nailed Mr. Briody in his ribs.

The result was that Mr. Briody sustained five broken ribs, but, ever the courageous athlete, so devoted was he to duty and our Cowboys that he finished catching the contest and took part in the celebration with his teammates before collapsing near the Cowboys bench and writhing on the ground in miserable, gut-wrenching agony. Shocked teammates gathered around the supine athlete to administer comfort and soothing words.

Working quickly, teammates Mox McQuery, Silver King, and team vice president Americus McKim hailed gallant policemen and a hack to transport the gallant Mr. Briody quickly to St. Joseph Hospital, where those devoted friends turned their groaning teammate over into the capable hands of Mother Celeste O'Reilly and our young physician, Dr. Jefferson Davis Griffith, who arrived in our fair city back in 1874 from New York. No doubt, Dr. Griffith took great pleasure in rendering medical assistance to a fellow brother of The Empire State. Mr. Briody hails from Lansingburgh, but has been quickly adopted by Kansas Citians, who love good sportsmanship, good spirits, and the greatest game on the face of the earth.

Dr. Griffith pronounced the broken ribs as serious but unlikely to be life-threatening. Immediately afterward, Mr.

Americus McKim departed via train in hopes of finding another catcher to sign to a contract to help fill in for Briody as the solid, eager player mends his ribs under the care of the Sisters of St. Joseph of Carondelet. Accompanying Mr. McKim, known for his generosity and his erudite handling of his barley and malt enterprises, was the Cowboys hurler, Master Silver King, who was so overcome with remorse that it was his pitch which felled the mighty giant that he insisted on having a hand in finding a capable replacement for Mr. Briody.

In the meantime, team President Joseph Heim announced that Mr. Briody will be replaced, for the time being, by Frank Ringo, a cousin of the famed gunman John Ringo who was involved in the scuffles in Arizona Territory with Wyatt Earp, who happens to be a friend of Cowboys shortstop Charley Bassett's father in Dodge City. We wonder if these two teammates, part of a grand Western vendetta, might be more prone to throwing lead at each other than a friendly game of catch. It should be fun to see, though, especially for our wild-and-woolly baseball fanatics.

Also, Mox McQuery, who Mr. Heim

cited for his baseball knowledge and peacekeeping abilities, will be replacing Dave Rowe on a temporary basis as manager of the Cowboys.

So stunned by the injury of his favorite catcher and one of his best friends, Dave Rowe fell into a series of apoplectic seizures, and was rushed, escorted by other members of our upstanding city police department, to the new German Hospital, which lies far out of our city proper at the old Henri farm.

Cheery mail and pleasant cards or flowers would be much appreciated by our felled athletes, but doctors confirm that neither Mr. Briody nor Mr. Rowe will be allowed any visitors for the near future. Watch these pages for any updates.

Of course, prayers are requested for our great catcher, Mr. Briody, and loving manager-center fielder, Mr. Rowe, and, especially, for our Kansas City Cowboys. May they continue their winning ways.

The Phillies have arrived from Philadelphia, and the first game of that tilt is scheduled for 2 o'clock in the afternoon today.

Although there were grains of truth in Mr. Whitfield's article, I do not recall the events after that ball game quite the same. What I remembered was that Dave Rowe would have shot Fatty Briody again had not Mox McQuery dived over the bench, one hand knocking the .32 downward so that the second bullet merely tore into the hard bench, leaving a splintered ditch, and lodged in the center of Cod Myers's new John Hillerich-designed bat. Which enraged Cod Myers so much that he jumped into the fray.

During my brief tenure in the National League, I had seen umpires maligned and even shot at. More than once, our police had to escort an umpire out of The Hole under armed escort. Otherwise, Americus McKim might have headed a lynch mob. Patrons at League Park had come close to rioting. Some umpires quit after one game in Kansas City. I remember one telling me: "You expect to be hissed and hooted at. But shot at?"

Another umpire told a reporter who printed this in the New York *Times*:

> I have often heard that an umpire's position was a thankless one, but I have never realized it before. It's bad enough to be hissed and called a thief, but in the West when the local club loses, an umpire is fortunate if he escapes with his life. Of all the cities in the league Kansas City is the worst.

I had never seen anything like this, though later I would witness an even more horrific Donnybrook.

Mind you, Mox McQuery had a great hold on Dave Rowe, and Cod Myers took advantage, pounding Dave with left and right punches. Americus McKim yelled for some of the remaining city policemen, who had been preoccupied with their task of rounding up their typical dozen or so drunks and hooligans they had shackled during the game, to come to our assistance.

During this time, I lifted Fatty's head into my lap while our mascot, Mert Hackett, whipped off his bandanna and plugged it against the bloody hole in our catcher's abdomen.

"If . . . ," Fatty tried. "If I'm . . . shot in the liver . . . I'm a . . . dead man."

"Fatty," Grasshopper Jim said softly, "if you got shot in your liver, the bullet's the one that'll be mortally wounded."

That managed to stop Fatty's tears, and he actually laughed.

"Thanks, Jim." Fatty coughed. I held my breath, exhaling only when I saw no blood leave Fatty's mouth, just saliva.

His eyes turned to me. "Get my key, kid. It's in my pocket. You might as well sleep at my place again."

"Fatty . . ."

"No. Do like I tell you. Or go home . . . where you belong."

My face hardened, and Fatty, groaning, got the key to his rat-infested slum out of his pocket. He placed it in my hand.

"How is he?" a feminine voice asked.

My head shot up. Cindy McKim was kneeling down next to me.

"Cindy," her father said, "you had best go home."

"Yeah," said Cod Myers, who had given up on punching Dave Rowe any more. Our manager had slumped into unconsciousness on the other side of the gunshot bench. "Ain't for no lady to see."

"Silver," Mr. McKim said. "Take my daughter home."

"No," Cindy said. "Silver's place is with Fatty. I'll go." She looked around, found Charley Bassett, and said: "Charley, can you take me home?"

Charley, mouth open, looked quickly at me. "Umm . . ."—then remembering that it was Mr. McKim who signed his paycheck—"well, is that all right with you, Mister McKim?"

"Yes. See her home. And for God's sake, don't talk to any newspaper reporters."

I watched our shortstop lead my love away.

"Blood ain't dark," Mert Hackett said.

My focus turned to our mascot. "That means?" I asked, fearing the worst.

237

"It's a good sign," Hackett said. "Bullet didn't hit the liver."

"And it's only a Thirty-Two caliber," said Mox McQuery. "He might make it."

"Jesus . . ." Mr. Joseph Heim had joined us, starting off with a fair impression of one of Dave Rowe's curses, and ending it with: "How in hell are we going to explain this?"

How, of course, they left to Mr. James Whitfield and his exaggerated prose with the *Times*.

Seeing what had happened, a police sergeant yelled for one of his coppers to fetch the paddy wagon—not a hack—so that Rowe and Fatty could be rushed to a hospital.

"Two wagons!" Mr. McKim said. "Take Briody to Saint Joseph Hospital."

"What about Rowe?" the Irish sergeant asked.

Whitfield answered: "The German Hospital. No one would look for him there. It's so far from here. But just in case . . . tell the doctors and nurses that no one . . . no one . . . is to be allowed to see Rowe, except McKim, Heim, or me. No one." Whitfield nodded at McKim, who promptly found his billfold and slipped the policemen several greenbacks.

While Mert Hackett continued to work at stopping Fatty's bleeding, two policemen dragged the unconscious Rowe out of The Hole, put him in the police vehicle, and took him to the hospital. I think, though, for Dave, it was more of a jail. Besides, I wasn't even sure the German Hospital had opened for business by that time.

It made sense, though. A couple of Germans named Schoellkopf and Spengler came to many of our baseball games, and they had formed this group that wanted to start this new hospital. The Germans then bought a three-story brick farmhouse well out in the country near Twenty-Third Street for $10,000. The remoteness of the facility might keep admiring fans or curious reporters from checking on Dave Rowe. I learned later that Mr. Whitfield told the staff at the hospital that should anyone come that far out of town to ask about Rowe, they were to speak German only, and pretend they could not understand English. I don't know if Mr. Whitfield had an alternate plan if the visitor actually spoke fluent German.

As we waited on the second paddy wagon to rush Fatty to St. Joseph Hospital, our team's three co-owners had other concerns—I directed all of my thoughts and prayers to my loyal, grievously wounded catcher and friend.

George Baker had been catcher for a few games for us whenever Fatty wasn't available, but he had broken his hand in a brawl two weeks ago, so he couldn't play.

"Mox?" Mr. Whitfield asked. "Can you catch?"

"Hell, no," Mox McQuery responded. "Especially if that son-of-a-bitching kid's throwing." He gave me a wink, and added: "I don't squat so good, Mister Whitfield."

"How hard can it be?" Mr. Heim asked. "Surely someone we have on this team can do it."

Frank Ringo was Mert Hackett's idea.

Mr. McKim and Mr. Heim began discussing the idea of signing someone quickly. Mert Hackett kept quiet, understanding that if he, a Negro, were to suggest a player, he would likely be considered "uppity" and fired on the spot. Besides, $5 a victory was pretty good pay for a cowboy turned animal slaughterer.

Likewise, I knew that the team owners would frown upon a suggestion from a rookie pitcher still in his teens, so I whispered to Mox McQuery. Having saved the franchise from a horrible scandal and Fatty Briody's life, Mox was being held in fine regard at the moment—even if he could not play the catcher's position. He had also batted four-for-five in our victory that afternoon.

"Do you remember a local boy named Frank Ringo?" Mox asked after I relayed Mert Hackett's suggestion to Mox.

The two owners turned and blinked. The name meant nothing to them, but it stopped James Whitfield from writing down any lies in his notebook.

"I do," the sports writer said. "Hailed from Liberty. Played with Peoria for a while, then some local clubs around here. Signed with Philadelphia two, three years back, but kind of disappeared."

"From everywhere but the saloons," Cod Myers whispered. Cod Myers remembered Frank Ringo, too, but Mox McQuery elbowed Cod, and Cod, having exhausted himself by beating Dave Rowe into oblivion, did not press his objections any further.

"Is he around here?" Mr. Heim asked.

Hackett nodded, which provided me enough information to nod, which caused Mox to say: "Yeah, he is."

"There's something about that name . . . Ringo," Mr. McKim said. "Wasn't he in some gunplay out West? Dodge City?"

With Charley Bassett escorting Cindy McKim home, the owners looked to me as the second-best expert on gunmen and cowboys and recent history in our Western territories.

"Tombstone," I said. That's all I wanted to say so I began wiping the sweat off Fatty's brow.

"Well," Mr. Heim said.

I didn't have a choice, so I explained: "Johnny Ringo was a gunman that went up against the Earps. Got killed a few years back." I tried to remember everything Dan Dugdale had told me about Wyatt Earp and Johnny Ringo. "They found him dead underneath a tree. Shot in the head. Never knew for certain if he'd killed himself or if Earp or one of his friends had killed Ringo in revenge."

"Revenge?" Mr. Heim asked.

"That shoot-out and all that bloodletting in that silver town in Arizona," Mr. McKim explained. "I remember it now."

"Wait!" Mr. Heim beamed. "Where's . . . ? Damnation, I wish to God, Americus, that you had not sent Charley Bassett away. Bassett might know of Frank Ringo. There might be bad blood between those two. And that . . ." Heim paused, seemed to be thinking, then brightened, saying: "By God, imagine the crowd *that* would bring in."

James Whitfield started scribbling in his notebook.

"Mox," Mr. McKim said. "It'll be up to you to find John Ringo and bring him to my office."

"Frank Ringo," Cod Myers corrected.

"Sure," Mox said. His face told me that Mert Hackett, who was nodding, and I had better not let him down.

"Well, that's settled," Mr. McKim said just as the police sergeant returned with an actual stretcher. It took two policemen and Mert Hackett and Mox McQuery to load Fatty and carry him out of the stadium. As the closest thing to kin Fatty Briody had in Kansas City, I followed, figuring I would be the only one at the Catholic hospital.

242

But I was wrong. Everyone, including Mr. Joseph Heim, followed us out.

A nun brought us coffee and cookies as the doctor and nurses attended to Fatty Briody. Mostly, we reminisced about our favorite Fatty Briody stories, but that troubled me for it felt more like a wake or funeral, and Fatty was still alive. At least he had been alive when the nurses and a young doctor had carted him down the hallway.

When Dr. Jefferson Davis Griffith returned hours later with news that Fatty Briody would likely survive the wound (barring infection, or heart weakness, or liver ailments, or unseen wounds, or internal bleeding, or simply The Will of God), we celebrated by helping ourselves to more cookies and coffee. A few of the men made the sign of the cross. As a Presbyterian, I merely thanked Jesus, God, and Fatty Briody's toughness. Then I remembered to thank Mert Hackett, and this I did out loud, for our black mascot had been the first one to go to work at stopping Briody's bleeding.

"Yes," said Mr. McKim. "That was fine work, Mert."

Mert Hackett nodded.

"Well, I have beer to brew," Mr. Joseph Heim announced as he rose as if to go home, and no one would have blamed him as, by this time, it was well after ten o'clock at night.

"Not yet." Mr. Whitfield flipped through the pages of his notebook. "Who do we have to replace Dave Rowe?"

"Frank Ringo can play outfield," Mox McQuery offered after I had related Mert Hackett's whispers.

"If he's sober," Cod Myers whispered, adding with a sigh: "But that means we need another catcher."

"Wait a damned minute," Mr. Heim said. "Two more players. That's costing Americus, Jim, and me a lot of money. Signing you ballists isn't cheap. And why can't Silver here play outfield? Or Pete Conway? Or any of you idiots? How hard can it be?"

"Why don't you try playing baseball yourself, Joe, if you think it's so damned easy?" Mr. McKim said testily. "We're winning, Heim. I'd like to keep that up."

Heim's mouth moved, but no words escaped.

"Besides," Mr. Whitfield said, "we have a mascot, and when John Ringo and Charley Bassett shoot it out, you'll more than make up what we spend on a couple of players."

"Frank Ringo," Cod Myers whispered.

Mr. Heim's mouth stopped moving up and down and settled into a smile.

That's when Mert Hackett decided to speak up, although not directly. "Say, Mister King," he said, thickening his accent again. "Don't you recollect that cowboy who used to hang out at the packin' houses. I think he played with Frank Ringo back in Peoria, ain't that right?"

"Why, sure," I said, although I did not know if Dan Dugdale even knew Frank Ringo, or Johnny Ringo.

"I ain't no ballist," Hackett said, "but he sure knows this game. Don't you think?"

"I think so," I agreed.

"Peoria is a long way from the National League," Mr. McKim said.

"So is our team," whispered Pete Conway.

I breathed in deeply, held it, before letting it out. "Yes, sir, Mister McKim. But this player you might remember. Dan Dugdale. Folks calls him Dug. He was playing for Denver's team in the Western League when we had that exhibition series in Colorado. Remember?"

McKim stared at me. I felt myself sweating. Mr. McKim had come close to tearing up my contract after my miserable performance against the Mountain Lions back in April.

"Catcher," Grasshopper Jim said. "Hit that home run in our last game over the center-field fence. Hell of a ballist. Knows the game, too."

"And," I told Mr. Heim, "Dug Dugdale is a real cowboy. You'd have a real cowboy playing for the Kansas City Cowboys."

"And Dan's not as prone to lushing as Frank Ringo," Cod Myers said.

Mr. McKim no longer looked at me. He stared at Mr. Heim, and then at Mr. Whitfield.

"This might work," Mr. Whitfield said. "If we can find Ringo. And I have read some good accounts of this Dugdale's baseball ability."

"I can find Ringo," Cod Myers announced in resignation.

"A cowboy," Mr. Heim whispered to himself. "Playing for the Cowboys. Why, we can break out those cowboy hats again!"

"Oh, God," groaned another Cowboy, echoing Shorty Radford's reaction.

"Mox?" Mr. Whitfield asked. "Can you manage the team until Americus returns with this Dugdale fellow?"

"Sure," Mox answered with eagerness. "Might be good training for me to become a policeman when my baseball career is over."

"It's a long train trip to Denver," Mr. Heim said. "And we've series coming up against the Phillies, Beaneaters, Maroons, Wolverines, and White Stockings."

"Y'all ain't got to goes all the way to Denver," Mert Hackett said. "I overhears a fellow at today's game. He says that 'em Mountain Lions is playin' just up the road in Saint Joe."

CHAPTER TWENTY

We had a problem, I thought, as Mr. McKim and I settled into our seats at the shabby ball park in St. Joseph. With both teams battling for the Western League lead, the St. Joseph Reds had tied the score at 4-all in the seventh inning—and Dan Dugdale was not catching for the Denver Mountain Lions. Instead, he played first base, and after Mr. McKim bought us some roasted peanuts and lemonade, the Reds' leviathan Edward Harting—appropriately nicknamed "Jumbo"—laced a ball just over Dan's outstretched hand, hit fair, that rolled to the fence for a triple.

Before scoring on Skyrocket Smith's single to put St. Joseph ahead, 5-to-4, Harting yelled across the field at Dan: "Dugdale, you stank in Peoria, and you still stink! You're a bum. Go back to herdin' sheep, you pathetic, cow-punchin' excuse for a ballist!"

"I don't know, Silver," Mr. McKim said. "I like this Jumbo better than your Dug. I've seen Jumbo catch before, and he's big and strong. Tall. He wouldn't have had to jump for that scorcher, and he would have caught it."

Every excuse I could think of sounded stupid, so I just cracked a peanut and took a sip of lemonade. My face flushed with rage at Jumbo

247

Harting, but Dan Dugdale ignored the St. Joe star's insults.

So I sweated through the rest of the seventh inning, all through the eighth, and felt relief when Dan Dugdale came to bat in the top of the ninth with two outs and runners on first and second.

"Well," Mr. McKim said, "let's see how your catcher who does not even play the catching position fare in such a situation as this one."

I crossed my fingers.

Dugdale swung at the first pitch and missed badly.

"Humph," Mr. McKim said. "Perhaps we can make this trip worthwhile, though. I've always wanted to see the home where Jesse James was killed. And I am certain I can sign Jumbo Harting."

Dugdale missed the second pitch, too.

"Perhaps Jesse James's mother is interested in playing for our Cowboys," Mr. McKim commented. "She has only one arm, I understand, but undoubtedly could hit better than Dugdale." In one of his vindictive baseball moods, Mr. McKim rose from his chair and yelled: "Come on, you worthless bum! You're a discredit to the game of baseball, you choking coward!"

Local fans filled the stadium, and those all around us cheered Mr. McKim, which fueled my boss and Cindy's father even more. He shouted more insults at my friend.

I tried to sink deeper into my seat. I had heard Mr. McKim's shouts during many of our baseball contests, but never had I sat so close to him. Now I knew what Cindy McKim meant when she said baseball turned her father into a monster.

The pitcher, St. Louis native Bart Grether, rifled his third pitch. I closed my eyes, but they shot wide open at that loud, solid *crack*. Leaping out of my seat, I watched, holding my breath as Bug Holliday raced from deep center field for the ball. He dived, as the ball hit his outstretched fingers, and fell into the grass. Yes, St. Joseph, Missouri, had grass in its outfield, while Kansas City, a team in the National League, had only dirt.

I cheered: "Way to go, Dug! Way to go, Dug!"

Those seated behind me showered me with peanut shells, but I did not mind. The runner on second scored to tie the contest, and the Mountain Lion on first rounded second, and looked back toward center field. Dan Dugdale, my friend, had reached first base, rounded the bag, and studied the outfield.

I had to give Bug Holliday credit. He came up on an instant, picked up the ball he had batted down into the grass to keep it in front of him, and threw the ball to shortstop Gus "Sherry" Sheringhausen. That's when Dan Dugdale raced for second base.

"Idiot!" Mr. McKim yelled, and followed that with some curses learned from Mr. Heim or Dave

Rowe. They certainly caused a few gasps from the ladies sitting behind us.

Sheringhausen had pivoted, but saw Dugdale's break for the bag. St. Joe's catcher, Al Strueve, yelled, pointing at the Denver runner now rounding third. Dugdale, however, kept running hard for second.

"Baseball," Mr. McKim said later, "must be like a gunfight. You have to make that shot count."

Sheringhausen dived, ball outstretched, and tagged Dugdale out.

"That's the player you want me to sign?" Mr. McKim said, and dumped more peanut shells on my cowboy hat.

"Mister McKim . . ." I gestured at home plate.

Reds manager Nin Alexander, being restrained by Al Strueve, yelled and cursed and kicked dirt on the umpire's pants, but the bald man shook his head with the authority of a hanging judge.

"What happened?" asked a Reds' fan sitting in front of me.

"The runner scored before Sherry tagged Dan out," I explained.

Mr. McKim, realizing this, sat down, then jumped back up. "Sherry, you miserable son-of-a-bitch! You dumb lout! You should've thrown to home to get that runner!"

Leaning back in my seat, I shook my head. "That was George 'White Wings' Tebeau running," I said proudly. "Once Sherry hesitated when Dan broke for second, his only chance was to tag Dug out before Tebeau scored. Dug knew what he was doing. So did Sherry. Close play. Good game. Great player." My smile beamed. "Yeah, a great player that Dug Dugdale is."

The players trotted to their respective benches, and Nin Alexander screamed at his players.

Mr. McKim sank into his seat, and said: "This contest is not over yet, Silver. I bet you twenty-five dollars that the Reds rally to win."

"Make it fifty," I said, and we shook.

Bart Grether grounded out to the pitcher, and William Frey struck out. I began to relax. But Joseph Herr singled and Sherry Sheringhausen walked, bringing Jumbo Harting to the plate.

"Now," Mr. McKim told me, "you will see what a real ballist does in the thick of battle."

Harry Salisbury's first pitch was again rifled straight down the first-base line, but this time Dan Dugdale knocked the ball down. It rolled into foul territory, and by the time Dan picked up the ball, Jumbo Harting stood at first base, safe.

Ever the sportsman, Jumbo Harting pointed at Dan Dugdale and laughed. That provoked the spectators to hurl peanut shells and curses and jabs at Dan.

My heart sank. Mr. McKim laughed.

Sighing, knowing that Skyrocket Smith now batting with the bases loaded—understanding that the Mountain Lions had not been able to get Skyrocket out during the entire game—I felt sick. Dan kneeled down by the bag, pulled on the corners, tinkered with this and that, and finally stood up. Harry Salisbury kneeled in front of the pitcher's lines and tied his shoes.

Skyrocket Smith tapped his shoes with his John Hillerich-made bat.

"Your star player," Mr. McKim said, "has just cost the Mountain Lions a victory and you fifty bucks."

Once Salisbury rose, Jumbo Harting took a few steps off first base. That's when Dan Dugdale reached under first base, produced the ball, and tagged Jumbo Harting.

"The runner," announced the umpire, who had been anticipating this play, "is out. Ball game!"

"What the hell?" Mr. McKim, and every person in the stadium, leaped to their feet. Art Strueve had to dive to tackle Nin Alexander from murdering the umpire. "That's . . . that's . . . he can't do that." Mr. McKim whirled toward me. "Can he?"

The man sitting behind us settled into his seat, moaning. "The hidden-ball trick," the St. Joseph man said, nearly sobbing, but he bounced back as anger replaced sorrow. "Jumbo. You dumb-arse bastard! Jake Beckley pulled that same trick against you for Leavenworth! Twice! And now you let Denver beat us with the same damned play!"

Once other Reds fanatics realized what had happened, they aimed their rage, curses, epithets, peanut shells, bottles, and lemonade cups at Jumbo Harting as he glumly walked off the field.

"You want me to play for you?" Dan Dugdale pushed his stein of beer away. "Kansas City?"

"I can offer you a contract," Mr. McKim said, "that will pay you eight hundred dollars for the remainder of our season."

We sat in a restaurant at the Occidental Hotel on Main Street.

"I signed with Denver, Mister McKim," Dan Dugdale said. "I try to be a man of my word."

"This is baseball, Dan," Mr. McKim said. "A man's word is worthless. But, seeing that you're a man of principle, I can buy out your contract." Which he did, I later learned, for twelve kegs of porter.

When Dan hesitated, Mr. McKim leaned forward, saying: "Confound it, man, this is the National League we're talking about. You'll be playing against Cap Anson, King Kelly, the best players in our United States, not miners, shopkeepers, and idiots like Jumbo Harting."

I found that a bit demeaning, especially as I remembered how badly we, the National League's Kansas City Cowboys, had fared when we had played Denver's Mountain Lions.

Mr. McKim smiled. He shook his head and

said: "But there's one thing I want to know, Dan. You had that hidden-ball trick planned the whole time, didn't you?" When Dan remained silent, Mr. McKim continued: "You could have had him out at first. Ended the game right there. Instead, you let him reach first base . . . to set him up. You wanted to embarrass him. Is that not the truth?"

This time, Dan shrugged.

"I like that kind of spirit in my ballists, sir. Do we have a deal?"

Dan looked at me, sighed, and reached across the table for the contract Mr. McKim had placed near his own beer stein.

A satisfied Mr. McKim gathered the contract and shook hands with both Dan and me, and then strutted out of the restaurant to make arrangements for our return to Kansas City in the morning.

"Did you really muff that hit on purpose?" I asked Dan.

Now he sipped his beer. "Never been one to take that kind of risk, Silver," he said with a grin. "Damned lucky I even knocked that ball down in front of me. Stopped Jumbo from winning the game for those Reds." His smile broadened. "But I was sure happy to shut that blow-hard up."

"I'm excited to be playing with you," I told him. "Thanks."

"Do you know a player named Frank Ringo?"

He had been lifting his stein to finish off his beer, but now he lowered it. "How many catchers is McKim planning on signing?" he asked.

"Umm. Well . . . our back-up is out with some busted bones in his hand, and we heard Ringo can play in the outfield, too. You don't like him?"

"I didn't say that."

"Your face did."

His head shook. "Playing in the National League has wised you up, Silver. Ringo had talent."

"Had?"

Dugdale finished his drink.

Remembering Cod Myers's comments, I said: "Was it his lushing?"

Dan Dugdale pushed himself out of his chair. "John Barleycorn's just one of his problems. It's the morphine that ruined his career."

We missed the Cowboys' 11-to-2 loss to the Phillies, and arrived home just after we won the next game, 12-10.

Our next two games proved dismal. Mox McQuery decreed that playing first base and managing taxed a person's thinking far too much, so he opted to play center field. That put Dan Dugdale at first base and Frank Ringo behind the plate. I pitched. "Pitched like a King," was how Mr. James Whitfield put it in the *Times*.

For some reason, I kept looking into the grandstands. It's hard to explain, but I wanted to see if Mother and Papa might be watching. I couldn't see either one, but Cindy McKim was there, yelling encouragement. Her father shouted profanity, but none of his curses had been aimed at me.

He screamed at Dan Dugdale, even though Dan made two fine snags at first base, and he screamed at Mox McQuery, who chased down four fly balls in center field. Mostly, however, Mr. McKim pelted our new catcher with curses. Frank Ringo, you see, committed five errors, struck out four times, and had to be carried from the field after our 3-to-0 loss. Those in the crowd threw bottles at our bench as we packed our gear—until Mr. Joseph Heim and Mr. Americus McKim arrived.

"That was pathetic," Mr. McKim said.

"The kid pitched well," Charley Bassett said.

"I don't need to hear from you, Bassett," Mr. McKim said. "If you want to do us a service, draw your Colt and shoot Frank Ringo in the head. You'll be avenging Tombstone and today's disgraceful performance."

"No," Mr. Heim said. "Wait till Monday's game against Boston. Shoot him then."

"I'm not shooting anyone." For once, Charley Bassett sounded as though he might be kin to a tough Dodge City lawman. "Especially a walking whiskey vat who can't even stand up."

"It ain't the whiskey," Grasshopper Jim said. "It's the morphine."

"My, oh, my . . ." Mert Hackett stared down at the unconscious, salivating, pale Frank Ringo. "I swan', Mister Ringo wasn't that bad last time I seen him. He was a right smart ballist."

"It's not your fault, Hackett," Mr. McKim said. "It's yours!" He pointed a finger underneath Mox McQuery's nose. "You suggested this worthless reprobate."

"I . . . uh . . ." Mox McQuery glared at Hackett and me.

"Get him off the morphine," Dan Dugdale said, "keep him away from the whiskey, he might come around."

"Jesus," Mr. McKim said. "You're not bad ballplayers. I know that. I read reports and saw that most of you played before I ever signed you to this team. It's September. The season ends next month. We have talent. Why in hell's name aren't we winning baseball games?"

When no one answered, Mr. McKim shoved Mox McQuery.

"I thought you were a manager. . . ."

"I tried, sir," Mox said. "It just ain't what I'm good at. Too much . . ."

"Thinking!" Mr. McKim snapped. "Yeah, I guess brains is not what you're good at. How about you, Dugdale? What's the problem as you see it? I know you have brains. That hidden-ball trick proved that. We have talent. Why don't we win?"

With a methodical purpose, Dan moved his bats into a bag, then placed his thin fielding glove and thicker catcher's mitt into the bag. After setting the bag on the bench, he pushed back the large sombrero Mr. Heim was making us wear now, and spoke in an assured voice.

"We have talent. We don't have a team," Dan said. "But I've got a remedy for that if we can catch the afternoon train to Atchison. We can be back in time for Monday's game."

"More money I have to spend on you wastrels?" Mr. McKim said.

"Consider it a tithe," Dan said pleasantly.

"Church?" Mr. McKim scoffed. "You're taking this bunch of rotgut-guzzling whoremongers to church?"

"My church," Dan said.

CHAPTER TWENTY-ONE

Everyone called the white-haired man Mr. Bill.

Bill Anderson ran the Diamond Nine Ranch south of Atchison, Kansas, with his three sons: Junior, McKay, and Shane. Mr. Bill and his boys—all grown men, sturdy, bronzed, and tall but not quite as tall as their father—met us at the depot in wagons and took us the seven miles to his small spread, where other cowboys busied themselves saddling horses tethered to a long wooden fence.

"Light down, boys!" Mr. Bill called as he set the brake of the wagon he had driven before hopping down from the box. Pushing back the brim of his dusty hat, he waited as we ballists stood awkwardly, taking in the bunkhouse, the wagons, the main house, the corrals, and all the cattle, which looked rugged and cantankerous, and the horses—already saddled—that seemed just as wild. Without speaking, Mr. Bill walked up to Dan Dugdale and Mert Hackett, shaking hands with both men, speaking a few pleasantries, and then telling them: "Find a horse that'll fit you, boys. I'll speak to our trail crew."

"Trail crew?" Shorty Radford whispered, and turned to Charley Bassett. "What the hell's a trail crew?"

"Be quiet," Charley said.

259

"I want you to know something," said Mr. Bill, ignoring Shorty and Charley and stopping in front of me before moving on. Years in the saddle had bronzed his face, which made his blue eyes more piercing and his brushy eyebrows more white. As he pulled off his deerskin gloves, I noticed the scars on his fingers, the roughness of his knuckles. His hands were huge, his legs bent into a bow. All of his sons wore belted pistols, but Mr. Bill went unarmed. Yet his mere presence told me that this man needed no six-shooter. He simply commanded respect.

"What do you see there?" He pointed a crooked finger at Mert Hackett and Dan Dugdale as they led a couple of cow ponies away from the fence.

"Dugdale," Jim Donnelly tried, "and the darky with some horses."

"Wrong." Turning, Mr. Bill smiled as Mert Hackett eased into the saddle, gathered the reins, and backed up his chestnut while Dan Dugdale swung onto a sorrel. "I see two *men*. I don't see any *color*."

He shifted back toward us, and put a hand on Donnelly's shoulder. "I'm no Abolitionist, son." He gave Donnelly a gentle squeeze and lowered his arm. "Served in Hood's Brigade out of Texas during the late war, if you want to know the truth. Left three toes at Gettysburg. Took my first cattle drive to Baxter Springs after the war, and a couple more after that. Bought this place after two trips to Abilene. Got sick of Texas, I guess. Fell in love with Kansas and the Atchison Antelopes."

He walked back a few paces, stopping in front of me again.

"But here's what I learned on those drives north. There ain't no black, no white, no Mexican, no Irishman, no nothing when you're trying to get two thousand beeves to market. You work together or you go bust. You don't got to be saddle pals, or best pals, or pals at all. You ain't even got to like each other. But you got to work together. McKay!"

His youngest son, a blond man with a thin mustache and his father's eyes, stepped forward and tossed Mr. Bill a baseball bat.

"Billy!" Mr. Bill called out as he settled into a batter's stance.

Before I knew it, Mr. Bill's oldest son was winding up and delivering a speeding baseball at his father's waist. The bat swung in a blur, cracked. The ball landed near the privy, where the middle son, Shane, who had dark hair and a brushy mustache, fielded the ball on the second bound, and hurled it all the way back to McKay. Shane's arm seemed like a Howitzer.

"Just like you got to work together on a baseball team," Mr. Bill said before he tossed the bat back to his youngest son.

"Now I know why this ranch is called the

Diamond Nine," Grasshopper Jim said, and we laughed.

"That's right, son," Mr. Bill said. "Saw my first game in Kansas City. Wild Bill Hickok himself served as umpire."

"My mother was at that game," I sang out. "With . . ."

Mr. Bill's eyes landed on me. I sensed them conveying something, but I didn't know what. I swallowed, trying to look strong. *Mother.* Even though I knew I had been in the right, I regretted those sharp words I had spoken to her, and I missed her. I missed my father, too. But especially I missed Mother's encouragement and . . . well, her coaching. I wanted things to return to the way they had been, only I wanted my mother to accept Cindy McKim—but that seemed impossible.

"Here's what we're going to do." Mr. Bill had moved down to the end of the line, where Frank Ringo shivered in his baseball shoes, and Mr. McKim looked bored. "You're going to find a horse. Let one of my hired men match you up with a good one. You're going to work cattle, and you're going to work *together*. You'll find a lariat on the horn. Don't touch it. Baseball players aren't good after they lose a finger. Show these Kansas City Cowboys your left hand, Nell."

The cowboy named Nell raised his hand,

which had only a pinky, thumb, and forefinger, the latter of which had been severed at the top joint while the other two fingers were completely missing.

"Any questions?" Mr. Bill asked.

Grasshopper Jim slowly raised his hand.

"Yes."

"Are we going to have to drive them cows to Abilene?"

A few of us laughed, as did Mr. Bill's sons, but Mr. Bill only grinned as he made his way back down the line. "They don't like Texas beef in Abilene anymore, son, and those are *steers*. Not *cows*. Besides, you have a ball game tomorrow against . . . ?" His eyes settled on me.

"Boston," I answered. "The Beaneaters."

"Isn't Old Hoss Radbourn throwing for them this season?"

"Yes, sir."

He whistled. "Saw him pitch for Providence a couple of times. Best pitcher I've ever seen. If you can beat him, you can beat anyone." With a curt nod, Mr. Bill walked to the end of the line. "All right," he said, then asked: "How many of you ballists have ever been on a horse before? And don't lie!"

A few hands lifted, including Charley Bassett's. Charley leaned toward me and whispered: "I'm lying, Silver. You know that."

"Then put your hand down, damn it."

"I can't. I'm supposed to be the son of a Dodge City lawman. I can't let anyone know I'm from Rhode Island. So tell me what do I have to know?"

"I'm not a horseman," I said. "Or a cowboy. Just . . ."—Mr. Bill started coming back our way—"just mount on the left side."

"Left." Charley's head bobbed. He flexed the fingers on his left hand. "I can remember that."

Mounted on a fine black mare with a white blazed forehead, Mr. Bill made his horse do things I never thought possible. He slapped his hat against his chaps, spun the horse in a tight circle, backed her up, went this way and that way, all the while barking orders at his sons.

They divided us into three groups—and that took some doing. Mox McQuery could ride pretty well, and Charley Bassett, bless his heart, happened to be put aboard a blood bay gelding that followed other horses naturally. Charley did not have to do much. Frank Ringo fell off his horse twice, once before it even took a step. But I give him credit, for he brushed himself off, as best he could with sweat cascading down his face, armpits, arms, and back, and got boosted back into his saddle.

I happened to be put into the group with Dan Dugdale, McKay Anderson, and two Diamond Nine riders—a Mexican called Pedrito and a grizzled old-timer with a reddish-gray beard named Duncklee.

"Here's the way this is going to work," Mr. Bill called out. He had ridden several rods ahead of us, and stood in his stirrups. "Shane'll take his men to the pond. You're picking up the herd and guiding them to the shipping pens. That's three miles. Back in the day, we'd make eight to twelve miles a day herding cattle from Texas to Kansas. If I were you, I'd make good time. Otherwise, you'll miss your game tomorrow and forfeit. To do that . . . get those beeves to the pens and you to your baseball game . . . you have to work together."

Junior's group had to ride the opposite direction. My team had to pick up the cattle grazing near the ranch house. I thought that gave us the advantage.

It didn't.

Pete Conway couldn't slow his horse, and the steers scattered.

"Slow down, slow down!" Duncklee bellowed, adding a few choice pieces of profanity and spraying tobacco juice with each word. "Runnin' cattle burns off fat, and fatter steers sell better!"

While I was trying to pick a steer to go after—like I had a clue what to do if, by fortune, I actually got close to it—Dan Dugdale trotted his horse over toward me. With a wide grin as he rode past, he said: "Give him rein, Silver. Horse does all the work. Like catchers in a baseball game."

I relaxed my grip on the reins, and felt the horse find a new gear. My rump pounded against the saddle, and I feared my shoes might slip out of the stirrups and leave me tasting gravel as Frank Ringo had. Except the Diamond Nine riders, Dan Dugdale, and Mert Hackett, no one actually wore cowboy boots.

We had no doubt who ran this operation. Dan Dugdale, Pedrito, Duncklee, and Anderson knew their jobs, but, to my surprise, we ballists learned fast. Or maybe our horses had the brains. I'm not saying we did everything, or anything, perfectly, but we managed to stay seated in our saddles. Even Frank Ringo, who got assigned to our group.

"Put them in a line!" Dan yelled from the point of the herd.

The barbed-wire fence stretched northeast. Despite the dust and the profanity directed at us, within a half hour we had our cattle moving.

Dugdale and Pedrito took the point, and I finally figured out the difference between "swing" and "flank"—swing being about a third of the way from the pointers, where the cattle began to swell a bit, and flank being another third down.

Pete Conway and Grasshopper Jim started out

at swing. Jim Donnelly and McKay Anderson took flank. I rode drag, eating a ton of dust, with Frank Ringo and Duncklee.

"Flank rider's main job is to make sure the beeves don't wander too far from the main herd," Duncklee explained while rolling a smoke, seeming oblivious to the dust the cattle kicked up and the wind blew into our faces. "Swing does some of the same. Drag riders, that's for the tenderfeet. We make the herd keep on movin', push the slowpokes along so we don't lose no cattle."

I had pulled up the bandanna over my mouth and nose to fight the dust. "You're no tenderfoot," I called out to Duncklee.

"No, but I'm paid to make sure you two keep up with the rest of us."

This made me feel like the lowest person on the cattle drive, although, at three miles, it wouldn't be much of a drive.

After Duncklee struck a Lucifer and fired up his cigarette, he continued explaining. "Here's somethin' you ought to know. On a drive, a real drive, 'em boys ridin' swing and flank and usually even point, they make a dollar a day. The boys ridin' drag, eatin' dust, gettin' blinded by dust, four to six months on the trail, they get paid the exact same. Because it's like that baseball game you and the boss man and his family is so fond of. Y'all gots to depend on each other. Boss man, he tells us . . . 'You're only as strong as the weakest man you got.' "

"That'd be me," Frank Ringo muttered.

"Bullshit," Duncklee said. "You got dusted twice before we ever left the damned ranch, boy. Weak man would've quit. You got right back in the saddle. Not once. Twice."

At that point, a brindle-colored steer bolted to the left, and before I knew it my horse had jumped out with it. The steer wanted to go back home, and although both Duncklee and Ringo reined in and turned in their saddles, neither did a thing to help me. They just watched.

I—or maybe it was my horse—blocked the steer's retreat, but this longhorn had no quit in him. He must have thought beating me had to be easy. I made myself ready, waiting for the steer to make its play. It bolted left, and I tugged my rein, feeling the power of the horse underneath me. Again the horse blocked the steer, and immediately it darted back to the right. I anticipated that ploy. So did my horse. This time, the spry mossyhorn turned around and trotted back past Ringo and Duncklee to rejoin the herd.

Duncklee took a final drag of his cigarette, flicked the remnants away, and grinned a toothless grin at me. "Good job," he said, adding a word that made my head swell, "cowboy."

CHAPTER TWENTY-TWO

The Boston Beaneaters pounded us 11-to-2 on Monday, September 6th, but when Mr. McKim and Mr. Heim came to our bench, screaming and cursing and pointing fingers, most of our players had a ready excuse for our bosses.

"My butt's bruised," said Grasshopper Jim, who had pitched that afternoon's game. "I can hardly walk, and don't even ask me to sit down."

"My thighs are so chafed it's not even funny," Cod Myers added.

Several teammates bobbed their heads in agreement, forcing our owners to glare at Dan Dugdale.

"Do you know how much that train trip cost us?" Mr. Heim said.

"Or how much that *Mister Bill* charged us for your little experiment?" Mr. McKim said.

Dan Dugdale simply grinned. "It's one game," he said calmly. "Besides, we didn't get off the train till four in the morning."

"Because you were so late doing your stupid experiment," Mr. Heim said. "Cowboys playing cowboys."

"Our boys did well *being* cowboys," Dugdale said. "Not *playing* them. And they weren't late. It was the train that was late."

"You're better at playing cowboys than playing baseball," Mr. McKim snapped.

"We'll beat Boston tomorrow," Dugdale said.

"They pitched Pop Tate today," Mr. McKim said. "He's not even a pitcher. He's a stupid catcher. That's how much contempt John Morrill has for us. He hurls a catcher against us. Do you know who he'll likely start tomorrow?"

"Joe Hornung?" Dugdale answered.

Hornung played the outfield. Neither Mr. McKim nor Mr. Heim laughed at Dan's joke.

"Radbourn!" Mr. McKim yelled. "They'll be hurling Old Hoss himself."

"And we'll beat Radbourn." Dan's smile vanished. "Or whoever Morrill pitches. Guaranteed."

"You better hope you do, Dugdale," Mr. McKim said, "or it'll be your damned ass."

When our owners stormed off, Mox McQuery came up to Dan. "Dug," he said in a whisper, "listen. You know this game better than me. And the way you just guaranteed our victory . . . well, I think you know, that, well . . . maybe you should be our manager. I'm a good first baseman. But I just ain't got what it takes to be no leader."

Dan shook his head.

"I mean," Mox said, "just till Dave comes back."

"*If* Rowe comes back," Charley Bassett put in.

"I'm no manager," Dan said.

270

"Hey," Cod Myers sang out. "What about Mister Bill? He sure made a fine trail boss. And he loves the game."

"Mister Bill loves the game," Mert Hackett said. "But he don't know it. He knows cattle. And men."

"Boys," Dan said. "I've got an idea for someone who just might be our answer to finding a manager. Come along, Silver."

We found Cindy McKim by the entrance to The Hole. Dan signaled a hack to bring his rig over for us. "Come on, Silver," Dan said as he climbed into the buggy. "And bring your sweetheart along, too."

The driver applied his whip, and the matched set of gray Percherons carried us away from The Hole. Cindy took my hand in hers as I said to Dan: "You once told me you never guaranteed a victory. Not in baseball. Said there are too many . . . too many in- . . . intangibles."

"You've a fine memory, Silver," Dan agreed from his seat across from Cindy and me, his back to the driver. "I did say that."

"But Mister McKim . . . he's a terror. . . ." I swallowed, having forgotten for a moment about whom I was sitting next to.

Cindy McKim, however, spoke right up. "My father's worse than a terror. And he will fire you on the spot if you lose tomorrow's game."

"We won't lose," Dan said.

"How can you be sure?" I cried out. "Boston isn't the best team in the National League, not by far, but Old Hoss Radbourn's one of the best pitchers we've see."

"I'm not so sure. Silver, this is baseball. It isn't life. If we lose, no one will remember my guarantee except McKim and me, and, I reckon, you. It's like a damned fool bet on a horse race, or the turn of a card, or a shooting contest. But I don't think we will lose. Because Mister Bill made us a team yesterday," Dan said matter-of-factly. "Hell, even Frank Ringo felt like a cowboy. He didn't even have a drink before or during today's game. We'll play together. Like we worked together yesterday. That'll be one difference."

"And another?" Cindy asked.

Dan pointed a finger at me. "Silver. He'll be pitching."

My throat had turned to cotton, but I croaked out: "Where are we going?"

"To get us a manager."

Realizing what street we had turned down, my stomach sank. "Who?" I was barely able to get out.

"Who knows the game of baseball better than anyone in this city, Silver?" Dan asked.

I knew the answer. I felt like throwing up. Cindy McKim knew the answer, too.

"You mean Silver's mother?" she said.

Naturally Dan had given the hack the address of our old house, so I had to tell Dan that we'd moved. He informed the driver of his mistake, and the old Italian muttered something to himself and then turned down the next street. He didn't seem to mind. A longer drive meant a higher fare.

"Sixteen hundred bucks a year buys a lot in Kansas City," Dan said as we neared our home.

"You're getting eight hundred," I told him. "For one month of baseball."

Dan laughed. "If I'm not turned loose tomorrow."

I could feel the sweat coming out of my pores and I became light-headed. I didn't know if I would vomit or maybe even pass out. But somehow I found enough strength to say in a hoarse voice: "It's right up here . . . on the left."

"Silver," Dan said when I stopped at the bottom of the porch steps. "If you don't want to do this, you don't have to. Mox can manage well enough."

Cindy squeezed my hand.

"No," I said, and climbed up to the porch, went to the door. I had never used the bell, had always just walked inside the house. I mean, it was my house. I had paid for it. But today I pulled the lever, and heard the bell chime.

It seemed to take forever before Mother opened the door.

• • •

"Coach?" Mother pushed her coffee cup out of reach. "You want me to coach . . . professional ballists?"

"Yes, ma'am," Dan Dugdale assured her. He sipped his coffee, washing down the piece of pound cake my mother had placed before him.

I wasn't eating.

Mother seemed unable to comprehend Dan's proposal, and finally shook her head. "Americus McKim would never allow that. Nor would Heim, that mean-spirited, flim-flam beer *meister*. And I am confident that the National League would never tolerate a woman on a bench in any capacity, other than maybe a mascot."

"Yes, ma'am," Dan Dugdale said.

"So then . . . ," Mother began, but paused, not knowing what to say since Dan was agreeing with everything she said.

"You sit in the stands, Missus King," Dan said. "Front row. You tell us what you think we should do, who should play, things like that. That's all there is to managing. Mox will do your bidding."

"That's . . ." Mother just shook her head.

"Ma'am." Dan gave Mother his most disarming smile. "I think you've been to The Hole enough to know that folks in those stands are telling us what to do and how to play all the time. We don't listen to them. But we *will* listen to you."

My mother let out a heavy sigh. "It'll never work," she declared as if no one could dispute her.

"Give it a try for one game, Missus King," Cindy said.

"Miss Cindy is right," Dan said. "If it doesn't work tomorrow, it really won't matter. McKim and Heim will have me draw my time. Mox, too. Most likely Silver here, as well. One game, Missus King. One game at a time. That's the way this game's supposed to be played, anyhow."

During our conversation, Mother had looked older to me than she ever had. But suddenly, in the last few minutes, her color had picked up, she looked brighter. She reached for her coffee cup, which I had to slide a few inches toward her. "I suppose . . . ," she said. A twinkle flashed in her eyes as she looked first at Cindy, then at me, her eyes finally settling on Dan. "Maybe it could . . . ," she started to say.

Dan Dugdale shot out of his chair before she could finish. "We'll see you at The Hole tomorrow before noon, ma'am." I started to rise, but Dan had already rounded the table, pressed his hands on my shoulders, and shoved me back down into the seat. "Come along, Miss Cindy," he said. "We'll wait for Silver out on the walkway while I try to get us another hack. I bet Silver and his mother have a lot to talk about."

Then they were gone, leaving me alone . . . with . . . my mother.

The sound of our old Seth Thomas clock, a familiar object from our previous home, filled the space between us. Mother studied her coffee cup, now empty. I stared at the door Cindy McKim had closed behind her.

"Papa," I said, thinking of an opening, "should be home directly, shouldn't he?"

"He has a masonry job on Twentieth," Mother said.

"Oh."

The sound of the Seth Thomas seemed to get louder.

"Silver." It was Mother who finally found the courage to bring up the subject that had been weighing on us both. "What you said . . . that . . . evening . . ."

"I was angry," I told her.

"With reason." Mother looked at the door. The corners of her lips turned upward into the beginning of a smile, a reflection, an absolution. "She . . . Cindy . . . she seems a very nice young . . . lady."

"She is."

Her hand reached toward mine, but stopped halfway. I stared at it. For a second I imagined it as a rattlesnake, but then saw it as the proverbial olive branch, and I took her hand in my own.

"You were my baby," she told me. "You will

always be my baby. My only child. Our only son. I never wanted to play baseball. Never wanted to be a boy. I don't think I'd be very good at either." Knowing how she was able, when the need arose, to use her charm, her smile, her iron will, I expected her to hit a home run. But she continued in an unexpected direction.

"If you want a horse, or a pony, or . . ."

I lifted my hand, giving her a moment to pause, to wipe away a tear, to regain that Samantha Koenig composure.

"Mother," I told her, "I just rode three miles on a horse yesterday. Probably closer to four or five miles, considering all the difficulties I had in handling the beast."

Her eyes narrowed. She stared at me, not comprehending.

I grinned. "A horse, I've learned, isn't all it's cracked up to be. And cowboying isn't the easiest way in the world to make a living. My backside hasn't hurt so much since that time Papa whipped me for busting out Mister MacDougall's window when I was seven."

This made me laugh as I recalled Mister MacDougall storming after me, yelling at the top of his lungs. Mother began laughing with me, but only for a few seconds before her laughter became sobs. Suddenly she was crying, the sounds coming from her akin to the noise the cattle made as we had herded them from Mr.

Bill's ranch. I came out of my chair, and reached for her. She buried her head against my shoulder.

"Mother," I said in an effort to comfort her.

"All I ever wanted was the best for you," she said. "Not me. Not your father. For you. I never meant to be . . ."

I pulled her closer. "It's all right, Mother. I love you." Telling her this seemed to make her cry harder.

It took her a long time to finally dam her tears.

"D-d-do you th-think . . . ?" my mother stuttered, and she never stuttered. She paused and wiped her eyes before continuing. "Would that . . . Cindy . . . would Cindy and you care to dine with us this evening? Dan Dugdale, too. Your father . . . he should be home before too long."

"I'll ask them," I told her.

It turned into a delightful evening. Papa, Cindy, and I retired to the back porch to watch the stars, to enjoy the early September breeze and those first hints of autumn. We swapped stories and jokes. Mother and Dan Dugdale remained at the dining room table. They talked baseball.

CHAPTER TWENTY-THREE

Dan Dugdale's plans did not end with the hiring of my mother—even if she earned no salary but merely an upgrade in where she and Papa would sit for our home games. That I learned on Tuesday morning when our players began arriving at The Hole.

Mother sat in her new seat and chatted pleasantly with Mr. Heim and Mr. Whitfield, while Mr. McKim stood near the visitor's bench, speaking to Dan. I sat doing my stretching, although mostly I was listening to Dan and Cindy's father, and keeping my eyes trained on home base and the man standing inside the six-by-three-foot batsman's lines.

"Dugdale," Mr. McKim said, "have you lost all reason? You've sworn you can beat one of the best pitchers in the National League today after you were trounced by a damned catcher yesterday. You've talked me into letting Silver's mother sit closer than I do at the very stadium that I helped to build. Not that I need a better look at the abysmal baseball you practice and just how horrible those sons-of-bitches the National League sends us as umpires actually are."

He was worked up, Mr. McKim was, and it

wasn't ten-thirty in the morning yet. We had three-and-a-half hours before the game started.

"Hire . . ."—Mr. McKim spat and pointed at home base—"him? Mert Hackett?"

"Center fielder," Dan said. "At least until Dave Rowe returns."

"Rowe could very well return tomorrow," Mr. McKim said. "If you don't win today."

"He's better than Dave Rowe," Dan said.

"You damned fool. If I signed that darky, the loaf Cap Anson would pinch would fill this entire hole. Don't you understand that?" While Mr. McKim increased his vehemence, Dan Dugdale nodded at Stump Wiedman, who threw a ball catcher Frank Ringo never had a chance to catch.

That loud, wooden smack of the bat hitting the ball caught everyone's attention.

Mr. McKim turned, but, by that time, Mert Hackett had rounded first base. Our vice president's eyes caught up with our mascot as he dashed toward third. By then, Mr. McKim was watching center field, where Shorty Radford sprinted to pick up the ball that had caromed off the fence.

Before Mert Hackett had crossed home plate, Mr. McKim had lowered his arms.

"Keep going, Mert!" Dan called out, and Mert Hackett started for first base again. Second. Third.

When Hackett picked up even more speed while heading home for the second time, Mr. McKim yelled: "By Jehovah, look at that little . . . *Cherokee* . . . run!"

"We can't hire him," Mr. Heim protested. "He's a . . . well . . . I mean. There's this understanding we all agreed on. And . . . well . . . he's our mascot."

"He's faster than King Kelly and he hits like Dan Brouthers," Mr. McKim said. "Besides, we'll call him a Cherokee."

Mr. Heim shook his head. "Seminole, maybe."

"No. Cap Anson would not allow a Seminole to play baseball. They are too dark-skinned and intermarried with runaway slaves."

"And Cap Anson ain't about to allow that ni- . . ."

"Cherokee." That came from Mother, sitting in her seat.

Our owners looked up at her, then at each other, then at Mert, Dan, and me.

"Jim Whitfield will put it in the *Times*. We're not only the Kansas City Cowboys. We're the Cowboys *and* Indians. Think of how Barnum would promote that."

"I don't know," Mr. Heim said.

"I don't, either." Mr. McKim whipped off his Stetson and slapped it against his leg—similar to how the Andersons and Duncklee slapped their hats against their legs. "But I'm damned sick and disgusted at losing. If this doesn't work . . . and it might not . . . then you can have your mascot back and I'll have my pound of flesh." His eyes landed on me. "Probably two pounds."

"Cherokee," Mr. Heim tested the word, the lie.

"Yes," said Mr. McKim.

"Well, why did we hire that Ringo fellow? I mean, how many more drunks and bone-headed ballists do we need on this team?"

"Enough to win," Mr. McKim said.

I added: "Besides, Ringo's a back-up for when Dug can't catch."

"Last time I saw Ringo behind that home base," Mr. Heim said dryly, "he couldn't catch a cripple."

"We're talking"—Mr. McKim pointed at Hackett—"about him."

With a heavy sigh, Mr. Heim shook his head and spit into the dirt. "You might be able to fool John Morrill. But this ain't ever going to flim-flam Cap Anson."

"Let's find out," Dan Dugdale said.

Our line-up that afternoon read as follows:

Leading off: Paul "Shorty" Radford. Right Field.

Batting second: Al "Cod" Myers. Second Base.

Batting third: Mert "Cherokee" Hackett. Center Field.

Batting fourth: Mox McQuery. First Base.
Batting fifth: Dan Dugdale. Catcher.
Batting sixth: Charley Bassett. Shortstop.
Batting seventh: Jim Lillie. Left Field.
Batting eighth: Jim Donnelly. Third Base.
Batting ninth: Silver King. Pitcher.
We faced John Morrill's Boston Beaneaters, who indeed pitched Old Hoss Radbourn.

Here's what you might have forgotten about Charles Gardner Radbourn. Back in 1884, when he was pitching for the Providence Grays, he had started seventy-three games, finishing with a record of fifty-nine victories and twelve losses. You want his record in the three years before that? Well, 25-and-11 in 1881, 33-and-20 in 1882, and 48-and-25 in 1883. The year before the Cowboys joined the National League, Radbourn had gone 28-and-21 and the Grays had sent him and Con Daily to Boston, likely figuring that Radbourn's arm just couldn't take pitching like that anymore.

His arm looked mighty fine on that September afternoon when our game began.

"What happened?" Cod Myers asked as Shorty Radford returned to the bench after striking out on five pitches in the first inning.

Myers dropped his bat in the rack at the end of our bench.

"Did you see that pitch?" Shorty answered.

"Well, no," Cod answered.

"Neither did I. Hell, I didn't see a damned one of them."

Cod struck out, too. So did Mert Hackett. After he jogged back to the bench to drop his bat in the rack and take off for center field, Mr. McKim began letting him hear it all.

"Cherokee! You play more like a damned squaw, you worthless, stupid, miserable little . . ."

Dan Dugdale pulled on his padded mitt, smiled, and said: "Let's get them, Silver."

"Radbourn," I told him, "just struck out all three of our players."

"He's a battler. Good pitcher. We've played a half-inning. Rules say we have to play nine. Or have you already lost this game?"

"Get out there, Son!" Mother yelled.

I glanced up at the closest seats, finding, to my surprise, Cindy McKim sitting next to Mother, and Papa, who must have gotten the day off from the packing house, on the other side of Mother. Drawing in a deep breath, I slowly exhaled and headed onto the field.

Radbourn led off for Boston. Since the Bean-eaters paid him $4,000 a year, I guess they wanted to get their money's worth.

I stepped inside the pitcher's lines, took another breath, and heard Radbourn call out: "High."

Then Mother's voice rang out: "Who can do it?"

Papa and Cindy lead the refrain: "Silver can-can!"

So I did my dance, and hurled a pitch that Radbourn grounded weakly to my right. I picked up the ball, dropped it, got a better grip, and sent it into Mox McQuery's beefy hands.

Right fielder Tom Poorman struck out, and first baseman Sam Wise flied out on a ball that should have been a double, but which Mert Hackett ran down easily.

Suddenly the cries of "Can-Can" had died, and now our spectators launched into a new shout.

"Che-ro-kee . . . Che-ro-kee . . . Che-ro-kee . . . Che-ro-kee!"

We hit Radbourn fairly well in our half of the inning, but left two runners on without scoring a run. Before we took the field, Mother stood, leaned against the banister and called out: "If Con Daily bats left-handed, Charley, do not shift over. He'll call low, Silver, so pitch him low. Low and inside."

Batting as a southpaw, Con Daily grounded out to Charley Bassett for the first out of the inning.

"Did you see that?" said a burly man in a sack suit, leaping out of his seat, and pointing at Mother. "That woman told 'em Cowboys what to do and they done it. A damned petticoat!"

"Shut up, Eli!" shouted another man as he pulled Eli back into his seat. "You're drunk."

I struck out Dick Johnston, and John Morrill sliced another fly ball into center field that Mert Hackett caught without even showing much effort.

"Che-ro-kee! Che-ro-kee! Che-ro-kee!"

That brought me first to the plate when we came to bat. "High," I called out, and Old Hoss Radbourn made his first mistake. He pitched me high, all right, but also inside. Mother always called that my "wheelhouse" pitch, I got around on it quickly. The ball flew off my bat, over third baseman Billy Nash's reach, bounced on the line, and rolled in the dirt toward the stands.

I stood on second with a double, and I remained standing on second after Radford and Myers struck out and Hackett flied out to Joe Hornung, who showed his own speed and caught the ball with a leaping catch.

In the seventh inning, Morrill laced a double that Mert Hackett could not catch. Dan Dugdale asked umpire Paul Grace for time to have a parley with me. Dugdale jogged out to me and said: "You're coming through the order for the third time. What would you think about stopping your dancing and throwing from the side like you've done before?"

"Is that from Mother?" I asked.

"It's from me," Dan said.

The game remained scoreless. Up until Morrill's hit, I thought that I had been pitching brilliantly. The only problem was that Old Hoss Radbourn had equaled everything I had accomplished.

"I don't know, Dug," I said. "I've had some success."

He grinned. "Did you see how hard he hit that ball, Silver? Damned near tore the cover off it. This isn't Chicago and it isn't Detroit. It's Boston. They'll be slightly ahead of us in the standings when the season's done, Silver. I don't have anything against Morrill . . . he's a good egg . . . but his blade wouldn't cut butter if you know what I'm saying. And he figured out a way to knock the hell out of your damned can-can shit. Side arm. Got it? Side arm. Or if you want, I'll go ask your Mother to come out here and tell you to throw that damned ball the way I tell you to throw the ball." He turned back, kicking dirt as he went, yelling at Paul Grace: "Pitchers! They're all just so damned stupid!"

So I picked up dirt, rubbed it in my hands, grabbed the ball, and glanced at the stands. I couldn't make out Mother's face, but I heard the fans all around her, all around The Hole, even on the hill from those cheapskates who sat over center field to watch the game without paying 50¢.

"Can-can Silver do it?"

"Yes, he can-can!"

The crowd went silent when I fired a side-arm pitch that Jack Burdock swung at and missed, falling to his knees.

"Criminy!" The Boston second baseman managed to stand, brush off his pants, and say something to Dan Dugdale, then Paul Grace, before settling back into his stance.

John Morrill was left standing on second base, too.

"Keep that up," Mother said when I trotted back to the bench after striking out three consecutive Beaneaters. "Forget that can-can. Your father and I have always preferred a good polka, anyhow."

Charley Bassett led off by ripping a long single to right field, Jim Lillie walked, and Jim Donnelly managed a weak hit back to Radbourn, who threw the ball well over Sam Wise's head. That sent Bassett to score the first run, and Lillie and Donnelly stood on second and third.

"Don't try to do too much!" Mother called down to me. "Radbourn's spent. That errant throw to first has rattled him."

She must have been right. Radbourn gave me nothing to hit, and I walked to load the bases. Radford and Myers struck out, but then that new rallying cry rang out across The Hole.

"Che-ro-kee! Che-ro-kee! Che-ro-kee!"

"Silver!" I heard Cindy's voice from my spot on first base, and I looked into the stands as Mert Hackett walked to home base.

"My father's yelling Cherokee, too!" she called out, and blew me a kiss.

It sounded like all of Kansas City kept shouting Che-ro-kee after Mert Hackett drilled a double over left fielder Joe Hornung's head that scored three runs. We were up 4-to-nothing, and Mother had been right. Old Hoss Radbourn was played out.

We wound up winning, 13-to-3.

The next day, Boston pitched Radbourn again. And after that game, in which we squeaked out a 7-to-5 victory, I caught up with him and asked: "Don't you ever get tired?"

"Rookie," he told me with a grin. "Tired? Tired from tossin' a little ball that don't weigh no more'n five ounces? Sonny, I used to be a butcher. Before the sun was up, from four in the morn till eight at night, I knocked down steers with a twenty-five-pound sledge." His head shook and he turned to walk away. "Tired? Golly. Tired from playin' two hours a day for ten times the money I used to get for workin' sixteen hours a day. Sonny, you sure make me laugh. Pitched a good game, though, your ownself. Are you tired?"

CHAPTER TWENTY-FOUR

In the Kansas City *Times*, Mr. James Whitfield called this "The Streak".

After winning two consecutive games against the Beaneaters, we played three games against the Maroons at The Hole. The first game, which went sixteen innings behind the brave pitching of Grasshopper Jim and Pete Conway, was called a 4-to-4 tie when it grew too dark to continue playing. The crowd at The Hole cared nothing for that, and Kerry Coffelt quit umpiring after that game when Mr. McKim led several other stalwart Kansas Citians.

"What I heard Mister Coffelt say," Mox McQuery told us when we had gathered at Mr. Bayersdörfer's place, "was this . . . 'I ain't afraid of their yells, but as soon as they pull their guns, I'm goin' to dust.' "

We followed that tie with 6-to-5 and 9-to-3 victories. On September 13th, the Detroit Wolverines came to Kansas City for four games. Manager W.H. Watkins, whose team was challenging Chicago for the National League lead, met Dan Dugdale in front of our bench as we prepared for the first of our games. Tying my shoes, I looked up to find Watkins glaring at the man sitting on the edge of the bench. The man, of course, was our center fielder, Mert Hackett, who was adjusting his black cowboy hat.

Watkins spit tobacco juice into the dirt. "Jack Rowe's wondering what happened to his brother. But now I see why Dave ain't here." Sarcasm accented his voice. "Are you baseball players, Dug? Or wranglers?"

"Wranglers work with horses," Dan corrected. "Cowboys work with cattle. And we happen to be both. That's Charley Bassett sanding the handle of his bat yonder. His pa's a lawman in Dodge City. Over yonder, drinking his coffee, is Frank Ringo, blood kin to Wyatt Earp, Buffalo Bill Cody, and Geronimo. Silver King sitting down on the bench, well, he just finished a cattle drive to Atchison. And that there's Cherokee Hackett and . . ."

"Yeah," Watkins said. "I've read all about this Cherokee in your newspapers." He spit again. "Hey, boy!" he called out to Hackett.

Hackett looked up, but said nothing.

"I hear you Injuns done a lot of scalping. So when you come to bat, boy, you prepare yourself for a little white retaliation. We might just scalp you, too. We're pitching the Kraut today, and when you come to bat, don't expect the Pretzel Twirler to throw you a bunch of curves and drops. He's gonna be aiming right at your head, Che-ro-kee."

That's when I stood up. That's when I realized

291

that Dan Dugdale was right. We had not been a team until that little lesson at Mr. Bill's ranch. Now we felt unified, like cowboys working on a cattle drive.

"I can say something about my sister," Cod Myers once told Dave Rowe. "But it don't mean you can."

Charley Bassett hefted his bat. Frank Ringo emptied his coffee cup, set it down, and found his own bat. Even Kentucky-born Mox McQuery walked up to Watkins, with Jim Lillie and Shorty Radford right beside him.

"One thing you ought to know about us Cowboys," Mox told him. "Working cowboys and baseball-playing Cowboys. We stick together. We play together."

"And," Shorty added, "we fight together."

Dan Dugdale gestured to the stands, which already had become crowded. "So do the folks who come to see us play. I know you've read about that in your newspapers, even in Detroit."

Watkins looked away from us and into the grandstands. Mother waved at him. Behind her, Mr. Bill Anderson, his three sons, the toothless curmudgeon named Duncklee, and a few other cowboys stood, adjusting their gun belts. I'm sure glad the Andersons picked that day to come watch us play a game.

The Wolverines came into that game with seventy-three victories. They still had seventy-three victories when we left the ball park, celebrating our 13-to-4 win. Perhaps Detroit's German ace, Charlie Getzien, should have thrown more fast balls after all—because the Pretzel Twirler's drop balls and curve balls did not drop or curve much on that afternoon.

We beat them, 9-to-4, the next day, and split the following double-header with a 14-to-13 loss but ending the series with a 7-to-5 victory. And if you're curious, Jack Rowe never asked anyone about the health or whereabouts of his brother. I don't think Jack liked Dave, either.

On Thursday, September 16th, however, we had to play the Chicago White Stockings, the best team in the National League. King Kelly and Jim McCormick. Jocko Flynn and Billy Sunday. Tom Burns and, of course, Cap Anson himself.

They were throwing John Clarkson, who had won fifty-three games in '85 and already had thirty victories this year. I would be starting for the Cowboys.

"This is what baseball's all about," Mother told me from her seat on that cloudy afternoon. "The best against the best."

"Mother," I told her, "Chicago is closing in on eighty victories already. That's double what we've won."

She shook her head. "For next year. We're building for next year. Small steps, Silver, lead to giant things."

I smiled. "You should be a manager," I told her.

Dan Dugdale had just walked up. "What do you think?" he asked Mother, who was about to reply when Cap Anson called out Dan's name.

Adrian Constantine Anson. Red-haired with a curled mustache, he stood six-feet-two and weighed north of two hundred pounds. They called him the "King of Kickers" because he could kick more dirt on to an umpire's shins than anyone in the game, and at The Hole dirt was in no short supply. We knew about Anson's intolerance for men of color. Back in 1883, in nothing more than an exhibition game in Toledo, Ohio, Anson had refused to take the field unless Toledo made its great catcher, Moses "Fleetwood" Walker, leave the stadium. He had refused to play against Newark because of their Negro pitcher, George Stovey.

When we turned around, Anson's eyes seared with hatred as he studied silent Mert Hackett, who was stretching his legs.

"When's Dave Rowe coming back, Dugdale?" Anson had walked right up to us.

"That's up to the doctors," Dan answered.

"You ain't playing that darky, Dugdale," Anson said, pointing at our bench. "We have an understanding in this league."

"Mert's a Cherokee," I lied.

"Red nigrah. Black nigrah. Nigrah all the same.

And he's no more red savage than my sainted mother. Get him off the field."

"You are a vile, wretched man!" Mother called out.

Anson spit. "And I've heard about her, too. You let a woman tell you what to do, Dugdale?"

"All the time," Dan answered. "Makes life easier."

"She ain't coaching this game. And he . . ."—pointing his finger angrily at Mert Hackett again—"ain't playing."

"The National League hasn't banned Indians from playing baseball," Dan said.

"Yet." Now Anson grinned. "But there's one thing I'm real good at. And that's reading minds." He spun around. "Hey, you!" he shouted, and when Mert looked up, Anson yelled again: "That's right, boy! Come here. Now. Now, I tell you!"

Mert Hackett stood, dusted off his pants, adjusted his cowboy hat, and walked slowly but surely to our congregation of men. By then, Mr. McKim had arrived to escort Cindy to her seat beside Mother. He came to the balustrade.

"What's going on here?" Mr. McKim asked.

"You'll see, beer-maker," Anson replied, and grinned the meanest smile I'd ever seen on a human when Hackett stopped and stuck his glove underneath his armpit.

"Take off that hat, boy."

Mert Hackett obeyed. I felt sick.

"Here's what you black-loving filth will learn about Cap Anson. No darky can ever lie to me. Tell me, boy, are you a Cherokee red devil? Or are you nothing more than a real black bastard?"

"Mister Anson, sir," Hackett said, thickening that accent the way he had done back when he was earning $5 a victory from Mr. Heim. He paused, though, no longer staring at Cap Anson but at me, and Dan, and Mr. McKim, and Cindy. Finally, he looked back at Cap Anson and grinned. "Cap," he said, and I enjoyed the shock and anger that registered on Anson's rigid face, "my mama picked cotton for Col'nel Dashiel Jones's plantation in Helena, Arkansas. Never knowed my pa. The col'nel sold him to a Baton Rouge merchant, I got told, for talkin' sass. Cherokee? I don't know. Hailin' from Arkansas and all, I reckon I might have some Cherokee blood in me. Besides, before the war, Cherokees owned slaves, too. But I'll tell you one thing, Cap. I loved my mama. More'n even I love cowboyin'. More'n I even love baseball. And I could never do nothin' that'd dishonor her and her memory. But I can lie to you, Cap Anson. I can say . . . 'You's a fine man, a credit to this game of baseball, and, even more, you's a credit to your race.'" He pulled on his hat, and closed in on Anson, who drew back as if to punch Hackett. But Hackett stopped. "Lay a hand on me, white man, and you'll never be able to even hold a baseball bat." Anson's face paled, and Hackett walked away.

That's when I heard hands clapping behind me, and I turned to find Mother and Cindy applauding Mert Hackett's audacity, and his bravery. Mr. McKim wasn't clapping, but his face had to be whiter than Cap Anson's. Dan Dugdale didn't clap, either, but his eyes shone with a fierce pride as he watched Mert Hackett shake hands with his teammates, gather his equipment, and start for the stairs. There's something else you should know. Most of my teammates likely felt the same as Cap Anson did about Negroes. But they were loyal to their teammates, and Mert Hackett had helped us win a few games. We were a unified baseball team. Like the cowboys of Mr. Bill's Diamond Nine, we all . . . black or white . . . rode for the brand.

That's when I started clapping, too, and that's when Mr. McKim did something that almost made me forget all his curses, all his anger, everything he did that angered Cindy, everything he did that ridiculed all of his baseball players, including me.

"Hackett!" he called out.

That stopped Mert, who was looking into the stands.

"Joe Heim pays you five dollars as our mascot

for every game we win, Hackett," Mr. McKim aid. "Take your seat on the edge of the bench. With the Kansas City Cowboys. Where you belong."

Anson whipped off his baseball cap, and pointed his ugly, crooked finger. "You play that black bastard and I'll run you out of the National League. You're finished in this league, anyway. You're all finished. And after we whip your ass . . ."

"Boston has a Negro white-washer as a mascot for its home games," Mr. McKim said. "You don't object to her."

"She don't play!"

"Neither will Mert. But one day, men of his color will."

"And I'll spin in my grave."

Dan Dugdale finally spoke. "I hope that's real soon, Cap. I really do."

Anson stormed to the visitor's bench.

The game everyone would talk about for years to come in Kansas City was getting off to a real friendly start.

CHAPTER TWENTY-FIVE

Catcher Lou Hardie, pitcher John Clarkson, right fielder King Kelly, first baseman Cap Anson, center fielder George Gore, third baseman Tom Burns, second baseman Fred Pfeffer, left fielder Abner Dalrymple, and shortstop Ned Williamson. Facing—after Dan and Mother had to tinker with our line-up at the last minute—third baseman Al "Cod" Myers, shortstop Charley Bassett, second baseman Jim Donnelly, catcher Dan Dugdale, first baseman Mox McQuery, left fielder Jim Lillie, right fielder Paul "Shorty" Radford, center fielder Pete Conway, and pitcher Silver King.

We won the toss, and decided to let Chicago bat first. Lou Hardie stepped over to the umpire, chatted a bit, and turned toward me. "Low," he said, before tapping his bat against his shoes, and settling into a comfortable position. Umpire Paul Grace gave me the nod.

Here's the crazy thing. I have to blame it on my nerves. I did not do the can-can routine, and I did not throw a side-arm pitch. I just chunked the ball. No wind-up. Nothing. But Hardie swung and missed. Then he complained.

"He can't do that, Grace. He didn't give me no chance."

"He did it," Paul Grace countered. "It was

299

exactly where you called for it. And you flat-out missed it."

Dan Dugdale had stood during that conversation, staring at me incredulously, but he just sighed and threw the ball back to me.

"Try that again, rookie!" Hardie called out.

That made Dan smile, and he gave me that nod that I knew meant . . . "If the dude asks for it . . ."

I was not sure I could throw the ball like that again. Didn't even recall how I'd done it the first time. Yet as I twisted my right foot in the dirt, a familiar voice called out from the seats just behind Mother's: "Hey, kid! How come you didn't never pitch that way when I was catchin' you?"

I turned, and gladness filled my heart when Cindy McKim and even Mr. Bayersdörfer, who was sitting in the next row, helped Fatty Briody stand up. He tipped his Irish cap at me, and the spectators around him, recognizing him, erupted in cheers and applause. If McKim, Heim, and Whitfield had been allowed to sell beer in the stadium, everybody there would have bought a round for Fatty Briody. And, knowing Fatty as I did, he would have accepted every nickel beer.

"Give me a pitch, boy," Hardie called out. "That ain't Buffalo Bill Cody in them stands."

I obliged Hardie. He missed badly. Did the

same on my third pitch, and Grace called him out on strikes.

Immediately Cap Anson began arguing and kicking sand across the plate and onto the umpire's shoes, but Grace was one of those players who always showed kindness to managers. He let Anson kick and scream, but when the Chicago bigot returned to his bench, Grace pointed at the plate and handed John Clarkson the little broom the umpire carried in his pocket.

"I didn't make that mess," Clarkson protested.

"But you're cleaning it up," Grace told him.

Those spectators close enough to hear erupted in more cheers.

I struck out Clarkson, too.

King Kelly did manage to get a piece of my fourth pitch, but popped it up to the foul line where third baseman Cod Myers snagged it easily, despite being peppered with peanut shells and curses from the White Stockings' bench.

I felt pretty good. My teammates patted my back as I settled onto the bench. I had thrown eleven pitches in the first inning, and only one player had made contact. This no-wind-up routine was doing something, and it would be only one of my weapons. I knew if they figured out whatever it was I was doing, I could go to my can-can routine, or start that side-arm delivery. This was just the first game of four against the National League leaders, I told myself. Play smart.

John Clarkson must have been telling himself something similar. He did not strike out any of our ballists, but matched my pitch count by inducing Cod Myers and Charley Bassett to ground out to second baseman Fred Pfeffer, and Jim Donnelly to pop up to King Kelly in left-center field.

Kansas City was a railroad town. Still is. And we got a lot of railroad workers to our games, including many folks from Chicago. For this game, there were quite a few Chicago fans in the stands by the White Stockings bench that kept cheering.

They booed us. Our patrons booed them. They cursed us. Our fans cursed them. All friendly, though . . . well . . . for the moment.

For six innings, that's how the game went. I kept the White Stockings in check, and our offense could not figure out a way to score against Clarkson. Mother told me how to pitch each batter, and what she told me worked. We did score a run in the fifth, but Anson drove in a run to tie the score in the sixth.

In the top of the seventh inning, my right elbow and shoulder throbbing, my fingertips raw from gripping and throwing the ball, I walked Abner Dalrymple and the power-hitting Ned Williamson. Then Hardie came to the plate.

"Can-can!" Mother called out.

God, how I wished she had told me to throw side arm or without any wind-up at all. I admit I had much success with that dance, but it felt so damned embarrassing. Still, it worked. Hardie popped up Mox McQuery for the first out.

As pitcher John Clarkson came to the plate, I looked to the seats for Mother's instructions. All I could see were several ticket-takers and Mr. Joseph Heim himself surrounding my mother. A burly man in a fine suit, with gold-rimmed spectacles and a thick, neat mustache, bowler hat in his hand, stood sweating.

"Silver!" Cindy called out.

Confused, I thought of something on my own. "Hey, Mister Grace?"

The umpire stepped toward me. "Yes?"

"Laces broke." I pointed at my shoes. "Can I have time to replace them?"

Lucky for me, Grace trusted me. He didn't examine my shoe laces, merely motioned me toward the bench, then went over to the fence and called out for a sarsaparilla from a vendor. Only Mr. Heim asked the umpire for a moment of his time.

Dan Dugdale went to the fence, asking: "What's going on here?"

"They're making Missus King move!" Fatty Briody yelled.

"Mister Heim?" Dan asked.

Our team president meekly pointed at the man

with the bowler, who had come to the balustrade and was quietly speaking with Paul Grace.

My stomach twisted. I didn't know what was going on. No one did.

"Boys," Mr. Heim said, "this is Nick Young."

That, of course, would be Nicholas Ephraim Young, Civil War veteran, former employee of the U.S. Treasury Department, one-time manager and umpire, and, for better than a year now, president of the National League.

"So?" I said.

"Well, this is the best seat we have," Mr. Heim said with no conviction.

That's when Mr. Bill rose, a move shadowed by his sons and cowhands.

"You kick a lady out of her seat?" Fatty Briody said with uncontrolled rage.

Mr. Bayersdörfer tugged on Fatty's arm.

That's when Mr. Bill's sons and hired men, back for another Cowboys game, put their right hands on the butts of their revolvers.

"No . . . no . . . no! None of that!" Mr. Heim's face paled. "We want none of that. Listen, we're just relocating Missus King to a shadier spot, to the coolest seat at League Park. That's all we're doing."

"Is that the kind of gentleman you are, sir?" Cindy, having joined the fray, said as she wagged a finger at President Young. The president ignored her.

"This stinks," Fatty said.

"What stinks," came a voice behind us, "is a baseball man who takes his instructions from a petticoat."

I whirled, and started for Cap Anson, who stood on the first-base line smiling smugly, only to be intercepted by Dan Dugdale and Frank Ringo.

"You got your laces fixed, Silver?" Paul Grace stepped up to diffuse the volatile situation.

Mother did the rest.

"It's fine," she said, and curtsied to President Young. "You will find no better seat at League Park than here, sir, and no better baseball team than these Kansas City Cowboys. Allow us to show you our Western hospitality." She held out her hand, and President Young stared at it as if she had handed him a deep-fried turkey leg. Gradually he lifted Mother's hand to his lips, and stepped aside as she moved into the aisle.

When Cindy started to follow Mother, she stopped and, turning to Cindy, said: "Please, Cindy, keep President Young company."

I understood what Mother meant: *See what he's up to.* My heart was pounding with anxiety as Mother disappeared in the crowd, followed by both policemen and ticket-takers. I looked at Mr. McKim, who did nothing but glower at his partner and President Young.

"Let's play baseball, boys," Grace announced.

Still smugly smiling, Cap Anson returned to his bench.

Dan Dugdale walked me back to the pitcher's lines.

"What's that about?" I asked. "Why would they make Mother . . . ?"

"You know why," Dan said. "Cap Anson's voice is heard back East."

"But Cindy's father could have . . ."

"Done nothing. That's the president of the league sitting there, Silver. Brought in, likely, by Cap Anson. Maybe Detroit's brass moaned some, too. And you know what those umpires and a lot of teams have been saying about us. Not us, but those folks who come to see us play. How rowdy things get. How umpires don't feel safe at games here."

"I don't feel safe in Saint Louis," I said.

Dan just tried to put me at ease. "We have one out. Two more." He pointed at John Clarkson. "Side arm. He can't figure that out."

He didn't. I struck him out, but King Kelly stepped up next. I knew I had made a mistake the moment the ball left my hand. Kelly swung hard. I grimaced, throwing up my hands and ducking, trying desperately to knock the ball to the ground before it had a chance to tear off my head. But I missed. The ball rolled to center field.

"Back me up!" Dan was screaming. "Back me up!"

I reacted, moving quickly past the plate, watching as Abner Dalrymple scored and burly Ned Williamson rounded third, trying to make it a two-run lead. Pete Conway had scooped up the ball in center field, and came up firing. I held my breath, moving behind Dan, watching, praying, seeing the ball skip on the dirt near the first-base-side pitcher's line, come up high and straight into Dan's big glove. Ned Williamson did not slow down, and Ned Williamson was no small man. He weighed better than two hundred pounds, most of that muscle, and he had a reputation for dirty, dirty play—which is one reason Cap Anson loved to play him. Williamson leaped, and I yelled, my stomach roiling, watching those big feet of Ned's tear right into Dan's left knee as he turned to make the tag.

"He was out!" Mr. Bill and Fatty screamed from the stands, but Paul Grace kept yelling: "Safe! Safe! The runner is safe!"

"No!" I shouted. "Williamson never touched home plate." Hell, I had a better view of the play than that umpire.

"You bum!" Fatty was yelling from the stands, and that was as polite as any Cowboys' fan got.

Then I saw something else. My focus was on Dan Dugdale. I ran as quickly as I could to him, feeling sickened by the way he was gripping his knee. I kneeled down as one of Mr. Bill's waddies was yelling at Paul Grace: "How the hell are you gonna get out of this Hole alive, you worthless bastard?"

"Gentlemen!" I recognized Mr. Heim's voice and glanced over to see him pointing to the sign someone had hung in center field a few months back: DON'T SHOOT THE UMPIRE!

But I didn't care about the run, or Ned Williamson's dirty play. I gripped Dan Dugdale's shoulders as he cursed and twisted his leg this way and that. Then Mert Hackett was beside me, cutting away Dan's torn baseball pants.

"Sumbitch . . . sumbitch . . . sumbitch," Dan kept repeating.

"Are you all right, Dug?" Grace asked as he stood over us.

"No . . . ," Dan groaned.

I looked around for my mother, not knowing where she had been moved, but I only could see the National League president trying to light a long cigar. I returned my attention to Dan, asking: "What can I do, Dug?"

Somehow Dan managed to smile, but only briefly. Grace had moved back to the stands, calling out to Mr. Heim and President Young: "Dug needs medical attention. It's his knee."

"I can't . . . stand," Dug muttered, before returning to his string of "sumbitch".

I watched as policemen and a doctor I recognized headed toward us. Dan saw them, too, and he reached up, gripped my shoulders, saying: "Finish this." For a man in such pain, the grip he held on my shoulders hurt like the blazes.

"Do you have a replacement for Dan?" our umpire asked.

I looked up at the stands again, and yelled: "Fatty!"

"No, damn it," Dan said as he gripped my arm. The doctor shifted Dan's leg, and Dan screamed.

"Fatty!" I shouted again, but Dan lifted his head and gripped my shoulder again. He hissed at me: "He can't play. Unless you want to kill him." His head collapsed back onto the dirt. "Ringo," he whispered. "It has to be Frank Ringo."

In the meantime, the crowd was getting restless for the game to continue. Chicago fans began chanting for the White Stockings. Cowboys enthusiasts cursed Chicago players and spectators. Our city policemen, who had grown accustomed to such rough play and rowdy crowds, appeared to be getting nervous. No. Not nervous. Scared out of their wits.

The Kansas City players had gathered around home plate. I stood and stepped back as the peace officers and doctor loaded Dan onto a blanket and carted him away. Mert Hackett went with him.

"Shit," I heard someone in the grandstands say. "There goes Dugdale. Shit!"

"Shit is right," his companion said. "Not

only is the catcher goin', so's our mascot. We're doomed."

Paul Grace said we needed a replacement catcher immediately. Those who had heard what Dugdale had said eyed Frank Ringo, who seemed to be growing paler as we stared at him in silence.

It was Charley Bassett who broke that silence. He came over, put his arm around the shivering Ringo, and said: "Come on, Frank. Let's get those two runs back and beat these bastards."

Mr. James Whitfield would write two columns about that incident. About how Charley Bassett, the son of a famed Kansas cow-town lawman, and Frank Ringo, his mortal enemy and a direct descendant of a notorious gunman named Johnny Ringo, put "their mortal feud"—Mr. Whitfield's words—aside for the spirit of baseball camaraderie.

It was horseshit, of course, but, hell, it sure was great writing. And Charley Bassett, while he might not have been anything close to a Western legend, he was a fine ballplayer and a great teammate. And that encouragement, that of putting an arm around Ringo, gave our replacement catcher a bit of confidence. He picked up Dan's padded mitt, found his spot behind home base, and gave me a powerful nod. We resumed out positions on the field.

"Let's play some baseball," Grace said, and

the crowd—more than seven thousand strong by that time—roared its approval. Even the White Stockings supporters cheered.

I managed to get Cap Anson, the bastard, to fly out to Shorty Radford in right, but the White Stockings led 3-to-1.

No runs in the eighth. But, somehow, I sat three batters down in order in the ninth. We had three outs remaining, and we trailed by two runs.

Cod Myers flied out to King Kelly on the first pitch. The crowd groaned. One out.

Charley Bassett walked, and Jim Donnelly came to bat. One ball. Two balls. Three balls. I held my breath. Grace called the fourth pitch a strike. The crowd booed. Then Donnelly hit a ball weakly back to Clarkson. He bobbled the ball, looked at second, knew he had no shot there, but threw hard to Cap Anson to retire Donnelly.

Two outs. A runner on second. We needed two runs, and Frank Ringo was stepping to the plate.

I closed my eyes. I even said a little prayer. I heard Frank Ringo grunt, and the crowd groaned. He had swung at Clarkson's drop ball, and missed. Strike one. Clarkson did his wind-up and threw again. Ringo did not swing. He should have.

"Strike two," Grace said.

I opened my eyes and looked at Frank Ringo. I wanted to give him some encouragement, but

311

as pale as Ringo looked, and as hard as that bat seemed to be shaking in his arms, I closed my eyes again. That's why I did not see that great hit until I heard what sounded like a detonation. My eyes shot open, and I saw King Kelly running as hard as he could for the center-field fence. Kelly leaped, but the ball tipped off his fingers, hit the wall, and bounced toward right field.

We watched as Charley Bassett scored easily, as Frank Ringo showed no signs of slowing down. I looked at right field. Kelly had reached the ball first, grabbed it, and threw it. Ringo was running around third. I screamed at him to stop, but he either ignored me or didn't hear. My eyes clamped shut. That's why I missed the fact that Cap Anson, beautifully arrogant and mercilessly evil, dropped the ball that Kelly threw to him. Had he managed to hold onto that throw, and had he done what he was supposed to do and relay Kelly's throw to Lou Hardie, the Chicago catcher would most likely have tagged Ringo out and the White Stockings would have won by a run. But Anson dropped the ball, Ringo scored, and we had tied the score.

Mox McQuery grounded out to Fred Pfeffer. Three outs. We were going into extra innings.

I worked my way through the tenth inning, my arm feeling as brittle as dried-out leather reins even though I did not feel tired. It was lucky I had foregone my wind-up through most of the game. As I sank onto the bench, Pete Conway said: "Silver, your mother wants to know if you need to come out?"

I blinked. "Mother?"

"Yeah. And, Shorty, Missus King says that if Jim gets on base, she wants you to just tap the ball back down the third-base line. Try to move Jim over."

All of our ballists were staring at Pete Conway, who smiled as he relayed my mother's instructions.

"Yeah, boys," Pete explained. "I'm standing in center field, and I hear her voice." He broke out laughing. " 'Pete do this . . . Pete tell Shorty that.' So I'm thinking . . . 'She's God.' Then I understand . . ." He gestured to the folks who filled the hilltop above the outfield.

We stared, knowing at last that my mother had outsmarted Cap Anson, National League President Young, and everyone who hated the rough and tumble Kansas City Cowboys. She had joined the misers on the hilltop to watch, and direct the baseball game.

Only Jim Lillie grounded out. Shorty popped out to Cap Anson. Conway lined a ball that, once again, King Kelly, even though well in his cups, caught with a diving leap.

Eleven innings. Twelve. Thirteen. Fourteen. I had to come out of the game by then. Even without a wind-up or the can-can move, I couldn't pitch anymore. Stump Wiedman came in to replace me. With two outs in the fifteenth inning, Cap Anson doubled into right field, scoring Kelly from first. Once again, the White Stockings had a lead. The score was 4-to-3.

I couldn't have felt worse. Sitting on the bench, arm aching, clothes wet with sweat, the crowd cheering, and feeling helpless, out of the game, with nothing to do but offer your teammates comments like: "Hang tough, boys," or "That's all right, Cod," or "Battle! Let's battle, boys!"

Stump struck out. Cod Myers walked, but was out at second on Charley Bassett's grounder to third base. Two outs. Down by one run. Then Jim Donnelly singled to right, moving Charley to second. We had a chance. Frank Ringo, probably more frightened than he had been at bat earlier, again stepped to the plate and prepared to face Chicago's new pitcher Jocko Flynn.

This time, I did not close my eyes. I lacked the strength.

Flynn wound up, and threw a fast ball. Ringo swung, walloping the ball between third baseman Tom Burns and that hard-sliding, meaning-to-maim, son-of-a-bitching shortstop Ned Williamson. Frank Ringo never ran so fast in all his life. The ball reached the outfield, but George Gore caught it on the second hop. He threw home. No, *threw* does not describe that cannonball fired by a mountain howitzer.

Catcher Joe Hardie caught it, but never tagged Charley Bassett, who slid safely across the plate.

I would like to think that Paul Grace just forgot the situation, and thought the play at home was a force out. But it wasn't. Hardie had to tag Charley to get the out, and that never happened. We had not only tied the score, but we now had Jim Donnelly on third base and Frank Ringo on first—with Mox McQuery coming to the plate.

I leaped up, cheering.

But then Paul Grace began yelling: "The runner is out! The runner is out!"

And in the stands, Fatty Briody saw something. He saw the National League president shake his head and give a solemn, Treasury Department do-as-I-say look at the umpire.

Paul Grace knew who paid his salary.

That's when everything registered as I heard the umpire shout: "Ball game! White Stockings win!"

Hell, Grace never should have said that.

Call it chaos, or insanity, a regular Donnybrook, whatever you want to call it, but no words can actually describe what happened. Benches clear in baseball games. More than a few times, I had seen it happen during that 1886 season, but never had I seen the stands empty.

Spectators leaped up from their seats.

Paul Grace ran for his life.

He started toward center field, but those non-paying patrons had headed down from the hilltop and onto the field. Paul Grace had nowhere to go but to join the Chicago players. That might have saved his life.

Cap Anson and the White Stockings had grabbed baseball bats to defend themselves, and soon they were defending Paul Grace. The Chicago railroad workers were running onto the field in an effort to defend their team. Those that made it to the bench, I mean. Others took to brawling with the Cowboys enthusiasts.

It's how I always thought Dodge City must be like when a trail crew pulled into town. Or some slaughter right out of the Old Testament.

"This is all your damned fault!" Fatty Briody was yelling as he punched National League President Young in the mouth. Mr. Bayersdörfer tackled Fatty. Mr. Bill's cowboys and sons surrounded the trio to protect them from a handful of Chicago railroad men, their pistols drawn. The railroad men turned tail.

Mr. Americus McKim was about to leap over the balustrade to join the fracas when Cindy McKim grabbed his shoulder. Mr. McKim turned, not realizing who was trying to stop him, to save him, and I yelled as that crazed father punched his daughter. Cindy somersaulted over the balustrade, and I dived, running faster than I ever had, some-how managing to catch her with my aching, battered arms. We toppled onto the dirt.

Gunshots echoed in my head as my heartbeat picked up speed.

Mox McQuery cried out: "Can't we all try to get along?"

Police whistles blew. More gunshots. Fists connecting to flesh. Curses. All those noises, while I just held my breath, staring at Cindy McKim, waiting for her eyes to open.

"Cindy," I whispered as I tried to cover her head with my body as beer bottles began pelting the field. One hit my back.

Then I could hear my mother's voice. I guess she had leaped down into The Hole in center field. "What are you doing?" she was crying out. "Look at yourselves! This is a game. A child's game. Stop it! Stop this!"

"Silver?" It was Cindy murmuring as her eyes fluttered open.

Then directly behind me, over the cacophony of the fight, I heard Cindy's father say: "My God, what have I done?"

CHAPTER TWENTY-SIX

In his room at St. Joseph Hospital, Dan Dugdale held up the *Times*, so Cindy and I could see the headline: CHEATED!

"You're taking this pretty well," I told him.

He shook his head. "Silver," he said, his voice now serious, "you'll learn one thing about baseball. It's a game. Not life or death. Not even real life. All it is . . . is a kids' game."

"That's what Silver's mother said," Cindy said.

"She was right," Dan said.

"Folks did not think so yesterday," I told them.

They most certainly had not. Cindy McKim's eye was black and blue, swollen, but the nurses and doctors at the hospital said she need not fear anything, that the bruise would fade, and her eyesight would not suffer.

"I think," she said, smiling, "I got my father back."

Yes, Americus McKim had stopped the riot, him and Mox and twenty or thirty of Kansas City's finest police officers. And Mother. Hell, Cap Anson and the White Stockings had done their part, too, keeping Paul Grace from being drawn and quartered.

A few years later, I would see that famous lithograph that some lithographer named Becker did of a painting called Custer's Last Fight for

Anheuser-Busch. And I wondered if Becker, or the original artist whose name I can't remember, had been at League Park that afternoon and drawn his inspiration from that mêlée. I can still close my eyes and picture Cap Anson and those ballplayers, eyes wide, staring at the horde charging them, believing they were about to die.

In the end, only fifteen men were arrested—nary a ballplayer among them—and ten were deposited at various hospitals. Most importantly, National League President Young agreed not to press any charges, providing we accepted his terms.

"Expelled from the league?" Dan Dugdale said, shaking his head as I told him Young's terms.

"They get to finish the season," I told Dan. "After we forfeited the remaining games against Chicago."

"Because," Cindy said, "the Cowboys were supposed to finish the season on the road, anyway. Mister Young didn't think there would be many problems as long as no more games are played in Kansas City. He said our team and our spectators are . . . are . . . hooligans."

"He's likely right," Dan said. "And Fatty?"

"McKim, Heim, and Whitfield had to release him," I said sadly. "No way Young was going to let Fatty off without punishment. But Fatty said it was worth it. He said he saw Young give Paul Grace a nod, and that must've been

319

a signal for Grace to make that terrible call."

Dan stared off into space as if he was deep in thought, and then it was as if he finally registered what I had said several minutes earlier. "You said *they* . . . 'They' get to finish the season . . . not *we*."

"I won't be going with the Cowboys, Dug," I said. I almost felt relief when I answered him, rather than disappointment. "Dave Rowe's back as manager," I added. "He told me to draw my time. And . . ."

Dan reached over to the table by his hospital bed and showed me a telegram in response. "He told me the same thing," he admitted.

My fists clenched, but Dan laughed. "Silver, don't take it personally. I figured this sprained knee would end my season with you boys. I knew my season was done." His face saddened. "Maybe my career in baseball, too. We'll have to see how this knee heals."

"Rowe said he'd use George Baker as catcher," I told him. "His busted hand's about healed."

"George is a good guy," Dan said. "You sure you're all right?"

"I'm better than all right, Dug," I told him, and could not contain a grin. "Mister Bill said that . . . well, once he and his sons and a few of his hired men get out of jail, that he'll put in a word for me with the team in Saint Joseph. I'll finish the season with them, I hope. See what happens after the season's over."

"You won't be in the Western League for long," Dan told me. "Another National League team will track you down. Trust me."

"That's what Mother says, too," I said.

"That was one hell of a game," Dan reflected. "Wish I could've seen the finish."

The nurse came in, reminding us that we needed to be on our way, so Dan could get some sleep. I helped Cindy out of her chair. Even with her shiner, she looked beautiful.

We were just outside the door when Dan called out: "Silver!"

Letting go of Cindy's hand, I stepped back into the room.

"Baseball season's almost over in Saint Joe, too." He patted his leg. "I got a case of the fiddle-foot, you know, but I got an idea." He paused and I waited, remaining silent. "When your season's over in Saint Joe, take a ride over to the Diamond Nine. That's where I'll be, and I bet I can get you a job for the winter. Play a little baseball. Nurse some cattle. Till the snows come."

I could not contain my grin. I had a girl. I had a loving mother and father. I had a great friend. And memories of a wild and woolly summer of baseball and cowboys. And all of those, I thought in my youthful naïveté, would last forever. And some of those did last forever . . . like the saddle sores that still cause me to limp.

EPILOGUE

So there you have it. We Kansas City Cowboys went our myriad ways after that 1886 season. After cowboying for the Diamond Nine in Kansas that fall and winter, I wound up in St. Louis the next year, pitching for the Browns in the American Association—had my best year in '88 when St. Louis won another championship. After that, I bounced around—Chicago's Pirates of the short-lived Players' League (where I threw a no-hitter, and lost, 1-to-0), Pittsburgh, the Giants, the Reds, took a few years off and went back to helping Papa with masonry, then came out to hurl a couple of seasons for the Senators.

Dan Dugdale did his share of bouncing around, too, mostly in leagues like the Western, although he did play some for the Senators in '94, but that problem knee shortened his career on baseball diamonds, though he could still ride a horse better than most men. He drifted from ball team to ranch and ranch to ball team. I think that's the way Dug liked it, wandering. He did turn into a pretty good baseball manager, I hear, back in his hometown of Peoria. Always lured by gold, Dug took off for the Klondike in '98, but he only made it to Seattle. Last I heard, he was managing a team there and doing well. I guess he finally realized that the only gold he'd ever find would be on a diamond.

League President Young did make sure the Cowboys got kicked out of the National League on the grounds of "hooliganism". He told Mr. McKim, Mr. Heim, and Mr. Whitfield that perhaps he might find a better fit in that "beer and whiskey league", and indeed the Kansas City Cowboys were resurrected into th American Association a few years later. But Mr. McKim never attended any of those games, although he kept baseball alive in Kansas City. He spent the rest of his life brewing beer, and doting on Cindy—guilt, I'd call it—and later spoiled his grandchildren.

Paul Grace never returned to Kansas City or the National League. He got out of The Hole that September day, though, and I read in *The Sporting News* that he became a lawyer in Baltimore. Last year, President Theodore Roosevelt appointed him to some highfalutin position in Washington.

Fatty Briody never quite recovered from that gunshot wound, or his drinking, or his weight. He did play for Detroit for a few games in '87, and returned to Kansas City the following year to play for the new franchise called the Cowboys, but that was for the American Association. I saw him some that year while I was doing well for the Maroons, and we often ate supper together after one of our games. Our paths never crossed again, and I was saddened to hear from Charley Bassett that poor Fatty had died in Chicago earlier this summer. He was only forty-four years old. Charley didn't say how he died. He didn't have to. Too many ballists have died from John Barleycorn, and I fear Fatty was no exception.

Liquor, though, did not kill Frank Ringo in 1889. Most people called it a suicide from an overdose of morphine. He had stopped drinking for a while, but never could keep that cure. Ask me, and I'd say Cap Anson, Paul Grace, and Nick Young had a hand in Ringo's death. They sent him back to lushing and taking morphine to forget about the heroics those bastards denied him. So don't ask me.

Mox McQuery moved over to the American Association for a couple of seasons and finally found his dream job as a police officer in Covington, Kentucky. I hope you read about him, and saluted him. I did. One evening about three years ago, Mox stopped a street car in Covington and tried to apprehend two murderers. They shot him down, and he died a few days later. I can't think about Mox without tearing up.

Most of my other teammates, and some friends I made with other teams, I've forgotten. Baseball does that. Like cowboying, I guess, at least the way Dan Dugdale used to say it went. You rode for a brand, made some friends, moved along, and probably never saw those friends again. Like Mert Hackett. Maybe one of these years, baseball will stop this ridiculous enforcement of keeping men of color out of America's greatest game. I doubt if I'll live to see it, though.

Charley Bassett moved to Indianapolis after the Cowboys went belly-up and spent three seasons with the Hoosiers, then three more with the New York Giants, and finished his season with the Louisville Colonels in 1892. He stopped pretending to be kin to a Dodge City lawman. In Indiana, New York, and Kentucky, no one much knew anything about Dodge City or the West.

Cap Anson and his Chicago White Stockings won the National League in 1886, and went on to play the American Association's St. Louis Browns in the World's Championship Series. I took great pleasure in the fact that the Browns, of that "beer and whiskey" league, won that series, four games to two.

Dave Rowe returned to Denver, and managed and played some ball around there. As far as I know, he's still in the game, though certainly you won't be finding him in this best-of-nine-game series that starts tomorrow that pits the National League's Pittsburgh Pirates against this new American League's Boston Americans in another one of these World Championship Series.

Cindy told me I should go. When she added that I should take Mother, I just laughed.

That got us talking about 1886 and my time with those Cowboys. Surprisingly, most of what I remember makes me smile.

We live on a few acres outside of St. Louis. We have horses—and not one damned cow or steer. I got my fill of those at the Diamond Nine. Mother and Papa live in the city, but come to visit us on the weekends. Papa tries to show his grandchildren how to lay bricks. Mother teaches them the finer points of baseball.

"What was your favorite year, Silver?" Mother just asked me.

"Well, that's easy," I told her. "It was Eighteen-Eighty-Six." I grinned and winked at Cindy. "When I met my beloved wife."

"I meant baseball," Mother said. "What was your favorite year in baseball."

"Same," I said.

"Why? You pitched better and your team won more when you played for Saint Louis."

"Yeah, but in 'Eighty-Six, I got to play baseball and I got to be a cowboy."

AUTHOR'S NOTE

"The history of baseball is filled with incredible tales of heroic feats and tragic twists of fate," Dashiell Bennett wrote for *Business Insider* in 2011.

The same, I think, is true of the West.

"Unfortunately," Bennett continued, "not all of those amazing stories happened quite the way that everyone thinks they did."

Just like stories of the West.

With that in mind, I tackled this novel. Nothing much about it is true.

The myth, of course, is that the Kansas City Cowboys were kicked out of the National League after the 1886 season because of "hooliganism". Yet while stories of umpires being harassed and threatened are factual, the Cowboys' 30-91 record and lack of money likely led to their ouster, not to mention how long it took teams from the East Coast to reach Kansas City by train. Things, however, indeed got Western in Kansas City. Kansas City police escorted an umpire off the field, and a cowboy did escort the New York Giants to the ball park.

In this case, the names weren't changed to protect the innocent. Most of the names come straight off the Cowboys' roster of 1886, but that's about the only resemblance to the truth you'll find. All right, Fatty Briody was fat, and Dave Rowe had a temper, and the story goes that Rowe actually shot at Briody—which might not be true, but it sure makes one heck of a story.

Silver King, who was born in St. Louis and did debut with the National League's Cowboys in 1886 at age eighteen (not seventeen), would go on to pitch ten years with various professional baseball clubs, playing his last game with the Washington Senators in 1897. I don't know if Silver's mother knew anything about baseball, and while his father was a brick mason, I gave him the extra job of working at a packing house to make Silver's introduction to Dan Dugdale more believable.

Dan Dugdale did play for Denver's Mountain Lions and was picked up by the Cowboys that year, although he might have been released by Kansas City first and then signed by Denver. I doubt if he knew a thing about cowboying, but his story about the design of those early catcher's mitts is pretty much in line with history.

As far as we know, baseball's Charley Bassett was not related to Dodge City's Charlie Bassett. Frank Ringo, however, might have been kin to gunfighter Johnny Ringo, and Frank definitely had substance-abuse problems that led to his death. Dave Rowe did spend time in Denver, and reportedly brought the Cowboys to Colorado for an exhibition in 1886. According to reports,

Mox McQuery was killed in the line of duty as a police officer in Covington, Kentucky, in 1900.

Parts of the other key figures in this novel are true, but not too many. For instance, the Cowboys did forfeit three games in a final series against lowly Washington, which did finish below Kansas City in the standings. The reason for the forfeits? It probably had something to do with the fact that they were scheduled to play seven games over five days, with three consecutive double-headers.

Mert Hackett was not black, but I wanted a black player to show the racism—and Chicago's Cap Anson was among the worst racists in baseball—at the time. The *de facto* agreement with major-league club owners began during this period and would exist, prohibiting many minority baseball players from competing in the big leagues until the Brooklyn Dodgers' Branch Rickey signed Jackie Robinson, who broke the major leagues' color barrier in 1947.

If you're interested in the true story of Kansas City's National League team, I recommend that you track down H.L. Dellinger's *One Year in the National League: An Account of the 1886 Kansas City Cowboys* (Two Rivers Press, 1977). I must warn you, it's hard to find.

I'm grateful to Cheryl Lang and the wonderful staff at the Midwest Genealogy Center, a branch of the Mid-Continent Public Library in

Independence, Missouri, for helping me with research and providing me with one of the rare copies of Harold "H.L." Dellinger's volume.

It was Harold who first introduced me to the story of the Kansas City Royals while we were attending a symposium on the James-Younger Gang in Missouri. I told him I was attending a Royals game after the event. We started chatting about baseball. He brought up the Cowboys, and the seed was planted for this novel. That was years ago.

Dellinger's other Kansas City baseball titles worth pursing—though equally hard to find—are *The 1884 Kansas City Unions: A History of Kansas City's First Major League Baseball Team* and *From Dust to Dust: An Account of the 1885 Western League*, both of which were also published by Two Rivers Press in 1977.

Other sources used in this novel include: *Unions to Royals: The Story of Professional Baseball in Kansas City*, edited by Lloyd Johnson, Steve Garlick, and Jeff Magalif (The Society for American Baseball Research, 1996); *The Western League: A Baseball History, 1885 through 1898*, by W.C. Madden and Patrick J. Stewart (McFarland, 2002); *When Baseball Was Young: The Good Old Days* by Gerard S. Petrone (Musty Attic Archives, 1994); *The Beer & Whiskey League: The Illustrated History of the American Association—Baseball's Renegade*

Major League by David Nemec (The Lyons Press, 2004); *Baseball* by Robert Smith (Simon & Schuster, 1947); *Baseball: The Early Years* by Harold Seymour (Oxford University Press, 1985); *Baseball in Denver* by Matthew Kasper Repplinger II (Arcadia, 2013); *Early Innings: A Documentary History of Baseball, 1825-1908* by Dean A. Sullivan (University of Nebraska Press, 1997); *A.G. Spalding and the Rise of Baseball: The Promise of American Sport* by Peter Levine (Oxford University Press, 1995); *Nineteenth Century Stars*, edited by Robert L. Tiemann and Mark Rucker (The Society for American Baseball Research, 1989); *The Great Encyclopedia of Nineteenth-Century Major League Baseball, Second Edition* by David Nemec (University of Alabama Press, 2006); *Slide, Kelly, Slide: The Wild Life and Times of Mike King Kelly, Baseball's First Superstar* by Marty Appel (Scarecrow Press, 1999); *Before They Were Cardinals: Major League Baseball in Nineteenth-Century St. Louis* by Jon David Cash (University of Missouri, 2011); *Turning the Black Sox White: The Misunderstood Legacy of Charles A. Comiskey* by Tim Hornbaker (Sports Publishing, 2014); *Comiskey: Remembrances of the Major League's First 37 Years of Baseball, 1876-1913* by Charles Comiskey, an Amazon digital reprint from *Pearson's Magazine* (Volume 31, Issue 6, Pearson Publishing Company,

1914); *Occasional Glory: The History of the Philadelphia Phillies* by David M. Jordan (McFarland, 2003); and *Green Cathedrals: The Ultimate Celebrations of All 273 Major League and Negro League Ball Parks Past and Present* by Philip J. Lowry (Addison-Wesley, 1993).

For Kansas City, I used *Kansas City: An Illustrated Review of Its Progress and Importance* (Enterprise Pub. Co., 1886) and *At the River's Bend: An Illustrated History of Kansas City, Independence and Jackson County* by Sherry Lamb Schirmer (Windsor, 1982).

For rules of the time, I turned to *Spalding's Official Baseball Guide, 1886*, reprinted by Horton Publishing Company in 1987, and *Playing Rules of the National League of Professional Base Ball Clubs, 1886*, courtesy of the University of Maryland's R. Lee Hornbake Library archives in College Park, Maryland.

I'm also indebted to the Kansas City Public Library's Missouri Valley Special Collections; the Negro Leagues Baseball Museum of Kansas City, Missouri; the Society for American Baseball Research (I've been a member since 2014); the National Baseball Hall of Fame Museum of Cooperstown, New York; the Denver *Post*; Baseball-Reference.com; Baseball-Almanac.com; and the Vista Grande Public Library of Santa Fe, New Mexico.

I should acknowledge some former professional

players for some tales that made their way into this narrative. Before I read Dan Dugdale's recollections of the meat-in-the-glove story I had heard it from my father-in-law, Jack Smith, who was signed to a professional contract with the Pittsburgh Pirates by the legendary Rickey. As a minor-league player in Waco, Texas, Jack was the real catcher who slid flank steak into his mitt to protect a bruised palm. Yes, the steak idea was still around sixty-seven years after Harry Decker had tested the idea in Peoria, Illinois. "I must've rotted out two or three mitts that year," Jack told me. Sadly, my father-in-law died while I was working on this novel.

Kent Anderson told me some lies—or maybe just slight exaggerations—over beers and moonshine while barbecuing during the Christmas holidays back in South Carolina. I think I remembered those stories right. Kent and I grew up together, and played Little League ball together. Except for some intramural softball activities in college and at the Dallas *Times Herald*, my baseball career ended there—at least until I started coaching and umpiring Little League games decades later. But Kent made it to "The Show", playing two seasons with the California Angels. We grew up a mile from one another, went to grade school, high school (playing on the football team), and college together. I even tweaked a few stories Kent's brothers told me to fit into this book. Butch played in the Philadelphia Phillies' minor-league system, and Mike spent most of his major-league career with the Phillies and St. Louis Cardinals. Yes, the Andersons of the fictional Diamond Nine Ranch in this novel are based on this wonderful family. The patriarch, Mr. Bill, indeed commanded respect. He died of a heart attack while Kent and I were attending college. As a newspaper reporter, I had a chance to write a lot about the Andersons. Because we've been friends forever, I won't tell you what stories of theirs I've used here.

Other stories came from games I've attended over several years, or from interviews I conducted as a sportswriter in South Carolina and Texas.

Finally, I finished the last draft of this novel a the home of Jenny and Julian Goodman in Naperville, Illinois, during the annual baseball trip my son and I make each summer—after a Chicago Cubs game at Wrigley Field . . . under the lights . . . in the bleachers (the Cubs won in the twelfth inning on a squeeze bunt, by the way). I coached Julian in Little League in Santa Fe. He and Jenny might even still remember the real bat-in-the-ribs story.

See you out West . . . or at the ball park.

Johnny D. Boggs
Santa Fe, New Mexico

ABOUT THE AUTHOR

Johnny D. Boggs has worked cattle, shot rapids in a canoe, hiked across mountains and deserts, traipsed around ghost towns, and spent hours poring over microfilm in library archives—all in the name of finding a good story. He's also one of the few Western writers to have won six Spur Awards from Western Writers of America (for his novels, *Camp Ford*, in 2006, *Doubtful Cañon*, in 2008, and *Hard Winter* in 2010, *Legacy of a Lawman*, *West Texas Kill*, both in 2012, and his short story, "A Piano at Dead Man's Crossing", in 2002) as well as the Western Heritage Wrangler Award from the National Cowboy and Western Heritage Museum (for his novel, *Spark on the Prairie: The Trial of the Kiowa Chiefs*, in 2004). A native of South Carolina, Boggs spent almost fifteen years in Texas as a journalist at the Dallas *Times Herald* and Fort Worth *Star-Telegram* before moving to New Mexico in 1998 to concentrate full time on his novels. Author of dozens of published short stories, he has also written for more than fifty newspapers and magazines, and is a frequent contributor to *Boys' Life* and *True West*. His Western novels cover a wide range. *The Lonesome Chisholm Trail* (2000) is an authentic cattle-drive story, while *Lonely*

Trumpet (2002) is an historical novel about the first black graduate of West Point. *The Despoilers* (2002) and *Ghost Legion* (2005) are set in the Carolina backcountry during the Revolutionary War. *The Big Fifty* (2003) chronicles the slaughter of buffalo on the southern plains in the 1870s, while *East of the Border* (2004) is a comedy about the theatrical offerings of Buffalo Bill Cody, Wild Bill Hickok, and Texas Jack Omohundro, and *Camp Ford* (2005) tells about a Civil War baseball game between Union prisoners of war and Confederate guards. "Boggs's narrative voice captures the old-fashioned style of the past," *Publishers Weekly* said, and *Booklist* called him "among the best Western writers at work today." Boggs lives with his wife Lisa and son Jack in Santa Fe. His website is www.johnnydboggs.com.

Center Point Large Print
600 Brooks Road / PO Box 1
Thorndike, ME 04986-0001 USA

(207) 568-3717

US & Canada:
1 800 929-9108
www.centerpointlargeprint.com